"Kirsten Dodge deftly connects two de[...] [...] immune systems and geopolitical identity—in starting and intimate discoveries made by a woman physician in Texas. *Let Me See* swirls with competing passions of science, mysticism, quests for survival. **It is an action-adventure tale with brains."** —John MacNicholas, author of award-winning play *The Moving of Lilla Barton*

"*Let Me See* is at once an exciting and a deeply serious novel. It tells the story of a principled and thoughtful woman . . . brought face to face with powerful forces, biological and natural, as well as psychological and personal, which threaten her existence as a professional, as a wife, and as an American. In telling this woman's story, Kirsten Dodge envisions a new and necessary female heroism, one that ties vulnerability and depth of feeling with courage, tenacity, and vision." —Pat Sharpe, author (with Frances E. Mascia-Lees) of *Taking a Stand in a Post-Feminist World*

"*Let Me See* is a wonderful book, full of excitement and deep meaning. Zoe Dempsey discovers what everybody else resists knowing: networks, like immune systems, come to function autonomously. She intuitively resists the pressure to conform and takes all sorts of chances, until she runs up against the lethal dimensions of normality in a thoroughly unforgettable climax. We leave her living in that liminal state, the blurred border of possibility where the world can be renewed." —A. David Napier, author of *The Age of Immunology*

"You will love this compelling and very contemporary book. I can't compare *Let Me See* to any other novel I've read—it can't be pinned down to one genre. The powerful characters and storytelling are not like anybody else's." —Joe Slate, professor of American Literature and Film, *University of Texas at Austin*

"An interesting tale from a strong, new voice. *Let Me See* balances a good story with some challenging, thought-provoking questions that will leave the reader at once satisfied and wondering." —Archer Mayor, author of the award-winning Joe Gunther series

"I love reading about the adventures of gutsy women, and I love encouraging new women writers. This book offers both." —Sarah Weddington, author of *A Question of Choice* and lawyer who won *Roe v. Wade*

"Zoe Dempsey, a Texas immunologist, seeks meaning beyond the sun-drenched homogeneity of Austin's medical establishment. . . **Zoe is a brave and smart searcher, a woman alert to how 'the truth might get bent.'"** —Pat Cusick, author of many books for children

LET ME SEE

A NOVEL BY

KIRSTEN DODGE

BASKERVILLE
PUBLISHERS

Baskerville Publishers, Inc.
2711 Park Hill Drive
Fort Worth, Texas 76109

Library of Congress Cataloging-in-Publication Data

Dodge, Kirsten.
  Let me see : a novel / by Kirsten Dodge.
    p. cm.
  ISBN 1-880909-67-7 (alk. paper)
  1. Women physicians—Fiction. 2. Autoimmune diseases—
Treatment—Fiction. 3. Fugitives from justice—Fiction. 4. Physician
and patient—Fiction. 5. Immunologists—Fiction. 6. Texas—
Fiction. I. Title.

  PS3604.O318L48 2004
  813'.6—dc22
                                    2004021198

Manufactured in the United States of America
First Printing, 2004

AUTHOR'S NOTE

Let Me See is a work of fiction. Events reported in local, national, and international news or posted on the internet during the time this book was written appear at times as metaphors and truths of the imagination, not as depictions of historical events. Names, characters, places and events are fictitious. The mountains and rivers, the sky and the desert of Texas and Mexico are as I have experienced and imagined them.

ACKNOWLEDGMENTS

Thank you to my family: my sister, Melody Davison (and her husband John, who provided a perfect phrase); my husband Richard Dodge, daughter Aina Dodge and son-in-law Steve Chapman; son Michael, daughter-in-law Beatrice Dodge, and grandson Alex, an avid reader if not yet of my books; Aunt Viola Brainard and cousins Honey and Larry Dodge, who truly see things differently.

Thank you to my friends, neighbors, and others who I have met only through the written word, who read the book in manuscript and discussed it with passion: Kevin Arnold, Annes and Ron Baker, Hal Box, Becky Bumpers, Mike Bryan, Rebecca Carrigan, Nancy Cihler, Paul Diehl, Sharon Draper, Janet Feldman, Kate Frost, Keren Johnson, Jane Howle, Cordy Lavery, Nancy Lewis, John MacNicholas, Beverly Manroe, Archer Mayor, Joe Maxwell, Kent McMillan, Kathy McTee, June Rainwater, Margit Resch, Kay Rogers, Pat Sharpe, Lucy Todd, Gary Treadwell, Janet Swaffer, Logan Wagner and Sarah Weddington.

I could not have done it without you: it's as simple as that. I'm especially grateful to Robert Gover, author and writing teacher, for incisive feedback and never-ending faith and enthusiasm. To my editor, Jeff Putnam: thank you.

For my husband, Richard

and in memory of
Jack Maxwell

It is noble I suppose to use the gift of storytelling, that peculiar power only humans have, as far as I know, to create a whole way of life from a strand of fact, a mundane incident quickly observed. Complete with the kind of guiding philosophies and dogmas that martyrs will die for, and in defiance of which heretics are put to death. No, I am not a story-teller, a maker of myths, a spinner of yarns, whatever you want to call it. My craft is blunt and simple, and much more honest.

Achmat Dangor, *Kafka's Curse*

LET ME SEE

Texas, Spring 1997

PART 1
THE MOUNTAIN

Chapter 1

From my office window on the top floor of the old building I can see my husband crossing the doctors' parking lot—even from this distance his bounding walk gives him away. I strain over the plants on the sill, following close enough behind him to smell the leather as he opens the door of his new Volvo. Where can he be going? We have a staff meeting coming up. Without taking my eyes off the car, I scramble for the phone on the desk behind me and punch his number. The mechanical voice intones: *the person you are trying to reach is unavailable.* Now ain't that the truth. I try his beeper, only to hear the tinny version of his voice refer me to another number for the on-call doctor. Shit. I sink down into my chair, afraid. How much will it cost me to find out the truth about Al's mysterious comings and goings? How can I ignore what I see? Too many unknowns. The phone buzzes, startling me. I push the button and bring it to my ear.

"Who is it?"

"It's Travis, Zoe. Who did you expect?"

"I was hoping it was Al. I just saw him drive off. We've got a staff meeting."

"He'll be back. I'll be there myself."

"What for?" As head of pathology, Travis attends all mortality reviews held behind closed doors and skips the routine gastro meetings. Unless he's on a crusade, like how we should call for more postmortems. "You still there?"

"Yeah, I'm still here."

"That's a comfort." Travis and Al were friends at A & M.

Travis switched to UT, where we met in our pre-med courses. Al showed up not long after; we all went on to med school in Galveston. "Why are you going, Trav?"

"Your old pal Glover's up to something. Bring your case notes on that patient of yours who developed pancreatitis."

"I didn't know her case was on the agenda." We practice a profession that would be impossible to bear alone. "Thanks for the heads-up." Travis grunts good-bye.

Glover's chief of surgery and I'm an internist in gastroenterology at Doctors' Hospital here in Austin. I cut my teeth on immune system therapy as a resident at UT-San Antonio a decade ago. The people who are now making research careers in the field of immunology are scary youngsters. Surgery's the treatment of last resort nowadays, which maybe explains why Glover makes an issue out of medical complications whenever he can. Al's an anesthesiologist on Glover's team. Howdy-do: complicated loyalties plague me.

I can't sit around all day looking out the window, waiting for Al to show up, so I go back out on the floor and lose myself in work for an hour. Travis is shutting the conference-room door when I come around the corner, going as fast as I can go without falling out of my clogs.

"Hey, hold it, cowboy," I shout down the hall. I forgot to pick up the case notes.

"Sorry, Zoe." Travis braces the door open while I do-si-do under his arm. He's dressed in his familiar jeans and boots, like a figure out of an old Western.

I latch the door behind me before stepping into the new conference room, where I catch Al's eye from the far end of the polished table. I quench his smile with a frown and am repaid with immediate remorse. If there were a third icon of the face, besides the happy face and the one on poison bottles, Al's would be it. The heavy vertical crease between his dark eyebrows and his wide mouth make his face habitually grave, while his blue eyes, holding you in unhurried regard, exert calm.

Massed thunderclouds turn the sunset over the hills west of

Town Lake into a theatrical backdrop for Dr. Frank Hawkins, chief of staff, who presides like a black Buddha from his place at the head of the polished conference table. Our board-certified gastro specialist, Cynthia Hagan, occupies her usual place to Frank's right. They went to medical school together at Penn, back in the day. Glover, never without his retinue, sits across the table, flanked on one side by the head of nursing and on the other by the new resident. He flips me a sour smile. Not all that long ago we fought side by side against the insurance companies in the battle over managed care. Maybe he blames me for ending up on the losing team. Lucky it's Al and not me who works next to him every day, hacking out parts of the intestine.

I mumble greetings to Dr. Owen Lerner, the psychiatrist, who plumps down next to me, dousing me with good will. Travis takes a place on the other side of him, leaning back perilously in his chair to wink at me from behind the old man's back. I drop into a trance while the bureaucratic wheels grind slowly through the Austin afternoon, longing only to get away to the mountains with Al and Iris, even though I've had a light load this year. When the Chief, who makes it his business to know everything, found out Travis was writing me scrips for Percocet (I'd nearly crippled myself doing a back flip into the cold spring-fed pool at Deep Eddy) he prescribed a year of 12-step meetings, making compliance a condition for keeping my job. The year has just now come to an end. It might have been worse: Frank could have taken me before a public board of inquiry and all that shit. Each profession has its taboo—for priests, sex, for stockbrokers, insider trading, and for us, drugs. I was a fool.

I tune-in to my surroundings when I hear Cynthia bring up one of her recalcitrant cases, an older woman suffering from long term CD. She's defending her profligate use of steroids, despite the risks of osteoporosis. I say nothing. Everybody here knows my views. Once Cynthia subsides, the new resident gets started, only to get trapped in a do-loop, going over and over his treatment of a maddeningly simple case.

My mind drifts to my friend Merla. She's been occupied with a new man in her life, one she claimed not to want to talk about.

But she couldn't stop herself. She told me this guy's married, but irresistible. When I shuddered, she jumped me for judging her morals. It didn't help telling her I was simply repelled by the notion of a man you could not resist. Everything I said to mollify her only made things worse.

Glover has been nattering on about gathering data, controlling the information flow, and the importance of generating probabilities—more or less his mantra—for some time, but I wake up at the mention of my patient.

"Excuse me, Dr. Glover," I interrupt, "could you run back over that again?"

Here's a man with a giant mind peering down through a tiny AMA-approved peephole on the whole vast world of body and spirit, a little troll with a large head, straight black hair, and pudgy body.

"Certainly, Dr. Dempsey," the troll responds with exaggerated courtesy. The room goes quiet. Al stops taking notes and glances up. My primitive nervous system, the limbic system connected to the lizard brain, rings its ancient danger note, a pain in the gut. "Permit me to fill in a little context here. Your patient Jordan Wilson's adverse reaction to treatment fits into a pattern evident since you came on board."

Glover unveils a flip chart on its rickety stand. He spends five minutes at fever pitch, showing his graphs, his curves, and his conclusions, while I watch as rapt as my colleagues. When the puffed-up little prick reaches a stopping place, I jump up.

"Without a broader context, this particular case means little. I've spent a lot of time with this patient . . ."

"Well, Dr. Dempsey," Glover cuts in, "maybe it would be better if you didn't."

"I'm sorry?" My face aches. I push my thumb along my jaw muscle.

"You get too involved with your patients," Glover says.

My whole body goes hot. Just barely back in good standing, I don't need Glover accusing me of transgressing the boundary between doctor and patient.

"Let's all take a moment to look at these materials," Frank says.

Before the words are out of his mouth I stride up to the front and stand in front of the graph, colorful in contrast with the monochromatic functionality of the meeting room and its inhabitants. Glover used standard measures to gauge recovery or remission rates. I flip a page and see he's done the same for patients suffering from all forms of IBD nationwide. It doesn't take an MBA degree to interpret the charts. We're not doing so well. Glover comes up and hovers next to me while I turn to the next page on the easel, with just two fat lines, one in red representing his patients, the other in black depicting mine. The man's whole body momentarily convulses in a spastic twitch while I study the chart. The red line for surgical patients wavers along without much change over time whereas the black line shifts up, up, up, for nearly two years, levels off for several months, then plummets down, down, down. Turning my head a fraction, I skewer him with a look. He's perspiring.

"Since we're both treating small populations, these statistics might mean anything."

"Dr. Dempsey steadfastly refuses surgery for her patients," Glover says.

"Nonsense. I'd never rule out surgery. The literature shows," I begin, only to be stopped in mid-sentence by a back spasm. Everybody waits politely. I lean the flat of both hands on the table until it passes. "Surgical intervention," I begin again, "can lead to fecal incontinence. The patient's a young woman. We're bypassing the gut with short-term TPN to rest the inflamed intestine and maybe save her from further resection." I leave an opening for Glover to object—total parenteral nutrition can be viewed as an invasive procedure with its own risks—but he says nothing. "The patient will be discharged tomorrow to continue with her therapy at home. I'm working closely with the nutritionist and nursing staff to prepare the family for home care."

"Just out of curiosity, Jeff," Frank says, making a deft gesture towards me with his chin to allow him to cut in, "is this just another turf battle?" Glover flashes the chief a manic look and flaps his arms like he's about to decompensate right in front of us. Frank points to the flipchart. "Why have you brought in all this ammunition?"

"I'm concerned about a colleague's clinical decision-making," Glover says, throwing his short arms out like he's being crucified. "Patients can't be allowed to entertain all the voodoo alternative quackery you see marketed to frightened sick people."

Frank turns to me with raised eyebrows.

"I make sure my patients understand the basis of the treatment I propose and grasp the attendant risks," I reply to his brows before turning to Glover. "Why does that trouble you?"

"I'm tired of the mumbo-jumbo. One of *my* patients got involved with that support group meeting in the basement, where everyone blathers on about *healing*. Weren't you instrumental in getting that group going, Zoe? It undermines my authority."

"Advocating personal responsibility for one's own healing is a key notion of PNI. . ." I begin, but back off when I notice my tone of voice and start over again. "Paying attention to the emotional and behavioral aspects of the immune response is simply good clinical practice." I sit down and glance at my colleagues. Their position on these issues can be inferred from when and where they went to med school.

With a prim nod in my direction, Cynthia explains her interest in psycho-neuroimmunology, and its close cousin psycho-neuroendocrinology. "Both are scientifically based medical approaches, and are no longer considered *alternative* medicine." Often both overbearing and ingratiating, like a flight attendant, she's going out of her way to support me.

I flash her my brightest smile. "Thank you for the clarification, Cynthia."

"Still, more and more of *us,* physicians who get sick, enlist at least some aspect of complementary treatment," Travis says. "It's a mystery."

Everyone turns to look at him.

"Maybe the mystery matters," he goes on, with a wide shrug. "I myself have examined some of these mysteries." Travis combines a high erotic charge with terrific control. The real mystery is why his girlfriends never stay around long.

"In baffling cases, we do have access to outside consultants," Frank says, "and I encourage you to call on them."

Glover jumps back into the fray, gesticulating with his short arms. "Dr. Dempsey's gone way out of bounds by giving her patients so much responsibility. She should be discouraged from playing outside the lines of accepted practice."

Frank gets up and turns on the lights. Everybody fidgets, ready to go home. He sits back down and points a finger in my direction. I stand up. Lerner angles his chair out from the table and leans forward with tense attention.

"Loss of faith in treatment can trigger a flare," I say, speaking slowly. "The immune response *is* the self. Autoimmune disease keeps proliferating, particularly in highly industrialized regions. Those of us sitting here intervene when the self mistakes itself for an enemy; still, we have to trust life in order to live it, and so . . ." I shrug and cup my hands, "if you want to get into the question of alternative healers, they have a place in the health care system."

"We're doctors, not faith healers," Glover says, shaking his jowls.

The nurse, Shaunna—small, blond, and energetic, like a high school cheerleader—raises her hand and waits for Frank's nod before speaking: "I'm sorry. I wasn't at the last meeting. Am I missing something? How did we get talking about faith healers?"

"Last week we reviewed a request, in writing, from Dr. Dempsey, asking permission for Lydia Flores to visit patients here in the hospital," Frank says.

"Lydia Flores is an RN trained in therapeutic touch—now taught in some nursing schools," I say. "She's also a recognized *curandera*, a healer in the Mexican folk tradition."

"I don't see any problem," the nurse says. "Nurses provide therapeutic touch when the patient asks for it. All the major faiths are allotted space in the hospital. Spiritual advisors are everywhere. Ms. Flores should be an asset."

"The problem," Glover says, "is that Lydia Flores neither works at this hospital nor is on our list of spiritual advisors. I object to her seeing patients on the premises. Dr. Dempsey's personal interests mar her judgment."

My head snaps around to Frank. Did he let on to Glover that I've been on probation?

"Everyone here knows Dr. Dempsey's my wife," Al says, "and that nobody is less in need of defending; but please bear with me. Dr. Glover has touched on three separate issues: one, the side effects of immunosuppressant drugs; two, the wisdom of sharing risk analysis and decision-making with patients; and three, our policy in allowing spiritual healing practices within the confines of this hospital. Let's remove Zoe as the target of our differing opinions."

"Well said, Dr. Clyde," Frank says. "Let's table these issues until we have time to look at them from the policy point of view." When Frank tables something it's usually gone for good. I have mixed feelings about Al defending me, but pleasure predominates. "One more thing. The internist from Australia will be here next week, funded in part by his hospital in Adelaide. He's expected to learn something, as well as help us out with staffing problems over the summer."

"Did you know Adelaide is Austin's sister city?" Cynthia asks no one in particular. Travis snorts out loud.

"Make our visitor welcome," Frank takes up from where he left off, "and make an effort to share your expertise with him. We're lucky to have him here, especially since Zoe and Al will both be gone next week, and Travis will be going to Mexico in a couple of weeks." Travis sets his chair back on all fours and salutes. Frank raises his immense head from his notes and looks around the table, catching each person's eye in turn. "Let's spare our guest any departmental in-fighting. Everyone can go on vacation this year knowing their position is covered." *Let's* is definitely the command form of the verb in Frank's mouth. Glover and I trade dirty looks.

"Y'all might look at the team dynamic we've got going here," Lerner says, his voice shaky. Nobody looks at him. He's older than dirt and goes unnoticed.

"Dr. Glover's stacked up some handouts here in front of me," Frank says, "for anyone who wants one." I raise my hand and he slides one down the table to me. Travis and Al also signal for copies. "I'll discuss with the chief of staff whether to add Lydia Flores to our list of spiritual advisors," he says, a worn-out joke meaning he'll make a unilateral decision. He glares around the table. "One last thing." Travis's eyes are turned to the ceiling, his hands folded in front of him. Al is standing. "You should have received an invitation to the spring party, to be held at the home of one of our most supportive board members. I hope to see you there. Do I hear a move to adjourn?" The motion's made and seconded. Everyone shouts "Aye" like we're getting out of school, then we head for the door.

Outside in the hall I hurry to catch up with Al, my heels thudding on the resilient tile, but give up pursuit when he starts up the stairs. Travis sails by with a wave while I go over to stand in front of the elevator with Frank.

"Don't take things so hard," Frank says with an assessing look. "We can't serve the sick while we're squabbling with each other."

"Still, that was dirty pool in there."

"I don't think so, Zoe," Frank says, stroking me with his velvet voice. "Dr. Glover's just covering his position, the same as we all do."

I start to protest, but am halted by Frank's right hand, palm out, long fingers upright and unwavering. "Look at the material. Make an appointment to meet with him in my office. You're in a public conversation with a colleague. Jeff Glover is not the enemy."

I relent. "I'll do that." The elevator stops in front of us for the second time. When Frank gets in, I peel off to take the stairs.

I run into Dr. Lerner, resting on the landing. "Why don't you take the elevator?" I ask. "Claustrophobia," he says with an apologetic downturn of his mouth. "But since we've met like this, may I have a word with you?"

I hesitate.

"Just one moment."

I'm trapped. I can hardly shove the poor old dear down the stairs. Without him on my side in the Percocet brush-up I might have fared worse than the year of purgatory.

"Tell me again about your research," he says.

"The complement system."

"Ah. If you wouldn't mind refreshing my memory on the complement?"

Maybe he really doesn't know. Medical schools didn't start teaching immune system functioning until the seventies, long after Lerner's time. "The complement's the part of the immune system ready to do business at birth; it doesn't need educating in the thymus and the bone marrow before recognizing pathogens."

He smiles and flaps his hand at me. "Go on."

"This inborn capacity to tell self from non-self at the cell level is set in motion by the right answers to a series of questions which culminate in a powerful cascade of proteins. Autoimmune disease involves mistaken identity, identifying the self as the other, as if it were some unknown pathogen to be fended off. My research stems from a question: *How do our own cells lose their identity papers? How can we forget who we are?*"

"My goodness," Lerner says. "Patients suffering from mental disorders are in the same quandary. We must never forget ourselves. An overactive defense system can make us miserable." I wait while he struggles with his thoughts. "But don't ever let your enemies make you choose between scientific and alternative medicine. They complement each other."

"What do you know about my enemies?"

He lifts his hands, palms up, and mimes juggling, a comical expression on his gnome-like face, while his eyes dart around at the imaginary balls. Without glasses, his cataracts are clearly visible. I reach out to touch him on his skinny biceps, as if I could palpate his concern. Around us, the wire-reinforced industrial windows marching up the outside wall of the stairwell make the whole space grim, more like a jail than a hospital. Lerner gives up juggling and bats his hand in the air in a gesture of bewilderment, like he's waving away a swarm of no-see-'ems.

"Never mind. I won't forget myself."

"No, of course not, of course. But make no mistake, addiction is a genuine form of malaise. Illness of any sort is nothing to be ashamed of."

I hold his gaze until he steps aside with a courtly gesture.

After making my escape I go to see Jordan Wilson. She's asleep, so I leave before my gaze wakes her up. I pull off the road on the way home to phone her mother about tomorrow's discharge. After holstering the phone I continue to sit in my car on the verge of the road, looking at nothing, until a fine rain begins to fall.

Chapter 2

First thing in the morning I hurry past the nurse's station with a nod and smile before stepping inside Jordan Wilson's room on Five West. She's propped up on the bed, her blond hair carefully brushed out against the pillow, a princess waiting for her prince to come.

"I'm sorry, Dr. Dempsey," she says, low and hoarse.

"What are you sorry for?" This girl could break your heart.

"For bothering the nurse. What can she do?"

"About what?"

"You starving me! I haven't had a morsel of real food since forever. You don't know what it's like!"

"So that's it." I sit down in the spare chair. "I'm sending you home to lie on your stomach in the privacy of your own patio and get some Texas sun on your bum."

"Go home, but still not eat," she says, measuring her words out dully.

"We need twenty more days avoiding the gut, monitored closely. I want you back on food as soon as feasible." I lean over to pinch her arm, checking for dehydration. She shakes me off. This girl has already fired her complete peds team, and won't even deal with the nutritionist except through me.

"Total nutrition, ha! Total nothing, that's what it is. Did you know fasting makes you psychotic?"

"Tell me the worst of it."

"It's like you're on a trip to nowhere. I dream about food, like I'm a prisoner. I never thought I'd get homicidal over a hamburger, but that poor nurse looked scared." She giggles, raking her fingers through her cloud of fair hair. "As if I'm a threat to anyone in my condition. *Me.* I'm in a state of suspended animation."

"You're not hallucinating, are you, Jordan?"

"Oh, I wish," she says with a foxy look. "At least that would relieve the boredom. Why can't we cut out the fistula, so I wouldn't have to put up with this awful pump?"

"That's still an option. The thing is, the fistula often shows up again after surgery. At the moment, your treatment shows good results."

"But how long until the next flare?" Her voice is so low I can barely hear.

"One step at a time. You're checking out of the hospital, and so am I." I stand up. "You knew that, didn't you?"

"Yeah. You're going on vacation." Her face brightens. "Where?"

"To the Davis Mountains for spring break. Back here in time for a gastro conference on the new Crohn's medication."

"Dr. Dempsey, I'm not going to get all worked up about new meds. I'm leaning more the other direction, to prayer and meditation. But go ahead and tell Mother. She's ready for the proverbial magic bullet."

"Your mother seems pretty tough to me," I say. "But I'm no expert on mother-daughter matters," I add when I see the look on her face.

"Now I'm eighteen, you work for me, anyway," she says. "Please don't discuss my case with my mother behind my back."

"We've never said anything outside your presence we wouldn't say in front of you." Her pale nostrils contract. "I'll heed your request," I interject before she gets started. "Now back to our goal here, getting you checked out of the hospital. You'll be coming in twice a week for the TPN outpatient care. What about giving the support group a try?"

"Maybe," she says, looking down at her hands, smiling. "What?"

"I've been surfing the internet," Jordan says in a conspiratorial tone, gesturing to the laptop computer on the tray table. "I'm learning about IBD from the Web. I've signed onto a digest, where you can talk back and forth. I've met some super people." She pauses a moment. "I forgive Daddy everything now he's brought me my computer."

"Wonderful." Her father has definitely been in the shadows; his work involves traveling. The same was true of my childhood—my father was always leaving home for his work, important work designing harbors all over the world. When my mother died and I went to live with my grandmother Anna, his trips back home dwindled until we lost touch altogether.

"So you're going to check out the IBD group that meets in the basement?"

"I'm not sure I'm ready to meet the whole group in the flesh. Doesn't it sound ghastly? A bunch of Crohnies in the same space?" She rolls her eyes to great effect, making me laugh. "How many toilets do they have down in the basement, anyway?"

"I can find out." I know already there aren't nearly enough.

"This guy Tommy Arbuckle. He started the basement group. Did you know that? Anyway, he comes to see me. Here. You would not believe him. He's hilarious. He's got ulcerative colitis—he just had surgery. But he's running around the halls, with all this apparatus still hooked up to him. He told me everything about his surgery—you'd think he was awake while they did it! Tommy says we're talking about the plumbing— why get all worked up?"

"I'm already enchanted with Tommy. But remember, colitis is not the same as Crohn's, even though they share certain factors. The colon's a tube, but the small intestine's not just a tube any more than a river's just a pipe; every inch has a job to do regulating the body's digestive, immune, and endocrine systems. Something like 70% of your immune cells originate in the gut . . ."

". . . my immune system's the origin of all my pain, not to mention the bleeding and diarrhea," Jordan says. "It unhinges me. Why can't we cut out the bad parts like Tommy did?"

"Surgery's a better option for colitis. We can't compare your case with his."

She shrugs her shoulder in a magnificent gesture of acceptance. "Tommy's a Buddhist. Can you imagine? He looks like a redneck. He says everything that matters resides either in your mind or in Big Mind. He's not totally consistent, come to think of it. He wants me to go on a special diet when I get out of here."

"I'll have to meet this guy."

"He fights with his doctor all the time. He calls her *Cynthia*. Truly, Tommy's had at least twenty doctors. He wants me to try the worm cure."

"The worm cure?"

"A far-out new treatment for what I've got. Some university hospital's come up with it."

"You're sure this isn't an urban legend?"

"No, it's real." She squirms around to sit up in bed. "Somebody noticed a third of the world's population still harbors all kinds of intestinal worms in their guts. In the developed countries we are worm-free." She beams at me. "What if our immune systems are geared up to fight worms, but there aren't any worms to fight?"

"The immune system attacks the intestine instead."

"Exactly. In the experiment, they feed people intestinal worms. Those in the study who ate worms had fewer flares!"

"That makes sense." I laugh. "I used to picture components of the immune system like Mafia soldiers. With no outside enemy in view, wars break out within the family. Anyway, we'll get your paperwork started for going home tomorrow."

Jordan doesn't say anything, but gathers her light back to herself.

"Your mom should be back any minute."

"Tell her to go home," she says, lying down and looking away. "We've run out of ways of entertaining each other."

"Hold on. I'm working on getting hospital privileges for

17

Lydia Flores, the *curandera* you were interested in seeing. But you could also ask her to come see you at home."

"Good. I'll tell my mother," the girl says, turning back. "It's killing me, the way I treated the nurse. Will you tell her I'm sorry?"

"It would mean more if you told her yourself. Now I must go."

Hesitating at the threshold, I turn back to see Jordan staring out the window into the darkening sky, where the rain has started back up. I duck out the door, return the chart to the nurses' station, and write the discharge orders, pondering on the new drug that had looked so promising in clinical trials. I can't forget how other drugs once hailed as cures ended up causing unexpected grief. I am more conservative than I used to be. This is not the time to introduce a new drug with no track record. Glover may disagree, even after chiding me publicly for Jordan's last drug reaction: surgeons see the worst gastro cases, and are often early adapters of new drugs in this field. Jordan Wilson has been missing out on the commotion of ordinary life, and now she's on the mend. I'm not going to let the clash of giant egos limit her chances for remission.

Chapter 3

I go to my office in a forgotten corner of the top floor of the old building. The tiny unused lab seems forlorn, and the plants on the black sink-top look pretty sorry, except for the mother-in-law's tongue. The place looked homier when Travis was using my lab for one of his pathology studies. Al used to join us here for lunch. Now Al uses his lunch hour to play squash at the U.T. courts with a lawyer who jogs over from the Capitol. My office has fallen into neglect along with the rest of my personal life. Sometimes I eat in the doctors' dining room, but mostly I exist on apples and granola. I settle down at my desk to apply myself to Glover's handout. Patients under my care, he claims, are now relapsing more quickly after leaving the hospital than they did at the beginning of my period in gastro. Five months ago the graph takes a dive, except for the one outstanding exception: Paul Lundy, sixty. With a gruesome past history of surgeries, he has been doing steadily better since I've been treating him. He's been pretty near symptom-free for the past eighteen months—longer than at any one time in the previous two decades. Thanks in part to the orthodoxy of an earlier time, and in part to the recalcitrance of the disease, Lundy's plumbing system has been severely compromised. Much of it is missing. His present good health, achieved with carefully calibrated doses of immunosuppresants, would seem miraculous to anyone who had a good look at his insides. Treatment, of course, can never be scientifically *proven* to be the cause of subsequent good health, which in this case may well be a testament to nature's fondness for over-engineering.

Next, I pick up the pile of film delivered to my office this morning and clip image after image onto the light board to peer at Jordan Wilson's intestines. It's not uncommon to see cutaneous expressions of disease in immunocompromised patients. We doctors are supposed to remain detached. Ha! Skin, perfect for its job—durable, flexible, loving and, in the end, terrifyingly fragile—is the largest organ of the body, our mask to the world, and the protection and expression of our being. Both internal and external manifestations of Jordan Wilson's fistula have been reduced. She's ready to go home. As for her having *almost died*, that's nonsense, and it was unprofessional of Glover to have made such a remark. We treated with a thoroughly tested drug to suppress an overactive immune system. Pancreatitis is a known risk—three to five per cent of those treated are susceptible. The pancreas is not an organ you want to fool with. As soon as the blood work indicated, we stopped treatment.

Glover has no grounds to fault me. I'd pointed out all the known risks to Jordan and her mother, including the chance of pancreatitis, which can prove irreversible. In other words, the patient can die from complications following treatment. Iatrogenic disease—unintended results from medical intervention—continues to soar. No treatment at all must always be considered a genuine option. But reciting possible side effects to the chronically ill is like reading off the Miranda agreement to a habitual criminal: We already know you're going to waive your rights and go for the plea bargain. Patients who repeatedly experience bad reactions are labeled drug-resistant and treated like naughty kids. Chronic disease makes special demands on doctors as well as on patients. Glover won't choose TPN over surgery because the healing process is far too slow. But none of this explains what's behind his attack.

Throwing the file on the desk, I stomp around the office. Shit. I pick up a dead violet and toss it in the sink, earthen pot and all, making a satisfying crash. How do we account for results in our battle against disease? War is the number-one metaphor used in medical school. Science proceeds by metaphor as surely as a poem, and the institution determines treatment strategy: we doctors are only tacticians. We always treat death as a surprise, just like the most primitive shamans. Dozens of variables could account for Glover's stats.

I clean up the dead violet and then sit down at the computer to retrieve the data Glover used to form his conclusions. I spend two hours searching, but I don't find what I'm looking for. Inexplicably, every path leads to a dead end. The computer freezes up, or asks for a password! I've never had these problems retrieving patient information. The clerical staff may be behind in entering all patient information on the computer, but it's not just recent case files that are missing. I am prevented from opening *anything* associated with any of Glover's patients, so turn up nothing. Without pausing to figure out why this is so, I come up with a way around the computer problem: patient files originally go to the morgue, where Travis reigns. I close down the machine and dig the phone out from under a pile of papers. But instead of calling Travis, I first call Merla.

"*Distraction Engineering,* Merla speaking," she answers, all perky. Merla has created her own little niche, marketing software and videos to the parents of privileged children.

"Merla, I've got to talk to you. I'm going out of my mind."

"What is it, sweetie? Are you fighting with Al again?"

I catch my lower lip in my teeth, annoyance flashing like sheet lightening all around me.

"Why does every damn problem in the world have to be a man problem?"

"You don't have to bite my head off—in my little corner of the universe it usually is. Since you're the one who called asking for help, you might try telling me what's the matter."

I loosen my hold on the phone and take a breath. "I'm sorry. It's not you. Something strange is going on here."

"Here where? At the hospital?"

"Yes, at the hospital, Merla, where else would I be this time of day? Oh, hell, I'm sorry, don't pay any attention to my mood. My patients aren't getting better."

"Correct me if I'm wrong, Zoe," Merla says slowly, grunting a little, "but aren't most of your patients people with chronic

21

illnesses? People who are going to stay sick for pretty much the rest of their lives?"

What other people call confrontation, Merla calls energy expressing itself. I pull myself together. "That's just it. Patients expect to get better faster, have fewer relapses, than if they were given no treatment at all." All I hear in response is rhythmic little grunts. "What are you doing, working-out?"

"Yeah, well, if you call flexing an eight-pound weight working out. Sorry, I'll stop. You were saying?"

"According to the numbers, my patients have been doing worse after they leave the hospital than they have in the past."

"Oh, that's a tough one. Isn't one of your doctor oaths to do nothing of no use?"

"Where did you hear that expression?"

"Don't know. Not from you?"

"Well, close. The first law of medicine is *primum non nocere:* first, do no harm."

"Isn't that the same thing? Never mind, back to your problem. Your patients aren't doing as well as expected. What's changed?"

"Good question. But since I'm dealing with real patients without the structure provided by clinical trials, there are too many variables for statistical analysis."

"You'll get to the bottom of it. Have you thought of consulting the *I Ching?*"

"Why do you do this to me, Merla? Why tell me to consult oracles before you've even listened to the parameters of the problem?"

"Better question: Why did you call me? You've got more doctors than prime time where you're at. If you have a medical query, ask them! Your cohorts in crime! If you wish to consult an oracle, get in touch!"

After she hangs up on me I hold on to the receiver until the electronic squeal comes on the line. Where else can I go for help? The queasy feeling in the pit of my stomach doesn't go away. From the outside, my life looks great. I've successfully diagnosed and treated many cases of recalcitrant IBD. I'm well matched in marriage and the mother of a beautiful child. Besides, I'm making a ton of money. Glover's observations may point out a temporary glitch, if not a trumped-up statistical anomaly. But in the practice of medicine, doubt carries a stigma.

Something's wrong when I treat Merla shabbily. I dial her right back, only to reach an answering machine. "OK, Merla, I give up," I say into the phone. "I believe in you, if nothing else. Cast a horoscope on me, on my patients, and on the hospital— whatever it takes. See if you can tell me why everything's going awry. I was born in Austin, June 1, 1962, at midnight. Thank you." I stop, feeling like an apostate to science, a candidate for a Carl Sagan re-education briefing. Too late to recant. I hang up and dial Lydia Flores.

"*Bueno!*" she shouts into my ear.

"Hello, Lydia...this is Zoe Dempsey."

"Oh, hello Dr. Dempsey. Sorry, I'm in a language warp."

"Call me Zoe. I've got some relatively good news for you."

"Now that's hedging your bets. Tell me."

"When your name came up at the staff meeting I sponsored your request to be placed on our list of spiritual healers. Dr. Frank Hawkins, our chief of staff, will have an answer soon."

"I'm very grateful to you. I'm eager to see your patient."

"I hope she calls you. The mother's an engineer. She may not be entirely behind Jordan seeing you."

"You're not totally convinced yourself, Doctor—Zoe!"

"It's hard for us left-brained scientific types to entertain a different way of knowing, Lydia." My jaw feels stiff.

"I'm sorry, you've been great . . ."

"It's hard for doctors to support the idea of patients choosing treatment. *We* went to medical school, after all." I laugh unconvincingly.

"A spiritual healing, what I do, fortifies her faith in connecting with her own vital energies," Lydia says in a level voice.

"Maybe you can help smooth out her immune system. Our problem is timing. Jordan goes home tomorrow, and I'm going

23

to the Davis Mountains for spring break. If Jordan doesn't call you directly, I'll get in touch when I get back."

"Will you do something for me while you're away?"

"As long as it's not too strenuous."

"No, of course. I need a plant, flowering in the mountains right now—root, blossom, leaf and boll. You won't have any trouble finding it. Can you bring it back?"

"Root and all?"

"A small chunk of the root will do."

"How will I know it when I find it?"

I drum my fingers on the desk soundlessly while Lydia describes the plant she wants. It grows tall, four or five feet, on the border between the shade from the hills and the sun in the meadows, sprouting yellow flowers with a strong lemony smell. She uses it externally, to brush away bad energy and revitalize the skin. Healers like to go on their own quest for the plants and herbs they need, she tells me, but she won't be in the mountains during this plant's brief flowering. She wants me to take over her quest. Her voice is warm and soothing. By the time the conversation's over I'm feeling unexpected pleasure that she trusts me. I'm happy to promise to look for the plant growing in the mountains on the border of light and shade.

Now I'm ready to call Travis and ask him for a favor.

Chapter 4

The day before we're supposed to leave the saturated green of Austin in a wet spring to embark on the long drive to West Texas, that mythic land known to the whole world from countless movies, Merla calls me back. She doesn't apologize for hanging up on me the last time we talked. Still full of cautionary advice, she tells me to watch out for bad weather and not to get mixed up in the ruckus going on in the mountains, where some people who want to create a sovereign Texas have been defying the sheriff. Since I never have time to read the papers, Merla fills me in. These separatists claim Texans never chose statehood, which was foisted on the citizens of the Republic of Texas by a resolution of the U.S. Congress—making all powers exerted by the present State of Texas illegitimate. Some of these folks settled in what they call their embassy just outside Fort Davis in the mountainous isolation of Jeff Davis County, a county of only two thousand people. The newcomers were tolerated for some time. The only excitement in the county concerned the upcoming centennial celebration until the separatists began filing liens on property, claiming they were acquired illegally. Land disputes in West Texas can turn ugly in a hurry. We'll be miles away from Fort Davis, I assure Merla, staying at Uncle Clayton's cabin. Nowhere near anybody else, since the cabin and the spit of land it sits on is in the middle of the large ranch where he worked most of his life.

After getting off the phone with Merla I hurry to look in on Frank, stepping across his threshold with a quick knock on the open door. He keeps his eyes on the paperwork in front of him longer than seems polite. By the time he looks up and gestures for me to sit down I'm getting agitated.

"Sorry to keep you waiting. The minutia of this office gets worse daily. It's all too easy to fall behind." He gets up and comes around the front of the desk and extends his hand. "Congratulations on your year's attendance at the 12-step meetings."

I struggle with my feelings as we shake hands. Since Frank gave me no choice about going to the meetings, he has more reason to be proud than I have.

"I won't trouble you more on this matter, Zoe. It seems to have turned out to be no more than a duty for you. Like my paperwork." He gestures towards the disorder on his desk.

"It seems to me like I was picked out for special treatment."

"And you can't imagine why, right?"

I don't reply. Everything I can imagine is demeaning to both of us. I'm afraid the bitterness in my throat will show in my voice.

Frank sighs and picks up a pencil from his desk, holding it end-to-end between his forefingers and staring at it like it was a puzzle to solve. "Strictly speaking, you're no more an addict than scores of doctors on the hospital staff. But with you . . . it mattered more." He drops the pencil with a clatter and looks at me with a face so fierce I pull back. "Drugs like Percocet separate the mind from the body, cutting off heartfelt participation in ordinary life. I thought the meetings might help you reach the same conclusion. But you're not going back."

"Well, no. I'm not in any danger of going back on the Percocet. Of course you're right, it's easy to get addicted to pain meds. We see it all the time. Chronic pain baffles us. I'm sorry if you're disappointed, but I fulfilled the obligation you required." I struggle to say something more profound, but fail. What was I thinking when I let Travis prescribe for me? The punishment could have been worse, I remind myself for the umpteenth time.

Frank sits back down behind his desk. "You're going on

vacation tomorrow?" I nod. "I hope you have a splendid time."
He reaches his hand awkwardly across the desk to shake my
hand once more. He's an enormous man, even sitting down, I
notice as I return his handshake.

"Thank you, we intend to. *I lift my eyes to the hills, whence
comes my salvation.*"

"Do you know the whole psalm?" he asks, shoving his chair
back, his face brightening.

"I don't know which one it is. Just that one line my mother
quoted."

"It's Psalm 121. The psalmist asks a question: Should I go
to the old gods of the hills, or to the one almighty God? The
speaker faces a choice between God and nature, the Creator
or his creation. The answer is unambiguous: '*My help cometh
from the Lord.*'"

"But surely, as doctors, we aren't asked to choose?"

Frank evades the question with a large gesture that reminds me of Dr. Lerner swatting at his no-see-'ems. We've all
got our own conflicts and accommodations.

We pull out of Austin after breakfast on Saturday in the
middle of a drenching rain, me and Al and Iris. My grandmother Anna stays behind this time. She spends most of her
days looking after us; she deserves some time to herself. We
get to stay at her brother Clayton's cabin while he's down on
the flat land, at a sheep ranch where he goes every spring.
When I was still a child I went from Austin to live with Anna
at Ft. Davis. By the time I was in high school I was known as
a brainiac. I latched on to the science teacher, hoping she could
show me the way. In the mountains, there's only one test: Can
you survive without unduly burdening others? People in the
Texas mountains have an ornery independence, like mountain
people everywhere. As a child I wanted desperately to be one
of them. I stayed long enough to be tolerated, because of Anna.
Slipping back to visit this place, unnoticed and undemanding,
keeps me sane.

The rain lightens up, but stays with us a good part of the

way driving west. I was looking forward to having some time with Iris, but she keeps her headphones on the whole time. Talk about addictions—Iris's pop music goes with her everywhere.

Al and I take turns driving. We munch on the road food we brought along so we won't have to stop. I drive the last leg of the trip, as I always do—thirty miles by back roads, through neighbors' gates with our own set of locks as well as their's. I am dead tired when we arrive at the cabin just after dusk. We unpack what we need for the night, come alive for a three-handed game of poker—Iris is just learning to play—and then all bunk down for the night.

I sleep without dreaming. In the morning I make an effort to go back to sleep after my usual wake-up hour. When I haul myself out of bed, the sun is out and Al and Iris already up. It's not often Iris beats me out of bed.

"The Davis Mountains are somewhere between twenty-four and fifty-eight million years old," Al's telling Iris, "the remains of a volcanic eruption. On that scale, a human lifetime does not register." He stops when he catches sight of me standing in the doorway between the cabin and the covered porch. Al always looks good in the morning, with his dark hair and intense blue eyes. He flashes a smile. Iris looks just like him—same sturdy build and serious face. She jumps off the railing she's been straddling.

"You don't have to move," I say. "You're too old to fall off anymore."

"That's OK," she says, flicking me a look.

"I'll make more coffee," Al says, brushing up against me as he goes by. I sink into the wicker chair he just left, as conscious of his touch as if I'd brushed up against a nettle.

Iris stands stork-legged in front of me in short shorts and shabby T-shirt. A string of knotted leather tied around her throat sets off her child-perfect skin, making her look heart-breakingly young—surely not her intent.

"I shouldn't have slept so long," I say. "The day's half gone. When I came up here with *my* mom I was a small child. The days seemed to last forever. I used to think it was this place.

28

Maybe it was just being a kid."

"It's this place," Iris says. "There's nothing to do."

"You had enough to do when you were little."

"I wish I'd known your mother," she says, catching me by surprise. She glances at me and then looks away quickly, bringing her gaze to her hands, which have begun a kind of intricate wave motion all on their own, etching something like the confluence of two streams in the still air. I can see why she and other girls her age find this new fad mesmerizing. "Didn't you say she drove a Cadillac?" Her hands fall to her sides.

"Yes. Mother could pull a two-horse trailer with her green Caddy. Everybody wasn't driving pickups back then."

"I'll go get your coffee," Iris says, and is gone, the wood porch squeaking under her bare feet and the screen door slamming behind her. I head down the steps and out into the wild to pee, keeping an eye out for snakes. Snakes like the same things we do—they are attracted to the cool shade and the promise of water.

"He was my man, but he done me wrong," I'm singing as I come back, locking eyes with Al, who stands at the doorway with two mugs of coffee. He comes out to set the mugs on the railing and hugs me, burrowing into the crook of my neck with a kiss. "You're tickling!" We've fallen out of the habit of touching each other.

Iris comes out of the cabin. "When are we going to get another dog?"

Al and I are standing hip to hip with our arms around each other. We're together on this. "Some day," I begin, "soon," he finishes. We look at each other with sly smiles.

"It doesn't mean we have to forget about Gus," Iris says.

"No, of course not, Iris," I say. Gus died about a year ago. I wonder if Iris came up with the idea of how we're grieving over the dog to explain what's gone wrong with us.

"If you're ready for a new dog, I am too. You can pick one out at the pound."

"Are you serious?" She sidles up next to me, linking arms.

29

Her ribs against my fingers feel as pliable as green twigs. Iris is fixing to start her periods any time now—none too soon from her point of view. Her peers are way ahead of her in this rite of passage.

"Get a puppy to bond to you," Al says.

"You guys decide what you want to do while I go shower," I say, letting go of Iris and turning into the cabin, "but if it's a puppy, don't ask me to be the one to tell Anna!"

"Grandma won't mind," Iris says.

"Not unless she's the one to end up taking care of it."

After my shower I walk back outside to the lip of the hill to gaze out over the unpeopled land. Out here the sky acts on me like a drug. I never get enough. I love this place, even the dirt. Iris and Al start looking around for a tarp to rig up a dew catcher while I get ready to go hunting for Lydia's plant, supposed to be blooming out there somewhere, putting a strong citrus fragrance into the air. Lydia told me she uses the flowers—stems, twigs, leaves, smell—for spiritual cleansings, or *limpias,* to sweep illness from the body. Hardly an orthodox form of treatment, but what harm can it do? She also told me *curanderas* spend three days fasting before gathering plants. I'm skipping that part, but not without qualms. In medicine it doesn't pay to leave out a single step.

When Al and Iris get busy rigging up the dew-catcher, I start out on my hunt, carrying a .30-30 out of habit, even though I'm after a plant. Once away from the cabin and out on the mountain, empty of all human habitation, I run carefully down a slope, holding the rifle across my chest with both hands like I was taught, following along the edge of a stand of mixed cedar and piñon pine that grows along the seam between the sloping sides of two mountains. I'm shrieking in pleasure, a sound taken up by two crows flying overhead.

Stunted oaks mixed with runty twisted junipers grow among outcroppings of red and black volcanic rock pushed into axe-blade or chimney shaped pinnacles, alternating with deep arroyos below the hold of the native grasses. Knowing my way around both peaks and valleys allows me to make good progress across country. Otherwise you wouldn't get far in a day.

The Chihuahuan desert, the country of no roads, lies at the base of the mountains, extending all the way south and west into Mexico. Every so often I stop to stare. The day, like the desert, stretches out at my feet forever. A black hawk, a kind we don't see around Austin, soars high and alone. I spend more time watching than walking. My first boyfriend, a born-again Christian, told me my love of nature was idolatrous. Possibly he was right. Maybe Frank was thinking the same thing when he was going on about the psalm. I'm not a kid anymore, and the hills are no longer animate with gods. But I love this spot of earth.

Large prickly-pear cactuses huddle in the lee of the mountain. I saunter along towards this familiar landmark before veering to make a sketch of a century plant in bloom. I must have a hundred drawings of this plant, but I hunker down to make another one. The trunk, topped with yellow flowers, towers at least fifteen feet from the thigh-high bulk of blue-green cactus forming the base. It looks more like a comical married couple than an individual.

On my way back I pass by a giant dagger yucca, a sacred spot where I once buried treasure. What if what I'm looking for is past flowering, and I can't see it among all the other small-leafed plants guarding against moisture loss? I end up back at the cabin, empty-handed except for the pocketful of tiny drawings.

Chapter 5

I ris rushes up to greet me. As soon as I've stowed my stuff she shows me around the elaborate fort she and Al have been working on—barracks, officers' quarters, camp kitchen, and guardhouse, all outlined with stones and branches. I admire and exclaim.

Iris beams back, sweaty and familiar. "Can I use a pillow-case for a flag?"

"Sure. Use one we brought with us."

I go in to shower quickly, saving water as I was taught to do. I notice I haven't given a thought to the hospital since we got here, and nudge this one right on by.

Iris has drawn a magic-marker lone star on a pillowcase by the time I'm back from my shower. Al builds a fire with wood we brought with us. After a supper of beans and franks Iris cajoles us into letting her sleep outside, hauling everything she might possibly need to her campsite, including a cot, flash-light, bottle of water, and radio. Al and I keep the fire going after Iris settles down. I'm sitting on a log close to the ground, Al on a stump a quarter-turn away.

"What's the matter, Zoe?" he asks.

"Why does something always have to be the matter?" I slide off my log onto the dirt, kneading the small of my back with my thumbs. I never did ask Al why he left the hospital that day of the staff meeting.

"Let me start over. I'm more interested in strategy, in *how* we can make things better, than in *why* things are like they are." He pauses. "How can I make you happy?"

"It's not your job to make me happy." I push myself to my feet, pick up a stick, and start poking around in the fire. "Or to take over mothering Iris."

"Whoa. Slow down," Al says, his voice laboring. "Isn't that what you needed from me while you were coming off the pain meds? To keep Iris occupied?" He gets down on his knees beside me. He starts working on the fire, methodically awakening the coals.

My mood covers me like blight. Everything I'd pushed out of my mind comes back. It takes me a while to answer. "Maybe I did need you to look after Iris. Forget what I said."

"No. I want to get a handle on what's bothering you." He gets up off his knees and squats down next to me, solidly balanced on his heels, his arms across his knees. He can stay like this indefinitely.

"More like what's tormenting me."

"The diagnosis sounds serious, but we do have treatment options, Zoe."

"Oh, Al, get real," I say, losing it.

"Me get real! You're the one playing some Hallmark-card version of yourself!"

"Good, Al," I laugh, glancing Iris's way. My laugh used to wake her. "That's good. You're usually not one for the metaphors. What other choice do I have but to play a part, with you supporting Frank's idea that I'm a drug abuser?"

"That's not fair. I didn't want to be roped into the intervention at all. I thought you needed somebody on your side."

"Besides Travis. He shared the hot seat with me." I jump up and move further from the fire.

"You have never once conceded you were addicted. Travis sure as hell will never admit he was out of line, writing you scrips. How could I help? You put me in a dilemma." Al stands up, silhouetted against the fire on the edge of darkness.

"It's everybody's fucking dilemma, Al." Alone together in the night, the stars shining down like friends, everything seems clear. "Official prosperity on the one hand, private terror on the other. Every solution accompanied by unacceptable side ef-

33

fects."

"God, Zoe, what's brought this on?"

"I'm sorry. I don't want to fight. I just want us to be able to talk to each other like we used to."

"You're the one who's not telling," Al says in a low whisper. He stops. I can hear his strangled breathing. A wave of anguish laps against me. "Try to get a handle on how strange that is," he finally gets out, "your keeping secrets from me."

My heart contracts in raw pain, the muscle closing tight as a fist before reluctantly cracking open for the next beat.

"No way!" I say. "There's nothing about me you don't know."

"You won't share your private standing ground," he persists.

My eyes drop away from him to the patch of ground between my boots, the fire-lit dirt, alive with shadows. I pick up a stick the fire kicked out to trace the lines flickering in the dirt. What kind of a treatment protocol can I devise for this marriage? My face heats up in the darkness. The fire is dying down to embers, but we don't make a move. We occupy the same darkness. I clutch myself to keep warm. "Nothing means more to me than medicine," I say at last. "Frank used that."

Now it's Al's turn to pick up a stick. He works intently on rekindling the fire, his back to me. He finally speaks, without turning to look at me. "Frank's doing his job. What's going on at the hospital is a separate issue from what's going on between you and me."

"Nothing's separate." My mind skitters to something looming on the edge of awareness, at the edge of the circle of light, a mental effort as physical as climbing one of the red rock formations on the mountain. I sit back down as close to the fire as I can bear.

"Did you get *anything* out of going to those meetings?" Al sits back down in the dirt next to me.

"I suppose. That's a big admission, one I refused to make when Frank grilled me. But it's a place where there's no taboo against telling the truth. Telling the truth changes things." I stare at the fire, wondering about the truth between me and Al. I shake my head and pick my words carefully. "How much truth is there in Glover's claims?"

"Glover's not on any quest for truth—he just wants his kingdom back."

"Every time I'm close to knowing what I'm looking for I run into a wall. Glover's a clue to what I don't want." I lose myself staring into the fire. Al settles down beside me. "If I'm looking for something, it stands to reason I've lost something."

"Tell me about the wall. Tell me what you think you've lost."

"It's like I've got a kink in my soul. If I could only press down hard enough on the sore spot, find words for the unspeakable, I could see what holds, what's true in all circumstances. But I can't do that. Something keeps stopping me. Like if I tell the truth, my life might get lost in the telling. Or the truth might get bent."

"I see what you mean. The uncertainty principle in action."

"Maybe I fear finding out that what I do doesn't *matter*. These days, any novice can use a computer program to diagnose and treat disease."

"You think my efforts matter more? As the gas man?"

"Maybe Frank was right. Maybe there's no path between my head and my heart."

"You used to let me love you. Before you got so remote. For some time I have felt deserted. "

Shaken by a back spasm reaching all the way up to my ears, I struggle to relax. "Let's not do this any more."

Al materializes beside me in front of the fire, standing on my own spot of earth, his arms around me, grasping me to him. My body's wound tight, but I don't push him off. He smells like wood smoke.

"Zoe. It's you I want. I miss you." He groans, a deep animal sound, touching my heart and stirring my womb. He tries to clamp it off, but the sound only changes register, cracking something in me. I start to shake. We stand holding on to each other, not speaking, his interior spaces gurgling against my belly, his cock beginning to stir faintly. Behind the roaring of my body I hear embers settling in the fire.

"I never want to love anyone else," Al whispers. "Please don't push me away. Tell me what you want from me."

He chokes on his words. We're molded together, clasping each other. I relax into his grip. I feel dizzy, like I'm leaning over a cliff. It feels sort of good, sort of scary.

"I'm weary, Al. I need more time with Iris . . ." I trail off, pushing myself free. "If Anna didn't live with us, we'd never manage."

We sit back down on the dirt. Al takes hold of my hand. My back squeaks with pain, my symptom of unfathomable grief, the trigger-event for all the drug misery, and all because of a moment's hubris, a stupid maneuver off a diving board. I take my hand back and stretch forward, concentrating on my spine between L2 and L4, willing the pain away. My hair, heavy and coarse and dark, hangs in the dirt, hiding my face from Al. He moves closer. We put our arms around each other at the same moment.

"You sure smell good," I tell him, my nose in his armpit.

"Let's go get in bed. I'll make you feel even gooder." He starts to nuzzle my arm. The promise of pleasure heats up parts of my body I thought had deserted me for good.

"Are we going to let Iris sleep out all night?" I'm not sure I want Al to know I'm becoming aroused.

"Let's go in. I'll check on her later."

"OK," I say. We used to be able to just say "let's fuck," but it's been too long for that. We get busy putting out the fire. When every last ember has been beat to ash and sand poured over the whole area, we stand craning our necks up at the night sky, brilliant with stars. A faint smear of light shows to the west. "What's that light from?" I ask.

"It's Zodiacal light. Leftover light from the sun scatters off the dust in the same plane as the solar system," Al says, his hand drifting to my thigh, the thrum of his energy heating a path to my crotch. "You only see it here in the Davis Mountains."

"I like that. Leftover light."

"The moon won't show up until after midnight tonight." He inclines his head to kiss me on the side of my mouth. My eyes drift shut. I concentrate on the sliver of my lip brought into awareness. Kisses no more substantial than hot breath pepper my cheek. His lips singe the creases of my closed lids. He whispers something in my ear in a voice too soft to decipher. I turn my mouth to him greedily. Instead of coming back to my lips, he kisses my neck where it curves into my shoulder and drops his hand as light as can be on my breast, making my nipples ache. I push against his hand. It seems like months and months have gone by since whatever's been keeping us apart has so kindly stepped aside to let us touch each other. I'd begun to wonder if Al had found someone else. Now the internal barricade set up against him comes tumbling down, collapsing with a stentorian groan I'm not sure is coming from me.

Incapable of holding myself upright a minute longer, I begin to sink to the ground, trying to pull Al along with me. He gets up on his knees and puts his hands under my knees to pick me up, making me laugh. "That's OK, Rhett Butler," I say, my face in his neck, smothering a laugh, "I can walk." Letting loose of me, Al stands up and grabs my hand to pull me up. I lean against him while we kiss some more. We let go of each other and I walk ahead of him to the cabin, leaving Iris to sleep alone in her sanctuary.

Chapter 6

Once inside the cabin I sit on the edge of the bed, limp as a tired child. Al begins to undress me, struggling to pull my T-shirt over my head. I offer no help. Once my shirt's off he strips off his own, then scoots me back on the bed so he can perch on top of me, kissing me with enthusiasm. I pull back, afraid to be so exposed. He rears up on his knees, straddling my hips. Even my body's wild need for this man, a yearning I give up trying to battle, can't entirely mask my fear.

"Can you see me, Al? You used to look at me and really see me. I want that back."

He drops back with his elbows propped on the bed, his body hovering over mine. He touches his forehead to mine, third eye to third eye.

"I see you, Zoe," he says, rearing back to speak. "I don't know what hurts you so. I see you grappling with it. I would do anything to make you feel how much I love you."

He starts kissing me again, his eyes open and glinting from under the shadow of his dark brows. He kisses me and watches me, like he's conducting an experiment. He drops a little kiss, a brush of his lips on my temple, while all the time peering at me. I stare straight ahead, my eyes losing focus.

"Is this what you want?" he asks, and asks again with every breath and touch, dropping tiny kisses over my entire face, warm rain after drought, missing my lips, kissing my neck down to my starchy, functional bra, sliding his tongue along the border between skin and cloth until I'm squirming in pleasure, starting to laugh, wanting him to hurry, beginning to moan out loud. He will not hurry. I arch my back, and he rears back to sit on his haunches, reaching beneath me to undo my bra. I'm making small urgent sounds but he goes no faster.

Al drops his lips to my sternum and kisses me while still grappling with the fastener of my bra. My sternum! Never before this moment an erotic spot. I struggle to turn over to give him a better shot at undoing my bra, but he clamps me between his legs and won't let me turn, so I switch tactics and rear up to take his head in my hands, trying to draw him down to kiss me, but he keeps working on getting the bra unhooked. When he does he throws it across the room and sinks back down on me to kiss me like I've been wanting him to. I can feel his erection hot against my jeans. So many layers of stuff still lie between us. I try to reach my hand down between his skin and his jeans, but he traps my hand with his abdominal muscles.

"Why are you so mean?" I pant, trying to win back my hand.

"How can you say that, Zoe, when I've been waiting for you, you don't know how long," he says, leaning away from me to look at me, his own face in shadow.

I reach up to undo the snap on the top of his jeans. He hops off me and struggles to get out of them, standing on the floor beside the bed. Still on my back on the bed, I watch him, holding my breath. He springs on top of me, turning and peeling my jeans over from the waist. I lift my butt up to help but the legs get stuck, so he gives up and pulls my cotton panties down and sinks his face into my crotch. His warm breath strikes me like a hurricane coming up from the Gulf, the sensation beyond what I can bear with my limbs constricted. I scramble to a sitting position, almost frantic.

"Wait. Wait," I say, "let me get my jeans off."

Al rolls off the bed and kisses my foot, then begins to tug my jeans off inch-by-inch, holding on to the cuffs. When I'm finally naked he leaps back up next to me, throwing himself full length on the bed on his back. His cock gleams in the moonlight. I bend my face down until I am very near but don't touch, just breathe, watching his cock bounce off the stretched drum of his belly. I shiver.

"What are you doing down there, lady?" Al asks in a comic head-of-the-department, found you padding your expense-account voice.

I look up to his face. "What I'm doing, sir, is torturing you. Payback. How's it feel?"

"Hard to tell. Could be ecstasy," he sings, bounding over and rolling me on my back.

How is it we connect our spirits by coupling our bodies? I've been waiting so long to make love. Even before the transubstantiation from flesh into spirit is complete, I'm wishing we were still outside, still on our way to that moment when we discover what we've known all along: we're not separate, after all.

We lie on our backs, my head propped up on Al's arm, fused together, sticky and happy. Al nuzzles my face with his. I touch his cheek, my eyes shut, intensely connected with the sensations of my body slowly lapping the boundaries of consciousness, listening in wonder as Al murmurs to me how all will be well. I lie awake long after he falls asleep. Maybe it's not too late for a baby. Maybe Al's right, maybe all will be well. All manner of things.

I wake to find myself ensnared with Al in a nest of sheets. After disentangling ourselves, I drop my nightie over my head, push my feet into my sandals, and tiptoe out into the night, stopping repeatedly to look up into the vault of night sky. Still no moon, but the stars are close enough to touch. Once beyond the compass of the cabin and Iris's campsite in the pungent night, I squat down to pee. I stand in the dark when I'm finished, imagining one of the sperm voyagers connecting with the ovum. The female gamete, the oocyte, must develop and be liberated—a lovely idea—before the mature ovum can be penetrated by the spermatozoa, which has gone through a similar (but somewhat simpler) process. The two together then form the zygote, the beginning of another creature. I laugh in glee. Before the pain pills, Al and I were hoping for another child. Even Iris got wind of it. Now she hovers on the far edge of childhood, eager to catch up with her peers in the race to grow up, while I get closer to the age when women have to seek out fertility doctors if they want to conceive. Anna's too old to help take care of another baby. But still, how grand it would be.

I lie down on the earth. For a moment I feel giddy, the earth rolling under me like a big animal getting more comfortable under my weight. I search the sky for a familiar constellation, one I can pin down with a name to keep me from floating off into nowhere. I look into the Milky Way, stars in laughable profusion and startling clarity, countless stars distinct from each other with googols more behind and beyond. Exactly like spilled milk, fresh and flowing, only one of all the thousands of other galaxies in space. Barely shifting my head, I can see Andromeda, not just another stout yellow star but a whole different galaxy. I feel I am being pulled up into the sky, like taffy stuck to the ground in one spot, then stretched and released, again and again, by some giant candy-maker in the sky.

A tentative wash of moonlight appears on the face of the mountain to the west. A moment later the crescent moon gains the peak of the mountain behind the cabin, teetering on the brink for a moment before floating free. Maybe the pain and craziness is behind us and we can be a family again.

Al's awake when I come back. I sit down on the bed next to him, peering at his face in the moonlight.

"You're cold," he says, reaching up for me.

"Not what you thought a little while ago." I let myself be gathered in, and tumble down until my face lies in the crook of his neck, breathing in his scent. Better than painkillers. I nibble at his neck. "Do you still think I'm cold?"

"I've been afraid of intruding on you. Of doing anything you'd interpret as forcing myself on you," he says, flopping over on me and pinning me down.

"You might say that's how come we're still married," I say,

pushing against his chest.

Al rolls off me to prop himself up on his elbow, his face touched by moonlight. He traces the outline of my mouth with his finger. I grab his hand and kiss it. When I let go he rests his head, warm and heavy, on the strong flat of my thigh, but sits up again after a few minutes and kisses me on the forehead.

"I'd better go tell Iris to come back in. She'll get damp if she stays out there all night."

I nod, turning my face up to him. He kisses me one more time full on the mouth, and then rests against me for a moment before separating. I resist the temptation to grab him and pull him back to bed. Instead I don't take my eyes away from him as he gets up to find his pants. He pulls them on, then turns and lifts the latch on the bedroom door. For a moment, silhouetted against the moonlight spilling through the porch all the way into the tiny living room, he turns back towards me, lying in the darkness. Then he goes outside to see about Iris. I don't hear him come back.

Chapter 7

In the morning, Al and Iris serve up kippers, black beans, tortillas and hot sauce. We eat from tin plates out on the screen porch. I'm still in my nightgown, my bare feet winter pale.

After breakfast, I go out on the mountain again, determined to range further than I did yesterday. The plant I'm looking for is covered with fragrant yellow flowers and grows to five feet at this time of year. How can I possibly miss it?

By afternoon the heat buckles down and increases pitch. Still empty-handed, I come back for food, rest, and company. Three low flying black helicopters ruin our picnic with their unbelievable roar. They circle again and again in ever smaller circles. Iris, excited, waves to the pilot; he's so close we see him wave back. Al and I look at each other, disturbed, and then give up and go back into the house. I follow him inside while he turns on the radio, tuning in a station that plays country music, thin and tinny like it's coming all the way from El Paso or from decades back in time. Finally the copters are gone and we turn off the radio.

I go back on my plant hunt, lugging the rifle with me. Uncle Clayton still believes I might run into a mountain lion up here, and makes carrying the .30-30 rifle he gave me, the one with the bluing worn off the barrel from all the years he carried it in his saddle holster, a condition for traveling alone. This is his place. He worked his whole life for the rancher who owned a good part of these hills south of town. When the rancher died not many years back, Clayton inherited the cabin he'd occupied as a tenant and the morsel of land where it sits. I carry the rifle like I was taught to do, but I never kill anything, not even a snake. Spotting a snake makes my heart beat wildly, but I deem it a privilege to share the earth with them.

I go slowly, stopping to sketch plants to compare with those in my Trans-Pecos field guide when I have a chance. I've been ranging these hills since I was a small child, watching out for the critters and admiring the birds, navigating by familiar features of the landscape. Close up I see piles of rock I got to know with a child's imagination. From a distance I spot the larger signs of civilization: the McDonald Observatory, very humble for its monumental task, and just a small turn of the head away in the middle distance, the white huddle of Indian Lodge, a 1930s CCC project and now part of Texas Parks and Wildlife. I wonder what the secessionists have in mind for it in their new Republic.

Before I lose the light I start back to the cabin without having found what I came for, feeling more alone than ever, hiking without a dog. Iris is right, we need a dog. Not a puppy, but a grown dog. At dusk the light shifts to an aching purple, a psychedelic bruise. The smells leach out of the earth and scrub to hang in the air like a presence. I fall out of myself and into nature, into this place, with no past and no future, just the mountain shade and the Texas sun, still hot and close even at this time of day. Rather than growing dark, it's like the light is getting denser, drawing my eye to the tremendous dome of sky, punctuated with clouds close enough to grab. I slow up, sniffing the air. Snake smell reaches a primitive receptor in the brain, raising the hackles, no matter how glad you might be to share the earth with them. But that's not it. Two steps further I recoil from the ripe smell of another person.

Pitching my ears for sound, I pivot around to walk with the wind, away from the smell. If whoever it is of the pungent odor doesn't know I'm aware of him, he won't have to declare himself. Too late. A man rears up on the uphill horizon, as big as a bear against the sky, his head uncovered, his arms wide against the setting sun, his hands empty. Heart pounding, I swivel my neck around to keep my eye on him while the rest of me keeps on heading downhill at a deliberate pace.

"Howdy, ma'am. I didn't mean to startle you," he calls out, a forlorn sound to his voice.

I plant my feet and turn back to him.

"Can I trouble you for some help?" he asks.

I dig in my heels. He's no more than twenty feet away from me in the gloom. Scared. I can hear it in his voice.

"I don't believe I know you," I say, drawing a breath, annoyed with his plea.

"Not likely you would."

He's sure to have been watching me longer than I've been aware of him. "Who're you visiting?" My voice comes out querulous.

"Well, I was over with some folks just outside of town," the man says. He sounds sorrowful. His big face is half obscured by a soft dark beard.

"I'm from over yonder," I say with a vague nod towards the cabin. The West Texas accent coming out of my mouth comforts me like a shot of whiskey.

He drops down to his haunches—a big man, used to being outdoors. He gestures to my gun: "You out hunting?"

"Just hunting for a native plant, something like a medicinal herb. It has a strong citrus smell, like limes or lemons." I stretch out my words while my mind speeds ahead. "You see any?" I'm breathing fast. Blowing smoke, really, while I recall the black helicopters hovering overhead. No doubt I am looking right at the man they were hunting for. "Run across anything smells like lemons?"

"Not since leaving California," the man says in a singsong. He stands upright and takes a step downhill towards me.

"Hold it!" I say, tracking him with the barrel of the rifle, slipping off the safety. He stops at once, teetering a little for balance. I don't feel afraid, just cold and unmoved. "Tell me what it is you want. Maybe I can help you."

The man exhales loudly. Moment by moment more light

leaches from the air. I'm beginning to hear more acutely than I can see. The stranger sounds as if he's out of shape.

"I guess you're not too crazy about talking to me this evening," he says. Then he laughs like he's just heard something really funny. "I understand that."

"My husband's waiting for me back at the campsite. What do you need?"

"I need water and some good directions."

"I can fix you up." I pat the water bottle hanging from my belt in its nylon sleeve. Again he takes a step towards me. "Wait, Mister." Again he stops, again I play the barrel of the gun at him, my knuckles steadying its weight and balance against my hipbone.

"Michael. Call me Michael," he says with the sound of a man calming a skittish horse.

"OK, Mike, but please stay put."

"Not Mike. Michael. Like the Archangel."

"Fine, Michael. You stay put and let me come to you. Maybe sit back down so we can visit more comfortably."

"That'll work. I thank you." He sits all the way down on the dirt, all at once, his legs sprawled out in front of him like a little kid.

"You're welcome to the water." I unhitch the bottle from my belt with my left hand and toss it to him. He catches it, twists off the top, takes a couple of swallows, and then recaps the bottle in a precise way, like a mechanic torquing down a bolt.

"Do you belong with the secessionists causing all the commotion over by Fort Davis?" I ask him like I'm just shooting the breeze, but my heart is racing.

"The people over at the compound don't call themselves secessionists."

"Well, whatever they call themselves, do you stay out there?"

"Used to," he grunts. "Not for long, and not anymore. Now I don't belong anywhere."

"Why is that?"

"Now there's a question I have given a great deal of thought to." He stops. I don't rush him. He still sits in the dirt. "You ever hear of Utopia?"

"Yes. It's an idea of the perfectibility of humanity."

"I think of it as a place. At least the possibility of a place where people can be free. Not interfere with each other. What Texas used to stand for, but now it don't."

"Human beings being what they are, perfection's quite likely nowhere to be found." My mind's busy on several tracks. The man's obviously at a breaking point, in need of help. "But it's the treasure we keep hunting for."

"I hear you. I came to Texas to satisfy myself there was no such perfect place this side of the hereafter. Do you mind if I stand up?"

"No. You go right ahead." I take a step back. He is unable to get himself up without turning over on all fours and getting some help from the hill.

"You won't make it far on foot. Not in these mountains, on your own."

"I appreciate that." He peers intently across the short distance between us.

"Maybe we need the idea of Utopia," I say across the distance, "even when no particular place pans out."

He laughs a long guttural laugh. "I used to think so. But I was a fool."

"There's more than one kind of foolishness. You might think of going on back to town," I offer without conviction.

"I've made up my mind to walk away from here. I'm in no mood to go back," he says, turning slowly around, his arms spinning wide, the fool on the hill.

"What happened?"

He shakes his head back and forth, stopping his manic spin. "At first I thought I'd found people who stood for something. Turned out I was wrong. So I walked away."

"Walking away could be misinterpreted," I say. "It might look like running."

"No matter. I've suffered bitter disappointments."

"I know just what you mean," I reply, surprising myself with the vehemence of my assent.

"Maybe you'd better be careful about going around helping people yourself." He's lifting his bearded chin in my direction.

The moment's charged with a lumpy energy, like the feel in the air foretelling a tornado.

I take another step back, and hold my gun with both hands. He laughs. "I had a hankering to help those folks back there. I was ready to stand by them." His voice has the keening sound of a hurt dog. The sound grabs at my heart. But not for a minute do I forget that hurt animals are dangerous.

"I told them I'd help them," he goes on in a thin thread of a voice. "Then they do something beyond foolish. No point to it. No sooner have they done it, they back down!"

"I haven't been paying attention to the doings in Fort Davis," I say.

"I told them not to do what they did. They said they would never back down on their principles, every one of 'em based on using the law. But they scuppered their principles. Nothing for it but for me to walk away." He shakes his head back and forth. He looks older than I first thought. Past his prime.

On the verge of asking him to come back to the cabin with me, I bite it off. He's heading into trouble. "I'm surprised you made it this far, to tell you the truth."

"How far have I come?"

"About twenty miles. Where are you trying to get to?"

"I've got a brother up north." He takes a sideways step, staggering.

"Did you hurt yourself?"

"I took a tumble earlier," he says. He looks around wildly as if he's forgotten something important.

"Let me see," I say, taking a step towards him. He backs away from me and I stop.

"I've got to be going. That's what I'm doing, keeping on going. Can you tell me which way to head out of here, staying off the roads?"

"Van Horn's on the way north, ninety-five miles or so." He obviously can't show up in any of the tiny towns in the county.

"But you're in no shape to travel there on foot, with the mountains between here and there. Mexico's seventy miles west." Moving back away from him some, I pull out the scrip pad and a stub of pencil from my pocket. Squatting down with the rifle across my knees, I hold the paper against the wood stock to draw a map.

"Look at what you're up against. Jeff Davis County marks the northern limit of the Big Bend region. Not many people, but not much cover, either. Just mountains and gullies and desert. Some springs here in the mountains, but you need to know where to find them. See here? The westernmost tip of the county touches Mexico. You have no business traveling even that far on foot." I look up. The man hasn't budged. I beckon him to come closer. "Here's the Rio Grande; Mexico; and the Pecos River over here. We're here." I turn the emerging map upside down. He squints at it in the fading light.

I draw a map of the immediate vicinity, tracing in pencil my mental image of the draw, Elbow Creek, the major ring of roads, and Limpia Creek to the east, identifying them as I go along. I make a dotted line along a possible route out of the immediate area, beginning just to the west of us before angling north towards El Paso.

"The dotted line follows the original San Antonio-El Paso Road—long abandoned. Not hard to make out in the daylight, or even in moonlight. Once you're on it you can see a trace, like a shadow.

"We're between the Baldy and the Blue mountains, at the base of Mt. Livermore, twenty-some miles from Fort Davis. McDonald Observatory's over there," I say, pointing. "You can see it from here if you're not behind a peak. Sawtooth Mountain's south of us," I go on like a tour guide. I can hear his breath, rasping. He smells rank. "Northwest on the old road you eventually come to El Paso, but that's two hundred miles away. I guess I don't need to point out how far that is to go on one bottle of water."

"I hear you. I've traveled by night before," he says, looking around. "I've been a soldier." He sputters a laugh, and then keeps on laughing, picking up the tempo, like being a soldier is the funniest thing you could imagine.

Maybe he's right. Nothing funnier than this unmoored solitary having been a soldier, a citizen protector. "You doing OK?" I ask. Stupid question. We're both playing the fool here.

"Yeah, fine," he says, cutting off the laugh abruptly. "The terrain's unfamiliar; lucky to run into a friendly."

"Evenings get chilly, but in the springtime in Texas you're not likely to suffer from hypothermia if you stay dry. It's still not too late to walk back into town." I take a deep breath. "If you like, I'll go with you."

"That's mighty kind of you, ma'am. But I don't think that will be necessary. Things get pretty simple once you've made up your mind. I've made up my mind."

I stay quiet, waiting to see if he's going to tell me more, afraid to hear any more from this man, whether lies or truth. I wait without hope.

"The only homestead light you'll see for miles will be ours," I say at length, when neither of us has made a move for some time. "This is all ranch land. I could show you where to find more than one spring around here . . . "

"I'd only need that, ma'am, if I was thinking about staying."

I'm within arm's length of him, holding the gun in my right hand, proffering the map with my left. "Give it up." The stranger reaches out gingerly for the map, as afraid of me as I am of him, but his fingers brush mine. He takes the map and fumbles it into his shirt pocket. "Nothing more for me to give up." He waves and starts walking away, painfully slowly, with a decided hitch in his gate. After a few steps he turns around and faces me, his shoulders slumped. "Do you think I placed too much faith in Utopia?"

"That I can't say." I hesitate, searching for a way to haul him back across a border he's already crossed. It will be dark soon. "Don't be a fool. I can take you back to town." He turns and goes with a wave of his arm, leaving me with the image of a grown man caught in childlike bewilderment in the face of overwhelming events.

Chapter 8

I whirl around and start running back to the cabin, adrenaline pumping, carving a path through the dark, leaping over bushes and swerving to avoid dark clumps of cactus until I plow into a bush, filling the night air with the odor of lemons on impact. Between urgency and exultation, my breath ragged, I rip at the plant with my left hand, stripping off flowers and pulling stems from roots in my haste, until I stuff the whole mass into the front of my shirt before moving on. By the time I reach the edge of the light spilling out on the cabin porch I'm winded, with a painful stitch in my side. Standing alone in the dark, I press my fingers under my ribs to stymie the pain and try to catch my breath. My lower back doesn't hurt at all.

Iris hurries down the steps and runs out to me.

"Where were you? What took you so long?"

Before unburdening myself of the plant I place the gun on top of the car and pull Iris to me, cupping my hand along the curve of her skull.

"Mom! You're a mess!" Iris says, stepping back.

I drag the plant in a bunch from my shirt and drop it on the ground at our feet, releasing the lemon scent that catches in my throat like a memory.

"You found what you were looking for!" Iris leans over and grabs a handful of the wild plant I scored. "Wow, Mom, that's great."

"More like it found me. Now you go find your dad." I open

the back door of the Suburban and shove handfuls of plant under the back seat.

I'm stowing the gun in the rack over the front visors when Al comes out, carrying a flashlight.

"Am I glad you're back; we were worried."

I turn around and take hold of him. He squeezes me against him with one arm.

"You're trembling, Zoe. What's the matter?"

"I met up with a man out there on the mountain. Someone I don't know." Leaning on Al feels mighty fine.

"You don't live around here anymore. You can't expect to know everybody," Al says.

I straighten up and let go of him. "Wait until you hear the story. But I'm all itchy; I've got to shower."

Stepping out of the rusty shower stall, I catch the sound of the radio news. I towel off quickly and pull on fresh jeans, all the while straining to hear. Standing on what used to be the back porch, I open the door in the weathered wood wall. Somebody fiddles with the tuning. The local DJ comes on loud and clear, reporting with unfaked excitement: *At this moment a couple dozen people from the Texas Separatists, holed-up in their embassy in the Davis Mountain Resort, are engaged in a stand-off with the sheriff and his deputies. The hostages, whose names have not yet been released, have been returned to their families. Those responsible for the kidnapping of local citizens have refused to surrender to the sheriff. Representatives from Alcohol Tobacco and Firearms have been required to wait at the barricades set up by the sheriff, along with members of the press and public. A mounting number of Texas Rangers and other local law enforcement personnel are on hand to assist the sheriff.*

My pulse quickens in response to the news. The radio sputters into static while I comb out my hair in front of the distorted mirror. Imagine the guys from ATF being forced to cool their heels. What the separatists call their embassy, and locals call the compound, occupies a few acres of land with a house and a trailer in the Resort, a land development cut out of the surrounding ranches. Not much of a resort, but just about the only place in the county newcomers can buy a small parcel of land. Uncle Clayton told me the sheriff let them folks be up until they started driving around with their homemade license plates and trying to swindle local citizens with bogus property claims. Nobody knew why the sheriff kept putting off serving a warrant he already had all written up—maybe so's not to stir things up. Back in Austin the Texas AG has been talking to the press, just itching for an excuse to clamp down on these folks. Sure sounds like he's got what he wanted.

"Did you hear that?" Iris asks the minute I come out of the bathroom, her voice high and excited. I nod.

"Why don't we go stay at the *Paisano* Hotel in Marfa," Al suggests, standing behind Iris with his hands on her shoulders.

"Are you serious? If we pack up and leave, we may as well go all the way home."

"This trip is for you, Zoe. We'll do whatever you want."

"No, Al, not just what I want. Tell me what you want."

"I sure don't want this kind of excitement. What about the man you met in the mountains? What did he want?"

"He asked me for a map. He was exhausted."

"He's *got* to be one of those people from the compound, on the run from the sheriff," Al says, slapping his forehead with the flat of his hand. "And I said you couldn't expect to know everybody in the county! Those helicopters—that's who they must've been looking for. Who did he say he was?"

"Michael. Like the Archangel."

"What's that supposed to mean?"

"Could be he's just colorful. Or maybe he's bordering on dementia. How do I know?"

"What's the matter, Pop? Are you mad at Mom?" Iris asks, coming in from the porch.

Al switches on the overhead light. "I'm not mad at your mom, sweetie," he says, trying to smile. He looks back at me. "Why don't we go home? Pack up and go back to Austin?"

I hesitate. How can I let Al know how drawn I was to the

man's plight? I link arms with Iris. "Come on, then. We'll stuff everything into the duffels and *bolsas.*"

"You said we could stop in Menard and see Uncle Clayton on the way home," Iris objects, pulling her arm from mine, "and we were going to go see Ft. McKavett."

"Fort McKavett's not nearly as grand as Fort Davis, pumpkin," Al says, flinging clothes into plastic carryalls. "You won't be missing a thing."

Iris and I stand eyeing each other. In the overhead light even she looks ghastly.

"I met a stranger out on the mountain when I was looking for my plant," I tell her.

"So?" Iris can pack a lot of meaning into one word. I raise my hand to my nose to see if I can still smell the lemon after my shower. Maybe.

"He doesn't have any business being out there. That worries your dad."

"Michael was the Prince of Angels," Al says, coming back with his arms full of bedding. "Maybe he's come back to fulfill the prophecy and do battle with Satan."

"Oh Pop, be serious," Iris giggles.

"This Michael was about to walk right away from here," I say, "not do battle with anybody." A pang of regret for not bringing him back with me churns my gut.

"This stranger, Iris, may be somebody the sheriff wants to talk to," Al goes on in an insanely rational voice. "Sorry things don't always work out the way we want them to."

"We'll get home tonight," I chime in, falsely cheerful, "and do something fun tomorrow. I promise. Now let's pack up."

Iris gets a canny look on her face. "Can I spend tomorrow with Amanda? She should be back home."

"OK with me," Al says, glancing at me for confirmation.

"Can I sleep over?"

"Give it a rest, Iris," Al says with uncharacteristic vehemence. Iris jumps visibly, but can't hide a sly little smile.

"I'll turn off the propane tank," I say, going back outside. Before long we're in the Suburban, heading into the night.

Chapter 9

We bump onto the pavement of State Highway 166, the loop around the town of Fort Davis, retracing our steps from three days ago. We haven't gone far when we run into lights and commotion—it looks like a major wreck, maybe one of the many eighteen-wheelers traveling too fast along this narrow road. A hundred yards down the road we're stopped by a dilapidated barricade, the yellow completely faded, with only the black stripes visible. I jump out of the car, hollering to Iris to stay put. I'm momentarily confused by the melee of flashing lights, cars, trucks, trailers, horses, and dogs. Al comes around from the other side of the car and touches my shoulder. The whole scene begins to look more like a carnival or rodeo than a wreck. A line of cars and trucks going nowhere stretches out on the other side of the road with lights on and motors running. Some people are out milling around on foot. We seem to be the only car heading this direction on the way to Highway 17, the road traveling southwest to Marfa.

A Texas Ranger strides up to us, dapper in his Stetson. Iris hangs out the window, eyes glittering. The Ranger, hardly more than a kid himself, asks politely who we are and where we've come from. Before I can reply his walkie-talkie squawks. He pulls it from its holster and answers. It sounds like he's talking to somebody at another roadblock. He switches off the radio and hollers to three cowboys in a huddle near a horse trailer, loaded with dogs, all making a hell of a racket. They obviously

55

can't hear him.

A bulky guy wearing a county sheriff's uniform strolls our way. "Zoe?" he calls above the din. The knot in my stomach eases up. "You can go on back to your posse. I know these folks," he tells the Ranger, who nods importantly and strides away.

"What's all the excitement, Gilberto?" Al and I ask in unison, then look at each other and laugh. Gilberto McDermott's half Irish and half Mexican, but all Texan. He was a year behind me in high school. His dad owns the hardware store in Fort Davis.

"We saw helicopters yesterday," Al says, shaking Gilberto's hand.

"We've got these nutcases, calling themselves separatists or secessionists or some damn thing. Busting their ass trying to get into a load of trouble," Gilberto says. He laughs—a rich, reassuring sound. "Finally figured out how to do it, all right—they took one of the neighbors hostage. Can you believe it? They weren't from around here, but still, I *know* these people! Homegrown Texas nuts. I swear we can handle 'em, but now we've got the ATF and the FBI here. I suppose you start talking secession, the Feds can't help but take an interest."

"That explains the helicopters," Al says.

"Yeah," Gilberto says with that boyish look machines evoke in men, "borrowed from INS. We may have the use of them again tomorrow. The hostages are safe and everybody's flushed from their hole except two ol' boys still wandering out there on the mountain."

"Two?" comes out of my mouth before I can stop it.

"That's what they tell me. Have you been staying over at your uncle's place?"

"Yes." About to say more, I freeze. Gilberto's pumped. Adrenaline brightens his handsome face. He hitches up his pants and waves at Iris, hanging out the car window.

"See anybody you don't know?" Gilberto asks, his voice studiously casual.

Rocking back and forth on the heels of my boots with my

fists stuck deep in my pockets, my heart starts to thud. If I breathe a word we'll be here all night.

"What do you think, Gilberto—can me and Iris go scout out the horses?" Al interjects. His voice sounds thin, like it's coming from a great distance.

A cowboy backs his horse out of a cattle trailer with the help of the headlights from his buddy's pickup. All around, the night's lit up in revolving flashes and alive with intention.

"Oh sure, let the kid out of the car."

Iris pitches herself half out of the front window and Al hauls her the rest of the way. They head over to the trailers. On the other side of the road, people at the end of the line are beginning to turn around and head back where they've come from. Gilberto surveys the scene with his back to me; his arms jut out to accommodate all his hardware.

"We'll make it home before breakfast," I say, "if we ever get back on the road."

"Well, let me get this barricade moved for you," Gilberto offers, looking around for someone to do the job. "We've got another road block up yonder." He turns to me and grins, his teeth gleaming in the dark. "You'll be the last folks to come down this road for a spell."

Al's moved no more than fifty feet away. I wave my arms like a cheerleader to get his attention. He looks straight at me without reacting. He can't see me. It's full dark where I stand, while he's surrounded with light.

"Just as soon as I can get my family rounded up we'll be out of here," I say.

"No rush. Let the kid look around. Nothing's going to hurt her. Your uncle down on the flat land?"

"Yeah. Sheep ranching."

Gilberto takes his cowboy hat off and slaps it against his thigh. "Mr. Dempsey's going to be sorry he's missed all the excitement. He's a walking history book on these parts."

"Sure enough," I reply, "Uncle Clayton's going to be sorry he was out of pocket for the big hoe-down."

Gilberto nods, tips his hat, and heads off towards a couple

of local kids who look to be Iris's age, dressed in clean shirts, dirty jeans, and cowboy hats. I can picture this posse confronting the stranger in the mountain—the man who doesn't belong. Unless he can adapt in a hurry, he's going to die. That makes me heartsick.

Gilberto splits off after talking to the kids. I can't think whose they are, but they look familiar as they hurry past me towards the barricade. Al saunters back while Iris stays to help. We just stand and wait for the kids to get the job done. Iris lopes up to us, leaving the boys to put the barricades back in place after we go through. She hurls herself into the Suburban with no warning. Al's glance meets mine as I take my place behind the wheel, and Iris's sweaty child-smell glues the three of us together.

Gilberto doffs his hat and waves us off. The night's charged with energy and resolution. Stopping people at night and chasing bad guys in the mountains sure beats selling hardware.

Headed back to Austin in a rapture of relief, no longer of interest to those left behind us at the roadblock, we all start talking at once.

"Maybe we should've said something to Gilberto about the stranger," Al says. His voice comes out somewhere between a shudder and a laugh.

"Oh no, not him again," Iris says, hunching over the console between us.

"Does anybody know where the water bottle went to? I'm parched." My tongue's practically stuck to the roof of my mouth.

"Pop can get it," Iris says, not taking her eyes off me, "I'm like totally squashed here. Those two boys asked me if I'd seen anybody. They're looking for the man you saw, Mom."

"Do you know those two boys?" Al asks. He's smoothing things over.

"They told me their names."

"They're about your age, aren't they?" Al prods.

"They're older but they're morons. We're in the same grade."

"Last chance to be a kid. Don't be so hard on them," Al says, giving up on the conversation and rummaging around in the back with one hand. He hands me a can of warm soda. I can feel his tension.

"Up here in the mountains you get to be a kid longer than you do in Austin," I say, noticing the speedometer and lifting my boot from the accelerator. I stow the soda in the cup holder for later. "So what did you say, Iris, when they asked you if you saw anybody?"

"I told them the truth. I didn't see anybody."

"What kept you from telling Gilberto?" Al asks me.

"Iris, try to find me some water," I say.

"Why doesn't somebody tell me what's happening?" Iris asks, her voice a forlorn wail coming from behind me while she makes a great show of looking for my water bottle.

"OK. OK," I say, picking up both hands and slapping them back onto the steering wheel. "I didn't say anything to Gilberto about Michael, the man I met in the mountains. On foot. Worn out. Needed water. Remember? You've heard all this before." I stop. My voice sounds defensive, even to me. I take a breath. I'm aware of Iris waiting for an answer as she hands me the water bottle. "There was no need to mention him to Gilberto. I had nothing to add, not a thing they didn't already know. The man might be a long way off from where I saw him by now. If I'd said the least little thing to Gilberto the three of us would've ended up sitting around half the night while all the hats came by to hear our story."

Iris, her body singing with the night's excitement, leans over my shoulder. "But Mom, who do you think he is?"

"A man who lost himself. He came all the way from California, to join up with some folks living on a piece of land out at the Resort, folks who think Texas ought to still be a free independent country, not part of the United States."

"That's dumb," Iris says.

"Maybe so, baby, maybe not," Al cuts in. "Let's delay judgment until we know more about other people's beliefs and why they hold them."

"Anyway, I wasn't ready to say anything more to the deputy. Those guys were on the scent. No good the pack of 'em shifting their attention to us."

"We haven't done anything wrong!" Iris says.

"Gilberto's not even a full-time deputy," I say lightly. "He's just got a badge and flashing lights to clamp on top his truck. I have a hard time thinking of him as representing authority."

"You ought to take the badge a bit more seriously than the bearer. What did you tell him after Iris and I left?"

"Nothing. He didn't push it, I didn't volunteer."

"If you already gave him a map to show him a way out from here, why would you tell the posse how to find him?" Iris asks. "What did he do bad, Mom?"

"I don't know what he's done. Looking at all those people, how much fun they're having—I wasn't about to help 'em out any."

"What if he's done something really bad?" Iris persists.

"More likely on the verge of doing something bad," Al says under his breath.

"Hey, you guys! Don't gang up on me. He didn't do anything bad to me. In our system of justice you're innocent until proven guilty."

"You didn't think he was dangerous?" Al asks.

"Mom's not scared of anything," Iris says, her tone implacable.

I squirm in the driver's seat, leaning over the wheel to peer at the road ahead. "Thanks for the vote of confidence, honey. Anyway, more to the point, the stranger was afraid of me. He must surely have considered me one of the hunters. If people consider you a threat—well, it's just not a good situation." I pat Iris on the knee before remembering she doesn't like to be patted any more. "So what kept *you* from saying something to Gilberto, Al?"

"I'm with Iris. I wasn't the one who met the man in the mountains."

"True."

"Well, it's not true nobody saw anybody," Iris says.

"You're right, Iris. Don't get the idea I think it's swell to lie. I didn't exactly lie to Gilberto; I just neglected to describe my whole day."

"Oh, right, fine. Next thing you know they'll come looking for my parents, asking me if anybody's stashed away anywhere they don't want to talk about," Iris says, alarm showing through the sarcasm.

"Gilberto and I've known each other since we were kids. But that's not what matters. The game between the hunter and the hunted goes on forever. You've heard the story behind Horse Thief Canyon. You know about the ongoing battle between INS and the illegal immigrants. When I was a kid we had what everybody called the Wetback Law."

"Folks were always crossing over the Rio Grande looking for a better life. Once here, somebody puts them to work," Al says.

"Yeah, but if they're caught crossing the river, they're deported," I say. "If they don't drown in a flash flood, weighed down with their clothes, or get shot."

"Mom . . . " Iris begins, but Al interrupts.

"You don't believe in borders? Or in the notion of sovereign states?"

"This land here in West Texas has been in the hands of a few families practically forever. Sometimes I just wonder how anybody else ever gets a chance."

"I know a girl named Amnesty," Iris says in a level voice. "Amnesty means something you used to not could do, but if you did, now you can forget."

"That's a good way to put it," Al says, his voice sounding more normal.

"All the Mexicans already in Texas when the new Amnesty law was declared, even if they had sneaked over the border, if it was a long time ago they got to stay. Now they're Texans," Iris continues to explain.

"That law was enacted right around the time you were born," Al says. "Accounting for your friend's name. But only people from Mexico who had already lived in Texas for four years were eligible . . . "

Iris begins to pummel him with her fists. "I know all that,

61

we learned about it in school."

"Hey, you guys, watch it, I've got to drive," I yell.

After about an hour, Iris falls asleep cuddled up against Al. With the long drive still ahead of us, the desire to probe the story of my encounter on the mountain strikes me like thirst.

"Do you think there's any chance he'll get away?" I ask Al with a dry throat.

"More than likely he's one of the guys they're after, Zoe."

"That's not what I asked."

"There's always a chance." Al reaches over the console to touch my cheek.

"Thanks for going along with me. I'm sort of surprised Gilberto didn't press harder."

"They're looking for an outsider. You and Gilberto are the natives around here. He expected you'd be sure to tell him if you knew anything."

"Treating a man to water in Texas hardly constitutes a crime. Even if you know for sure the law's after him. But thank you, Al. Thanks for backing me up."

"Never mind, Zoe. It's behind us."

Something tells me that whatever it is, it's just starting.

PART II
THE RIVER

Chapter 10

My eyes open to the morning light penetrating the wall of window an arm's reach away. A dream departs while I lie still, automatically checking over my body to find out what kind of day it promises to be. A cardinal flashes red across the yard outside the window, disappearing into the saturated foliage. The air itself looks green under the cloud cover.

Al swoops down like a bird of prey, thudding to his knees behind me on our giant bed and arching over me, his face upside down.

"Geez, Al!"

"Sorry, Zoe. Did I hurt you?" He steps over me to squat down on the floor between me and the light. His face looms close to mine.

"No, I'm fine. Give me a minute."

"It's Saturday and not a drop of rain," he says, studying my face.

"Well, maybe a drop," he corrects himself, jumping to his feet, "we had a shower around daybreak. Today seems to be our day to run the river."

I sit up and swing my legs over the side of the bed. I remember I promised Iris we'd do something. "OK. Shower. Coffee. River."

He reaches out his hand to pull me to my feet. "I'll check it out with Parks and Wildlife."

The hot water puts me into good working order. Al reports the river is up, but not to the danger level. Unless we get more rain today we should be fine. Iris sits at the kitchen counter,

65

fixing herself pop tarts and talking on the phone to Amanda. Practically littermates, they have been closer than ever this past year. Merla's agreed to drop everything to go canoeing the first chance we get, even on a weekday—a bonus of being part of the shadow economy. I take my coffee into the bedroom and call her, waking her up. She says she'll be ready by the time we are. Al packs up the river gear while I retrieve sandwiches Anna fixed and left in the refrigerator, papered with sticky notes. She doesn't trust us to manage our own food. Anna talks about moving back to Ft. Davis, but I know she won't go before Iris gets out of high school.

All in a rush despite our combined efforts, I pry Iris off the phone to help. Outside to check on the weather, I reflect on the possibility I'm pregnant. The zygote, if there is one, will barely have begun its trek down the uterine tube. It is way too early to start obsessing. The rain continues to hold off.

We take two cars south on the Interstate to New Braunfels, an old town settled by German farmers towards the end of the Texas Republic in the 1840s. Al and I are in the Suburban and Iris follows behind with Merla in her ancient Datsun. In just over an hour we leave the Datsun at the pullout spot, seven miles by road from where we'll put in, and all pile into the Suburban to go back to rent the canoes. We are on the river by midday. The sun wavers out, lifting my spirits with every degree of light. Al and Merla, with a tiny bit more canoeing experience, are chosen to be the leaders. Iris goes with Al and I get in with Merla.

Soon we're drifting between the warmth of the sun and the steady pull of the river, Merla bright in the bow of the canoe, her red hair charging out from under her straw hat, her eyes the same luminous green-brown as the river. Her bare arms are covered with freckles, the rest of her with a woven Mexican dress over a bikini. From the stern I practice steering, one of those right-brained sorts of task, like backing a trailer. We've already practiced paddling in unison with so much gusto we've pulled way ahead of Al and Iris.

"Tell me what's going on with you. How's the patient you've been so worried about?" Merla asks in a loud voice, holding her paddle up, drifting with the current.

"It's unprofessional to worry about a patient. The one I'd be worried about if I weren't so professional is hanging in there."

"Good, good." She hesitates. "Glad to hear it. I did your chart."

"And?"

"Well, you don't give astrology much credence. But watch out for surprises. You're about to come under the influence of a malefic aspect of Uranus. Be ready for unprecedented events, unpredictable outcomes."

"How can you get ready for the unpredictable?"

"Good question. Just hold yourself in readiness. You're likely to encounter life-altering experiences. That sort of thing." She flourishes her paddle back and forth in the air.

"Define readiness," I say to her sturdy back.

"Go with the flow. Don't try to push the river. OK?" She turns to get a look at me, her face serious.

"Fine, Merla. Don't sweat it. I'll get in sync with the Tao."

"I hope so," she mutters. "And Al? You two getting along?"

"We're getting along great," I answer, annoyed. "Not good enough to paddle in the same canoe, but that's OK, the distinguished Dr. Alwyn Clyde glories in being Pop."

"Al's Irish, isn't he?"

"No, Welsh. Alwyn means 'well loved,' and Clyde means 'loud-voiced.'" My own voice sounds strident.

"What did I say to make you crabby?"

"Dunno. Maybe waiting for you to ask me if he's a good lay."

Her spine stiffens and her paddle comes straight up out of the water, to hang suspended for a moment before plunging back in, causing our paddling to get out of sync. We work together without speaking for three or four strokes to get our rhythm back.

"Do you think sex is all I ever think of?" she asks. "Don't answer that! Back to Iris of the loud dad, loved by all the little

67

Lolitas—how's the little muncher?"

"Iris isn't so little anymore. She spends a lot of time hanging out with Amanda and listening to pop music. She's getting too big for her pony, but she still wins over fences. Al schedules his surgeries in the morning, horses around with Iris in the afternoon, and tries to get to all her horse shows."

"Don't you think Al should have some life of his own, instead of being a full time horse-show father?" Merla asks, not taking her eyes off the river.

"Oh, Merla, I don't know what I think." I pause to adjust my peevish tone. "Everybody else seems to think it's wonderful. I'm busy at the hospital. How can I go to horse shows? Not that I want to."

"Didn't you do barrel racing?"

Nodding at Merla, I suddenly feel ourselves sluing sideways.

"Paddle hard," Merla yells, digging her oar in the water. I do what she asks and soon we're back to drifting, indolent in the high water of late spring.

"I told Iris we'd start looking for a horse for her whenever she's ready to sell the pony."

"But she's still hauling home the ribbons?"

"Yes. Makes Al happy. He likes to win."

"It's not as if you don't," Merla says, ducking her head to miss a branch hanging over the river. After I steer us around the tree, Merla stops paddling to get a sandwich out of the cooler. She clutches her food in one hand and tears at it with her teeth like she has to subdue it first before swallowing. Her perfume, flowery and female, cuts through all the conflicting river smells.

"Oh crap! Steer over to the bank, Zoe," Merla hollers, starting to paddle strenuously, grunting with the effort.

Once close to the bank she slings off her shift and jumps into the water to haul the canoe further up the bank. I steady us with my oar planted against the limestone river bottom.

"What're we stopping for?" I ask.

"Have you ever been down this part of the Guadalupe?" she counters.

"No. I've only canoed with Al on the San Marcos."

"I've never been in this section either. Didn't you see the sign hanging over the river? It says 'Portage Your Canoe' in mile-high letters. Best check it out."

I get out of the canoe, stepping into the water in my river shoes. How could I have missed the sign? We pull the canoe further up on the bank. Merla goes back to read the sign.

"Slumber Falls is coming up," she says when she gets back. "There's always a hydraulic after a falls. Have we got everything tied down? We'll need to turn the canoe upside down to portage."

"Everything's tied down. Do you want to wait for Al and Iris?"

"What for?"

I lift one shoulder in a shrug. "How far to the falls?"

"How do I know?"

We pull the canoe all the way out of the water; it takes considerable effort. When we start to turn it over we find everything's not tied down, so we heave it back. Merla stops to put on shoes that fell out when we tipped the canoe. We tie down everything that's loose. The heavy cooler's in the middle, where it belongs. To portage, Merla gets under the front and I go to the back. We grunt and giggle until the thing's hoisted up over our heads. Merla settles her head inside where she can't see anything. I carry my end on my left shoulder.

We get started with a good rhythm, Merla calling out cadence in a muffled voice from the front. She can't stop laughing. She picks the canoe up straight-armed and frees her head, then sets her end on her right shoulder. Now we're out of line. We almost drop the damn thing. I holler for her to stop while I shift my end to my right shoulder. We walk like that maybe fifty paces when Merla yells out in outrage. We put the canoe down and go over to the riverbank to check out the falls.

"Fuck. We're killing ourselves for nothing," Merla says.

The river falls over a long stone shelf, dropping off maybe two feet, three at the most, going the whole way across the river. It doesn't look intimidating. The roil of water after the falls can be seen quite clearly, close to the falls and not very big around.

A canoe with two young guys, college types, comes shooting out over the ledge as we watch, shouting as they go over, a small sound compared to the sound of the river. Their canoe hits the water hard, front first. The guy in front paddles like fury while the guy in back picks up his stroke as soon as he can get his paddle back in the water. They continue on down the river. Merla and I exchange looks. Another canoe with an identical set of males follows. The shouting dies off when they come within a whisker of capsizing. They manage to right themselves when the man in the bow lunges across the canoe and stabs the water with his oar.

"We could've done it," I say.

"Yeah. For sure," Merla says. "Let's get back in. You take the bow this time. I'll steer. After all, that's the easy part."

I suspect if that were true we wouldn't be switching, but I don't argue.

"Just keep up a steady pull with your paddle. We need power to steer," Merla instructs. "Doesn't matter which side you paddle from, unless I tell you. If I tell you to back-paddle, put everything you've got into it. It takes some muscle, but you and I together can keep this canoe in place in any rapids we're likely to meet today. When the river's this high the rapids are weenie, but we'll get some white water before we're done. We can't do any worse than those college kids."

We get the canoe flipped back and take our new places. We haven't gone a hundred yards when we see the boys who had gone ahead of us standing on the bank, sucking down beers. They yell at us, beckoning us wildly with manic arm movements, but we just laugh and wave and go on. We're practically old enough to be their mothers. They keep yelling after we've gone by until the roar of rapids, louder than I would've thought possible, drowns them out. I throw a glance back to Merla, who scouted ahead.

She's yelling what I take to be "Paddle!"

We come around the left-hand bend of the river to a roar of

sound that assaults me and stops my heart and, momentarily, my paddle. The river disappears in front of us. Merla is yelling instructions, but already I'm back-paddling furiously. The river drops off to nowhere in front of us, flowing over the edge of the world. Pulling against the river for all I'm worth, my heart beating fit to burst through my chest, the river inches us closer to the edge, tugging at my loins like desire. My brain mutters to my will, commanding my muscles to hold the bloody canoe in place by paddling still more fiercely. But it can't be done. The river hooks into my navel, tugging us closer to the drop-off. Merla's useless shrieking enflames me. I can't distinguish her words over the roar of the water and can't afford to twist my head to see her. I watch the line between water and thin air coming closer.

The rear of the canoe kicks up like a bucking bronco. My head snaps around and I take in Merla ditching the canoe, flinging her body away and up in a swan dive, stunningly free of gravity. Unencumbered of her weight, the canoe begins to dive. I face down towards the water, my paddle gone, crammed up close to the bow clutching both sides of the metal prow. I crab-walk backwards at the moment the canoe begins to slide over the edge to hover suspended over nothing, held motionless by cartoon physics.

Time halts long enough for me to take in everything around me, the panoramic view like a concert hall for the force and sound of the river beating into my body. I've got time to wonder if this is the last thing I'll see in this lifetime and then all at once the canoe lets go of the edge and plunges down into the falls. Something tells me to let loose of my hold before hitting the water. It takes the entire force of my will to undo my grip and kick off from the canoe, losing the sky and aiming my body down towards the whirling water, waiting until the last instant to draw breath, only to be whacked in the side of the head just as I enter the water with less than a lungful of air.

The momentum of my launch from the canoe plunges me deep into the river. I keep going down, farther than imagination, deeper than thought, before I lose the first force of my fall and begin to slow up, making me think I can start back to the surface. I make a move to fight the downward thrust, pulling strongly with my arms and paddling hard with my feet. Nothing happens. I don't start to go up. For a moment I go nowhere. I absolutely cannot go up, but instead I find myself moving laterally. Increasing my efforts to get up to the light has no effect. Inside this moment I hear Merla's voice: Don't push the river.

Fear lets go of my mind enough for it to start functioning. An inner voice instructs me: *You can't go up. Let the river take you down*–a voice as commanding as the earlier whack in the head. I quit fighting. Holding my breath takes all I've got.

As I give myself up to the whirlpool I'm somersaulted over and over, swept around and around and down. Looking up, my head lolling back, my arms wrapped around my body, I see the sun hitting the surface of the water, filtering down like substance, real gold falling, glints and speckles and debris of light. Whirling away from the light, I find myself suspended, released from ordinary measures of time, my body drawn still deeper into dark water. Oxygen, the computer function of my brain registers, is in finite supply, but there's no pain or fear to accompany this bulletin. Part of me yearns to be back up there with that sunshine, but the dark holds its own allure. Nothing can be done but submit to the fall.

Nature's picked me up and slammed me down. One more time I return to the shallow depths in a lateral spiral, spending a far longer time than a land animal was ever meant to stay under water, the current of the river pulsating through me. I'm under water long enough to yearn back for the surface, the membrane separating me from oxygen and the world of everyday life and all my past and all my future. In my mind's eye I can see Al and Iris coming down the river, portaging all the way. I know my husband. Gratitude for Al's sanity acts like an extra shot of oxygen. As my breath pries against my lips to relieve my lungs I clamp my mouth shut, filled with euphoric knowing—for this moment it's only me who struggles, only me who needs saving.

For a fraction of eternity I'm held in suspense, ready to die here in the river. I stare back at the surface membrane bright with sun and leagues away, an opening not to the real world but to a stage setting filled with the props of my former life. Everything I thought was real seems a comical illusion that fills me with mirth. A tiny bubble of air escapes my lips before I can summon enough will power to button my mouth closed, still enjoying the joke.

With this last effort to trap life and air I hit the river bottom and thrust against the rock with all my might, scraping my toes, yanking my elbow away from something dragging at it, digging in and pulling ahead with more force than I knew I possessed. I swim one, two, three strong breaststrokes and powerful frog kicks, not up towards the surface but along the bottom of the river, going downstream with the current, away from the whirlpool. I was a diver, not a swimmer. Now I'm a star.

Clear of the sucking power of the vortex, I claw the rest of my way to the surface, my throat and lungs searing. The used-up air explodes from my lungs in an exultant shout, a sound like giving birth. I take in the fresh air, gulping a ton before my head goes back and I'm tumbled further down the river in a flurry of white water. I have all I can do to flip on my back and prop my feet in front of me, stubbing my bare toes against rocks. A laugh rumbles up from my belly, glee bubbling along with the oxygen soaking into my lungs. The river's stripped me of my shorts and cheap river shoes. I'm practically naked.

Beyond the whitewater the river flows quietly. I propel myself, panting and croaking, over to the bank on the east side of the river, squirming into mud like cake frosting, brown and glossy and enveloping, rare in this limestone-bottom river. I slither in it, pulling myself along by tree roots until I'm far enough out of the water to fasten my arms around a good-sized rock and rest my head on my arms, my legs churning to keep the river from reclaiming me. Too tired to do this for long, I push on further until I'm all the way up on the bank, out of the river, half under the roots of a tree. When I open my mouth to holler, not a sound comes out.

I open my eyes. Merla envelops me, clutching my arm, shaking me none too gently. "Hey, girlfriend. Sorry I bailed on you," she says, her voice a cascade of gratitude.

"I nearly drowned in the whirlpool, Merla."

"Yes, I know," Merla says, cupping her hand to wash the drying mud off my face and neck with river water. "I'm so sorry, I should have known. Geez, it's like I did know and shut it out. You were under the water so long. It was awful. But you'll be fine."

What looks like another woman seems to peer down at me, the light making a halo around her head. I reach up and touch her face. "Benita?" I speak my mother's name.

"It's me, Mom, it's me, Iris," more impatient than scared. "Pop's coming with the canoe. I swam over. He told me not to but I did anyway. What's the matter? Did you hit your head?" She pitches herself against me, hugging me, then lunges away, holding on to a root.

"Oh, Iris, you looked so much like my mother. I'm sorry, my head's fine, baby." I struggle to sit up. I've lost my place in the ordinary world and am still somewhere in the back of beyond. I don't want to lose what I found in the river, but I'm afraid if I linger too long I'll lose my chance to return.

"Hey, Mom, you look like a crocodile!" Iris's eyes flutter over my nakedness. She closes her eyes as she struggles over to kiss my cheek. This is always the way with our family: to see and to touch at the same time seems too much to bear. Iris and Merla in their bathing suits are nearly as covered in mud as I am.

Al splashes over to our little eddy. He struggles to say something, pushed to the verge of stammering before getting his voice. "You could've drowned. I'm sorry I let you get so far ahead." He stoops down and helps me up. We lurch up the bank.

"It wasn't up to you to let us, Al. It's not your fault."

"That's Slumber Falls where you wiped out," he says, stripping my clothes off, rubbing me briskly. "It's notorious." He helps me into a dryer shirt.

I can't believe you did that," he says, switching his attention to Merla, his face going blotchy. "Didn't you read the sign? Did you see the number of people who died at Slumber Falls? I thought you knew this river."

"We thought we'd already gone past the falls," Merla answers. "We made a mistake." When nobody says anything, she goes on. "Actually, it's not the falls but the hydraulic that causes the problem."

"You could both have been added to the number painted up on that sign," Al says, shaking his head.

"I didn't go back to look at the sign. We thought the next drop-off was what they were talking about."

"That stone shelf stretching across the river was nothing. I should've known that's not what they meant," Merla says, "but that's what popped up first thing. The sign needs to be closer to the falls. Don't blame Zoe."

"I'm not blaming anybody. Least of all Zoe," Al says.

"I'll go get the car and bring it back. OK?" Merla walks off along the riverbank.

Al goes back to dick around with the canoes. Iris and I sit slumped together on the bank. I feel a huge warmth glowing inside me; I no longer feel lost or alone. "I'm glad you're my kid, Iris," I say. "Don't ever forget."

"I'd like you even if you weren't my mom," she says. Her child's mouth twists into a grown-up smile of reassurance. "Here comes Pop," she adds, her eyebrows rising, speaking in that female voice of collusion.

Al comes back from securing the canoes to squat down next to us on the bank, the sun behind him making a halo. Iris moves away to explore along the bank. Al sinks all the way to the ground and pulls me up against him. I wiggle in next to him, my back against his chest, warming up. I turn around to look at his face, a face I know better than my own. I reach up to kiss him, smearing his face with mud in the process.

"Mom! Pop! Check this out," Iris yells. "There's a snake eating a frog!"

"Not now, Iris," Al calls back. He looks me over with a diagnostic squint. "We've got to keep your mother warm and

75

dry."

"I'm OK. I'm not cold."

I'm in no pain. My endorphin load must be out of sight. I don't even feel like the same person. That witch Merla did promise unprecedented events.

Since Merla drives herself back to Austin in her Datsun we don't have a chance to talk about how soon her prophecy was made good. Iris doesn't listen to music on the way back, just snuggles up to me in the back seat. Again and again she asks me to describe what it was like in the river. In return, she relates to me what she and Al were doing the whole time, and how she knew all along that I was going to be all right. Al keeps looking at us in the rearview mirror. I don't faint or go into shock or anything—I just glory in being alive.

Chapter 11

Once back home, we are soon falling all over ourselves to tell Anna, the tireless witness to our dramas, what happened on the river. She exclaims over every detail of our ordeal, asking questions, determining each critical moment in the unfolding action from beginning to end. Our adventures could have turned out worse. I'm stunned with gratitude.

Later, as the others sleep, I listen to the water from the onslaught of another storm. I imagine the water beginning to climb high up the face of the dams forming the string of man-made lakes controlling the flow of the Colorado River. This Colorado, not the same one that courses through the Grand Canyon, forms Town Lake in the middle of Austin before continuing east. If the water climbs too high and the gates must be opened, houses along the banks are flooded. I drift into sleep and dream of water coursing down the river, and of light not leftover or forgotten. The sunlight flashes on the water, the membrane between me and the rest of my life. In the dream I struggle once again, longing towards the light. Over and over I hit a wall of terror. Finally I let go, and drift down to the dark in massive relief. Towards morning I dream of me and Al and Iris twined together in the mud. I awake at first light to find Al leaning over me, propped up on his elbow, peering at my face.

"You were thrashing around and calling out," he tells me, his sweet face scrunched up.

"Who did I call?"

"Me," he says, rolling on top of me. We make love with exquisite fury. Sweet muffled sounds come from us like none I have ever heard before, amidst sensations I'd give up the next world for.

"Is this all there is?" I ask when we lie twined together like snakes sunning on a rock.

Al mistakes my meaning. He turns to me again with a surprising intensity. What he has to tell me with his body is something I've never heard before. Concentrating entirely on telling me this story he wants so desperately to tell, the flood of sensations he evokes from my body obliterates time and alters the sense of the *I am* until it gives up directing and scolding and frees the rest of me to go with Al to wherever he wants to take me, somewhere I've never been, where the dark of the deep inks the light coming from the other side. My body becomes the channel through which the river rushes, a sensation so intense that the present moment, the dream, and the reality are confounded. Al is the river and I am its banks. My mind stretches beyond comprehending, and I hold on to Al for dear life as he plunges inside me.

He falls asleep muttering my name over and over. How could we have lived so long apart? Something happened in the mountains to break the spell that had sundered us. Once again we can tell each other with our bodies what can't be formed into language. We may have already started a baby. It may be getting ready to make its way into the uterus to float free for a couple of days, in touch with eternity and indifferent to the future. I fall asleep. No dreams before I wake to the blessing of ordinary daylight.

"I'm softening at the edges," I say when I see Al open one eye. "Some knot in my center is dissolving."

"Don't you worry, my pretty," he says, his voice low and gravelly, theatrically sinister, "I'll hold you here, and keep you on the planet for my enjoyment." He encloses me in his arms, his hairy body friendly and familiar again.

"Thank you. Thank you," I breathe. Al sinks back into sleep while I lie awake, my arm going numb under his neck, and my cunt—ah, how that wonderful word stops the mind— secret of secrets, satisfied.

Al and Anna are sitting together at the table when I come in the kitchen. Iris isn't up yet. Anna hands me my coffee with a quick look of concern.

"What's the matter, Anna?" I ask with a twinge of guilt. We haven't had a chance to sit down and visit for what seems forever. She just looks at Al, who passes me the paper with an odd look on his face.

I don't have long to wonder what's up. While we were canoeing the Guadalupe, my man in the mountains has become front-page news. I scan the article quickly, my pulse racing: A man carrying a Texas Separatist ID was killed in a shoot-out on Monday. The Texas Rangers and the sheriff of Jeff Davis County had only wanted him for questioning. No charges had been brought against him in Texas, and there were none for his role in the standoff in the mountains. The man's brother has been contacted. Asked to account for his brother's actions, the grieving man speaks of his brother's vow to die fighting rather than be returned to California, where he was wanted on a year-old arrest warrant for violating probation by leaving the state. He had been in a dispute over the inheritance of a piece of property. He felt he had been treated unjustly by the government, a grievance similar to those expressed by others living at the Embassy over the past several months.

Somebody from the Texas Rangers says the fugitive started the shoot-out by first firing on the hounds. The posse who hunted for him numbered in the hundreds, made up of members of three different law enforcement bodies. He was tracked to a camp-site by helicopter, where he was shot. The law enforcement agency responsible for the shooting has not yet been made public.

"He wasn't packing when I saw him," I say stupidly. Anna gives me a sympathetic glance but Al shrugs, a sardonic expression on his face. Not seeing a gun means nothing, *nada*. Of course, he's right, but the gesture annoys me. My connection with the man on the mountain has something to do with the part of me that repels Al. I bunch up the newspaper and throw it on the floor. "He was found close to where I left him. He didn't even try to get away."

"Not surprising," Al says. "With the copters, he couldn't even move around at night without being seen. He must have finally given up." He stands up and starts to pace.

"Well, no, if he'd given up he wouldn't be dead. It was foolish for the man to die. Preposterous and unnecessary. I hate it." I pick the paper up and smooth it out, noticing something else to fill me with disgust.

"If you two will excuse me," Anna says. She's gone before I have a chance to respond. I sure don't want to alienate Anna, but I seem to have lost the knack for ordinary social behavior.

"He was shot in the back," I say in a dull voice, "in all likelihood by one of the good ol' boys I've known all my life. Biggest moment of his life."

"Don't blame the sheriff. Your friend joined a bunch of people carrying guns, taking hostages, and shooting back. In the end, he was on a suicide mission. He picked his way to go: suicide by cop."

"Al, please. I know. But why do you suppose a man would do a thing like that?"

Al sits down next to me at the table, looking out the huge window facing east to an oak tree taller than the house. "He'd have to be totally fed-up with the world the way it is. At a loss for any way to make a difference."

"If you'd seen his face, Al—etched with bewilderment. A look you see reflected everywhere. The poor bastard didn't know how to register his sense of revolt."

"And ended up dead," Al says. "Maybe if he'd thought things through . . . I'm sorry," he interjects when he sees the look on my face, "but it's not your fault. There's nothing you could have done."

"Maybe somebody could've listened to all the things he'd thought through before shooting him in the back. That's what could have been done."

"Up on the mountain? If the man had wanted to do any

80

talking, he'd have come back to the cabin with you."

"I didn't invite him back to the cabin. I told him I'd take him into town."

"No difference," Al says. "But we'll never know why he did what he did. It makes me wonder what I'd be willing to die for. You and Iris, I know that."

"Would you, sweetie?" I stroke his cheek. His jaw is rigid. "Mine might've been the last friendly face the man saw before he died."

"That's the way I want to go," Al says, making a grab at me.

I push him away, smiling and shaking my head. "Iris will be up soon." I pour us more coffee. "I can't shake the image of the man's face."

"Are you sure this isn't just a case of how ladies love outlaws?"

"I don't think so, Al. It's not just the defenders of liberty who have gone haywire. It's as if the whole country suffers from an autoimmune disease—we label bits of ourselves the enemy so we can attack."

The *Austin-American Statesman* moves the story of the Texas Separatists off the front page. The weather becomes the front-page news. The river authority opened the floodgates on the dams above Austin, releasing tons of water and destroying homes built too near the lakes. Residents are urged to watch for rising water and when in doubt to seek higher ground.

Despite the warnings, in three days of interminable rain several people die needlessly at low-water crossings. Texans worry more about drought than flood, despite the great rivers. South, west, and north of Austin the state is dry. In East Texas, pine forests segue into the rest of the South where the black dirt turns into red. In Central Texas around Austin, where the Great Plains peter out, it's green and lush due to the man-made dams and massive tree-planting over the last century. But this year the rains have overwhelmed the dams.

Some folks say the dams have done all the good they're going to do—now they're over fifty years old and have started
doing harm. Massive problems seem to stem from solutions to
earlier problems in many different arenas of human effort. After reading news of the weather I read of the arraignment of the
secessionists who the stranger left behind at the compound, holding hostages. Those people who surrendered and saved themselves from being hunted down now face the consequences of
actions the rest of us find hard to comprehend.

For awhile I try to keep tabs on what's happening to the
people in custody while their fate is debated daily in the back
pages of the newspaper. One young man is still at large. How
did he manage to get away while my guy didn't? Maybe I should
have tried harder to look at why he was limping.

Despite my unease over such questions, work keeps me occupied. I tell Anna to just let the newspapers pile up for me to
look over when I can grab the time to brood over the fate of
strangers. Off and on, feelings of foreboding dart through my
mind like a fish.

I go by the hospital early so I have some free time before I
have to meet Cynthia for our foray over to City Hospital for
the presentation on the new Crohn's drug. I stash the plant
from the mountains on top of the file cabinet in my office and
call Lydia Flores. I leave a message on her machine, telling her
to come get the fragrant bundle; if I'm not there Shaunna or one
of the other nurses will let her in my office.

With time to spare, I look up the Texas Separatists' website
and discover a story of grassroots political organizing. A mission statement is followed by arguments by various authors
concerning the original annexation of Texas by the U.S. Congress in 1845. I skip the section devoted to copies of original
documents from Texas history, flip through what appears to
be private exchanges between different factions of the movement, and proceed to the meeting times. They meet once a month
in Austin and more frequently in small Texas towns. I jot down
meeting times and locations before switching off the computer.
Maybe I should go find out if people are still meeting, and find

out what they think about what has happened. Maybe they can tell me more about the man who met his death.

Maybe I've been focusing too hard on my work, or maybe it's true that the body politic can't tell the difference between self and not-self.

Chapter 12

Cynthia drives us back to work after the dazzling intro on the new drug. Doctors from out of town are making a day of it, but neither of us accepted the offered entertainment from the corporate types of the proud pharma. I'd also been invited by some old cronies up from Galveston to go listen to jazz later at the Elephant Room on Congress Avenue. I decided not to waste an evening watching them ebb into inebriation, so begged off. Cynthia's face looks tired and naked without the mask of professional authority she normally wears. She flips the radio to KUT. The sun tries to struggle out from behind some high clouds just in time to set.

I call Anna. She says Iris wants to sleep over at Amanda's so they can study for a test tomorrow. I say OK with a twinge of guilt. Anna leaves the phone twice to tend to the new dog they brought back from the pound a few days ago—a spayed female Anna has already named Grendel, after the man-eating monster in Beowulf. Anna was a high school English teacher before she married my grandfather, the doctor. Traffic flows by while we talk, mesmerizing me. I'm not used to being a passenger. After saying good bye to Anna I'm suspended in a lull between worlds. My mind drifts; I wonder what it would be like to have another child. For a moment I can remember the feel of Iris as a featherweight infant tucked close to my bare skin as she nursed, her translucent blue eyelids quivering, and almost smell the aroma of her breath.

An over-the-counter pregnancy kit could tell me what I want to know.

Cynthia lets me off at a side entrance of the hospital and goes on to park. I go up to my office to shed the stack of conference materials. There's a note sticking out from under the mother-in-law tongue: *"Sorry I missed you. I gave your plants a dose of energy while I was picking up the Tickle Tongue. One of the nurses, Shaunna—what a sweetie—let me in your office. Thanks for everything. Lydia Flores."* All by myself in the empty room, I laugh out loud: fancy thinking of our indomitable head nurse as a *sweetie.* I'm glad for my plants, although a little water might have prevented the need for mystical intervention. You don't have to be a *curandera* to treat living plants better.

I check out the action on the gastro floor before going home. The doctor from Down Under seems to be coping, and my intern hasn't foundered yet. I decide to see if I can unearth Travis, and find him in one of his hidey-holes—smoking a cigarette in a cubicle behind the defunct radiology unit in the basement. He's sitting with his boots off, one bare foot crossed over his knee at the ankle.

"I can smell that cigarette halfway up the corridor."

"Everybody knows I smoke. There's a difference between keeping something secret and not flaunting it," Travis's lip curls around the cigarette in the corner of his mouth, a ringer for the Marlboro man.

Staring back at him, I try to get a handle on his uncharacteristic belligerence. Travis has always been as close as a brother, but lately it feels like he's grown up and left home.

"What's the matter?" he asks without taking the cigarette out of his mouth.

I flap the smoke away, feeling my face pinch up into a frown. At least with Travis I don't have to pretend to be nice.

"When did you find out what Glover had up his sleeve?"

"You're like a hound dog, aren't you? Never give up the scent. I've been looking after your interests. That little porker was going through the path-lab files on your cases." He takes a long pull on his cigarette.

I purse my lips and suck in secondhand smoke while squeezing in next to him on the tiny bench. "What do you think he's so hacked-off about?"

Travis adjusts his body to give me room and sighs heavily. "He's not of a mind to hand over power."

"Yeah. His dick might fall off. I'll check out the stats on *his* patients. There might be more than one story to tell."

"There should be a boatload of data on Glover's patients. One thing I can't fault him for, he does more post-mortems than anybody else; many of them he does himself. Go for it."

"Yeah, well, that would be dandy, but it seems my computer's blocked."

"Blocked?"

"Well, the last time I worked on this matter the sucker either froze up on me or popped out weird requests for passwords."

"Do you have enough memory?"

"For the morbidity and mortality tables? I download high density images from Medscape all the time."

"Security codes to access patient records aren't given out automatically anymore. Did you fill out all the forms you got in your in-box? Is your authorization up to date?" Travis takes the smoke into his mouth and rolls it around before exhaling.

"Shit. Maybe not." I slap my head in exasperation. "My mind's fried."

Travis finishes his cigarette and stubs it out on the underside of the bench before dropping the butt on the floor.

"At the end of the day you'll have quite an unsanitary little wad there," I point out.

"Wrong. I police my own area."

I stare down at my clogs, hiding the curl of my toes. "What's got your back up?"

"What's going on with you and Al?" he counters.

"Why do you ask?"

Travis makes a loud popping sound with his tongue on his palate. "I saw him with your red-headed friend. He didn't invite me to join them."

Blindsided, I try not to let it show. "So what? They're friends." He gives me a strange look. "You and I are friends, Travis. We could be seen together. Like now." He shrugs and turns his head away. "So where did you see them?"

"I shouldn't have started this conversation."

"Well, you did. So answer. What's wrong with friends seeing each other?"

"Look, Zoe. You, me, and Al are friends. Merla—well, Merla's a witch. As far as where I run into people . . ." he stops.

"So where was it, some place I'm not supposed to know about, like off-track betting or the dope house?"

"We've gotten way off course here. Let's just get back to why you were looking for me."

I look at Travis from under my lashes, swiveling my body in a vampy pose. "I'm only after your little old computer files, honey."

"Cut it out. You look ridiculous," Travis says. He gets up, a sour look on his face.

I feel a wave of heat. "What's the *matter* with you? My hero has been turned into a pig."

"Oh hell, you're right. I feel like a whole herd of swine. But I do not have time to get involved in all your problems, Zoe."

"Fine. Let's go back to where we started, something we might be able to fix, the problems with my computer. Yours works and mine doesn't. Perhaps what I'm looking for is buried under the *need to know* protocol. Can't you give me your password?"

"The number of passwords required to search for anything has multiplied. Plus, every keystroke on every computer becomes a matter of record. Nothing's ever erased. Even if it were, there are ways to retrieve it." He grins, a fake leer, showing a sliver of gum recession.

"This sounds like one of the non sequiturs you collect. I'm not following."

"Some flunky could take down all the information from *your* use of *my* computer, then hand it on to Frank, who could look for certain patterns. Then he could turn his interpretation of events over to the Board or to who-all else upstairs in Admin might ask for it. Why should I get myself in a pile of shit by giving you my code book?"

"You're paranoid. Why would anybody be interested in your

research?"

"You sound like I'm just some sort of cadaver-carver in the basement," Travis says, pulling on his socks. "My research constitutes a record of the comparable success of different treatments by different doctors of a host of conditions."

I jump up and stand in front of him, swiping the cube-curtain back and forth on the short rod. He digs around to collect the butts, and then sheds the tiny changing room like he's been wearing it. He pulls the curtain from my hand and lets it fall behind us. "I don't suppose it'd be any use telling you to forget it?" he asks, grunting while he bends over and pulls on his boots.

"No."

He stands in front of me, all booted up. "If I give you access to the files in the lab, can you finish up in a week?"

"No problem." Whenever Travis and I spend any time together, Al's the third who walks unseen. We used to contend for first place with Al, at least until Iris was born. But it seems like Travis still calls some plays in whatever game we've got going on.

"Come see me in the path lab," he says as if every word is costing him. "I'll help you find the records you need. Do it soon, before I go to Mexico."

"I wish I could go with you."

"It's not a vacation, Zoe."

"Well, in some ways it is. Don't be stuffy." I know all about Travis's work with the Outreach Clinic, founded by doctors from both sides of the border to treat children in at-risk populations. The health-care system in Mexico delivers modern health care to more people than ours does. Outreach brings translators along with the doctors who immunize children in far-flung communities where nobody speaks Spanish, much less English.

"You have to obey instructions from the clinic supervisors, no matter how grand you might be back home," Travis says, eyeing me.

"Sounds like a stretch. I'm surprised you keep going back."

"My work in Mexico is something like an expiation."

"For what?"

Travis looks down at his boots, his face sallow in the basement light. "For working with the dead instead of the living. Or maybe for writing you prescriptions for narcotics. How do I know? Our least sins are probably those we can name."

"You astonish me. I can't see what treating my back pain has to do with immunizing Mexican kids."

Travis jerks his head up and looks at me intently. "I knew better. I am not as naïve as you are. I should have been watching your back for you. You're not immune, you know, Zoe."

"Immune from what?"

He looks around him, like he's waiting for the answer to appear in the ether.

"What are you talking about? Just the short answer will do."

"About the stranger you met in the Davis Mountains. About what you said and did not say to the sheriff."

Al must have told him. I sure didn't. "What's that got to do with Mexico?"

"The indigenous people are experiencing great hardship. They have been expelled from their villages by the army. They have had to flee their homes pursued by thugs in uniform called paramilitaries. They live in poor conditions, prey to disease. I'm a doctor. I want to help them. I don't particularly want to get involved in some very complicated politics. But sometimes to help somebody is to oppose somebody else. And it is always dangerous to oppose those in power. Now do you get it?"

"No. Too cryptic for me."

Travis sighs. "I'm just warning you to watch out for your impulses."

"What about you? If you're so worried why do you still go to Mexico?"

"Indigenous people don't trust doctors. To be effective, you need to keep showing up. To be allowed to go back, you have to conform to the rules. If immunizing the children is all I can do, fine, even though clean water's more important than shots, and half the children have worms and various GI problems."

"What about what you said—how helping one side means opposing the other?"

"The Mexican government lets Outreach use foreign doctors because the international spotlight's been on Chiapas since the Zapatista uprising on New Year's Day, 1994."

"I'd like to go with you." I try to hide my surge of excitement.

"Maybe next time." Travis shakes his head and grins at me like he used to. "For now, I'll round up the files your buddy Glover's so interested in."

"Add the files on *his* patients, the ones I couldn't find because somebody's hexed me."

"You got it."

Chapter 13

While consulting with the radiologist I get a call from ER telling me Jordan Wilson has shown up with a gummed-up TPN catheter. I take the elevator downstairs and stride down the hall, opening the double doors to hear Glover's commanding voice issuing instructions from behind curtains as ineffective in blocking the telltale meat-locker smell of a gastrointestinal bleeder as they are in stopping sound.

I slip through the gap. "Can I help?"

"We got it covered, Doc. We are on our way upstairs," the resident chants from his post at the head of the gurney as he begins edging it into the corridor. I stand back to let them by.

Glover passes close enough for me to see his jowls quiver, his gaze intent on his patient, whose scared eyes are locked to his. "You're in the right hands at the right hospital at the right time of day," Glover booms, rat-a-tat-tat. "Relax and enjoy the ride."

When I reach Jordan, the intern and the nurse have already cleaned out the catheter. Jordan complains of severe abdominal pain, and even more vehemently objects to the smell and the noise around her. I decide to admit her. Her mother talks to someone from the business office, and Jordan's soon settled into a suite of rooms on the ground floor, new and swank. We spend the whole day testing and imaging to discover if something critical has developed in her intestines, but find nothing.

It's after dinner before I get to Jordan's room. I'm eager to tell her about her excellent test results, but find the room empty.

She must not be back from the children's floor where I said she could go to read to the kids.

Mrs. Wilson pops in the door before I've made a move. "I cut short my meeting and got back early," she says with a frown. "Is Jordan still undergoing tests?"

"No, she's done. She went to read to kids just out of surgery. Transportation was supposed to have her back by now."

My words conjure up a large Samoan nurse's aide with an angelic face steering Jordan back into the room in one of the sleek new wheel chairs. Mrs. Wilson drops a kiss on the girl's fair hair and exchanges a few words before heading for the door, even before Jordan's settled in the bed. She calls out apologetically over her shoulder that she needs to make a quick call.

"The kids were great, Dr. Dempsey," Jordan says after she's settled in. "You don't know what it's like. I bet you've never spent a whole week in bed in your life."

"Well, not alone," I say without thinking.

We stare at each other for a moment then erupt into laughter. She laughs and laughs and keeps on laughing until she rolls over on her side and hangs her head over the edge, retching. I grab the emesis bowl from the cupboard and hold it under her mouth. Saliva and thin foul-smelling bile drip into it. Nausea's a common accompaniment of TPN, but Jordan has been pretty well free from that nasty side effect. I help her back to the pillow. Her eyes are wide with exertion, her skin clammy. Tears trickle into her hairline. I hold a glass of water to her lips.

"How bad is the pain?"

She shrugs.

"How much?"

She holds up three fingers.

"OK. You'll be fine. Your tests look good. You only have one more week to put up with the catheter. We'll keep you here overnight. In all likelihood you can go home tomorrow."

"This equipment makes me feel like Frankenstein," she says, touching the newly installed feeding tube and grimacing. "Being sick is a full time job. That's who I am, the sick girl."

"Not at all, Jordan. Your essence shines through. You're a

brave girl."

She nods, wiping the back of her hand against her mouth and dismissing me by closing her eyes.

By the time her mother comes back in the room Jordan has recovered her spirits. I repeat what I just said about the test results.

"What about the new drug?" Mrs. Wilson asks, her face tight and expectant.

"Everybody's talking about it on the Internet," Jordan says, "but I haven't seen any testimonials yet."

"The drum beats with something to report this time," I say. "The first drug specifically designed to treat Crohn's has cleared clinical trials. Something to keep on the option list."

"You don't sound very enthusiastic," her mother says, her voice accusing.

"I don't look for magic bullets. The drug is much too new to . . . "

"Tell us how it works," she cuts in.

"It's in a class of its own—a by-product of the new genetic research, designed to block one of the proteins causing inflammation."

"Can't you be more specific?"

I hesitate. This woman is an enigma to me. I don't know if she's interested in testing my knowledge, or truly wants to know how the drug works. "The drug itself is a synthetic antibody. The specific protein affected is Tumor Necrosis Factor-Alpha." With most families all this would be information overkill, but this woman has been doing research on the immune system since Jordan was diagnosed eight years ago.

She nods, hope creeping back into her face. She seems to find comfort in having names for states of disease, to break down what's happening to her daughter into smaller and smaller components. I did at one time, too.

Jordan speaks up, her face as fresh as a flower. "How safe is it? How much good does it do? Compared to, like, seeing the *curandera*?" She looks at her mother and laughs, clearly excited.

"Whoa, girl. That's what I'm saying about waiting. We've got the time to watch for the drug's safety record."

"Has the drug been tested the whole nine yards?"

"Yes; it's just been FDA approved. The patients chosen for the study were very sick. Many patients suffered with fistulas; none were in remission; and all had long histories of drug treatment and surgeries. People who had experienced little relief from their symptoms with standard treatments."

"Worse than me?" Jordan asks.

"Certainly worse than you are at the moment, responding well to your current regimen. You can see the protocol for the clinical trials and check the Crohn's index values."

Jordan eyes me, her face young and hopeful. "What are the typical results following treatment?" she asks, mimicking the language and tone she hears spoken around her.

"In some trials, eighty percent improved, and fistulas closed, but far fewer improved in other trials. The big differential in outcomes could be worrisome. I suggest waiting until we have more data from clinical practice."

"How's the drug administered?" Jordan asks. "How long does it take?"

"Intravenously; in the hospital. It takes a couple of hours."

"What's the worst that can happen, so far?"

"Possible side effects during infusion include severe allergic reaction, but the incidence is small."

Jordan shoots her mother a smile of complicity.

"Anybody die?" her mother asks, taking a step towards the window and looking away.

"No deaths. Less than one-percent experienced a severe allergic response; all those patients responded quickly to adrenaline. Mild allergic response somewhat higher, occasional hives, handled routinely with antihistamines during infusion. Severe headache, mild fever, body aches are all common post-infusion. I could show you the tables I've done calculating risk/benefit according to the treatment profile we've established for Jordan."

"Give me the gist," the mother says, with a sharp look. "Any other downside?"

"If the patient has fistulas, three infusions are required, at two- and four-week intervals after the initial dose; the possibility of allergic reaction and post-infusion headache increases with each infusion." I pause. "It's expensive; the techies are just learning how to infuse it. Minor matters. My only objection is simply our lack of long term experience."

"You want to wait and see," Jordan sighs.

"Yes. If we wait a year, we'll know far more."

"While I'm missing out on the end of the semester!" Jordan says, her face flushing. "I'm already older than the other seniors. Except for the morons."

"My daughter Iris mentioned morons. Is there an epidemic or something?"

Jordan ignores my comment. "Tell me again what you want me to do."

"It's always better to wait for new medications. Your situation is stable."

"I'm so sick of being sick." Her face is set, her arms crossed in front of her chest.

"I hear you. But take your payoff for your weeks on TPN. You are on the mend. If it's not broke, don't fix it."

"Oh spare me, Dr. Dempsey." She crosses her eyes at me.

"Sorry," I laugh. "One more thing. Even if we fall on the fat side of the statistics and have few bothersome side effects—we don't know how long the treatment will last."

"How long did you say it takes for the whole course?"

"Three infusions, four weeks. It can be done on an outpatient basis."

"OK. Just to be fair, tell me the upside."

I can't help smiling. "Patients report they feel normal." Some people who have been sick as long as Jordan become bitter, but she's acquired an implausible, street-wise sweetness, a combination of Buddhist monk and biker. "There are people saying they got their life back."

We're motionless as lizards. The room is utterly quiet. Not

much more than a week ago Jordan was all ready to consult a *curandera*. Now she hopes technology will save her. Maybe Glover's right: it's not fair to expect patients to make rational treatment decisions. I feel like I hold this young girl's future in the palm of my hand.

"Tell you what: let's wait a month. If you're not in remission by then, let's reconsider."

She sighs. "OK. I go home tomorrow? And get rid of the rig in a week?"

I nod. Her mother and I both keep our eyes on her. Despite everything, she's beautiful. We've told her. She knows what we think. What we think doesn't matter. She's eighteen and wants that fistula gone.

"The cost is not a consideration, as I'm sure you know," the mother says.

"Yes. Make an appointment to meet at my office to look at the studies."

"I don't want you two going to your office and talking about me and my life," Jordan says. Her voice is soft and her tone weary, more effective than if she shouted. "I'll decide."

"Are you sure?" her mother asks.

"It's a lie to say I make any decision myself, even about my body. This body doesn't even feel like it's mine," Jordan says, one hand clawing at the IV line. Chronic disease fosters mood swings even without steroids.

I move next to her, clucking, fussing with the lines. Her mother doesn't move.

"You're right," says Mrs. Wilson. "You're old enough to make the decision for yourself. You go ahead. I've got to get back to work." She leaves the room without a backward glance.

Jordan sinks back into her pillows with a look of relief. "She's tired of me being sick."

"Would you and your mother like to get a second opinion on treatment?"

"Who from?"

"What about Dr. Hagan? You know her. She's looked in on

you before."

"She's OK, I guess. Tommy likes her, even though he sometimes calls her the Old Hag. Sorry," she says, clamping her hand over her mouth. She removes her hand but can't hide her smile. "Please don't tell her."

"I won't. But it wouldn't shock her. She's been called that since medical school."

"I don't need another doctor, or more medical opinions. I need to call the *curandera*, Our Lady of the Flowers."

"Lydia Flores. Yes. Let me find out whether the chief has added her to the list of spiritual advisors. In any case, I'll give you her telephone number. We'll have you on real food and back in school before you know it. For tonight, concentrate on getting some sleep."

"Yes, ma'am," she says, shutting her eyes.

Her composed young face, feigning rest, imperfectly masks a harrowed look not consistent with her medical work-up. "You'd tell me if you were experiencing any unusual pain, wouldn't you?"

"Yeah, sure," she says, without opening her eyes, "but I've forgotten what I'm supposed to feel like."

I lift my eyes from her face and look out past her through the window, thinking of the world beyond the hospital, waiting for this girl to pick up her place in it. *Should* I recuse myself from this case and let Cynthia Hagan add her to her caseload? If I do, Jordan will be destined to start the steroid symphony. True miracle drugs that demand careful handling: sooner or later steroids turn on you. I will continue to be the one to make treatment decisions for this patient.

Pain is the body's messenger. Maybe it performs a similar function for the soul. I recall the moment in the river, a boon I did nothing to earn. Since the river, the anguish that's been so much a part of my life has receded. If Jordan wants to see Lydia Flores she must be allowed to see her. I turn to speak to her again but she's asleep. When the nurse enters the room I put my finger to my lips and get up to follow her out.

PART III
THE DESERT

Chapter 14

It's been my job for over a decade to intervene when death stalks another human being. Yet up there on the mountain I was fooled by the stranger's naïve views of his own powers and prospects. He compared himself to the archangel Michael, the angel the Bible promises will *bring justice with a sword* at the end times, when the faithful find redemption. I'm a medical practitioner, trained in science. I have no experience with the whole idea of redemption. We are part of nature, the little added fillip of consciousness explicable in physical terms.

I carve out a chunk of time to go to a meeting of a group of people who had once been allied with those who took hostages up in the mountains—people who believe Texas should regain sovereignty. I try to get Al to go along with me, but there's no way, he's totally against me having anything to do with them. Next I try Travis, who also turns me down, but without prejudice, as he phrases it—grant-proposal language meaning I can apply to him again some time for a different favor and he may say yes. I don't dare call Merla—who knows, she might decide to join them.

I'm sure not ready for the sea of gray hair I encounter on walking into the meeting of separatists taking place in the community room of an apartment complex the size of a small town, somewhere off the MoPac expressway in far north Austin, halfway to Waco. At least I've nailed the dress code—in my blue silk blouse and beige pants I look like everybody else in the room, male and female, old and young. A man who looks to be in his seventies, his leathery skin a litter of moles and age spots, threads a path through the small crowd of people to stop in front of me.

"Hello. I'm Eli Norton. Glad to see a new face. Where are you from?"

"Hi. I'm Zoe. Dr. Zoe Dempsey," I say, shaking hands.

"We need to get you a name badge," he says, gesturing to the hand-printed name badge pinned to his polo shirt.

A man in a Western-cut suit, not nearly as ancient, comes up and slaps Norton on the back. He turns to me, shaking hands briskly. "Hi. I'm Duke Rainwater. Glad you could come." He turns back to the older man. "You need something, Eli?"

"Make Dr. Dempsey here a name badge, if you would be so kind."

"Let me get Nancy to find you one," he says, loping off.

"Where are you from?" Norton asks me again.

"From here. Austin."

"A lot of people come here from other chapters. Welcome to the Texas Separatists. Glad you could make it." Norton's dark eyebrows waggle, giving him a comical Groucho Marx expression, an old man bristling with energy and good health.

Rainwater comes back accompanied by a tall woman with a commanding presence. "I'd like you to know my wife, Nancy Rainwater."

"Zoe Dempsey," I say, offering my hand.

"We're from Amarillo," she says, returning my handshake in one swift motion and taking a nametag from her pants pocket, resting it against her knee, writing my name with a magic marker, and pasting it on my shoulder. "What brings you here?"

"I met a man associated with your movement who was killed in the mountains."

"You did? Where? At the compound in Fort Davis?"

"No. Out on the mountain."

"On the mountain!" she echoes "What mountain? When?"

"In the Davis Mountains, between Baldy and Blue. The day before he was shot."

She whirls around to Eli. "She met . . . somebody out in West Texas. One of us."

Eli contemplates her with a *not in front of the children* look.

"He told *me* he didn't really belong anywhere," I say.

"You were with the posse?" Eli asks me with a little grunt.

"No." I want to tell this man NO! with thunder, to tell him how I lied for the man who I took to be one of *them*, someone with a cause he ended up dead for. "No, of course not. We were staying at my uncle's place in the mountains."

"You just ran into him?" The old man's brows reach up to his white hairline. As old as he is, he's not wearing glasses.

"Something like that. I'm not trying to be mysterious. There's nothing much to tell." From Eli's imponderable face I can see I'm not going to find out anything from him.

"I never met the man, myself," Nancy Rainwater says. "From what I heard he just showed up at the Embassy and offered to help. They put him on guard duty; he'd been in the Army. Most of the folks at the compound were among the original founders. Not him."

"None of us really knew the man from California," Eli says. "He latched on to the wrong bunch. Those of us you'll meet tonight adhere to the rule of law. I can show you minutes from the meetings . . . those folks were no longer part of us." Eli looks at me, his face mottled, the color drained from behind his age spots.

"Well, now, that explains a lot," I say. What it explains is that those folks are in big trouble with the authorities and these folks aren't.

"The man whose name was Michael appeared out of nowhere," Nancy says. "He was chasing a dream."

"Curious you should say that. He said he was looking for Utopia. I told him Utopia was nowhere to be found." Is that what I told him? I can see his anguished face as clear as those in front of me. The silence gathers. "He said his name was Michael, like the Archangel."

"Ah, yes, justice with a sword and all that," Rainwater says, looking around the group with the easy assurance of a

103

large man. "He was a security guard at the compound. Now he's a martyr to the cause of liberty."

"Hell, Duke, he was a nutcase," Eli says. "Our cause would be better served without folks like him. Anybody with a serious disagreement on how this country's run is already labeled an outlaw. We have a good case for reclaiming the sovereignty of the original Republic of Texas. People in power have misused the law and we can prove it. We don't need any of this Utopian business in our deliberations."

"What do you think of the sheriff?" asks Nancy. "You're from out there."

The urge to say more about my part in all this has faded fast. "He's approachable. You might talk to him yourself."

"We should give the danged sheriff a medal," Eli says, pulling on his ear lobe, as twisted and hairy as a root.

"What for?" Nancy and I ask simultaneously.

"For not making things worse," Eli replies. "Our goal is to reestablish the original Republic of 1836. Texas has *never* legally been a part of the United States. What was done in 1845 was not done with the consent of the people. We need to prove our claim, not go around kidnapping people and getting in gun fights with the sheriff. It's as simple as that."

"Me and Duke support political activism," Nancy says to me in a low voice. "Our bookstore in Amarillo attracts like-minded people, like the Texas Separatists. That's how come we're here."

"So why do you think secession's the answer?" I ask. Everybody looks at me.

"Well, Doc, that depends on your question."

"My question is why would a man sacrifice his life . . ." I hesitate, searching for words, "on the unlikely chance of founding a New Republic of Texas?"

"Dunno," Eli says. "He wasn't even a Texan. I hear he had a few grievances against the federal government. But all of us here have our own personal reasons. I'm for establishing government by the consent of the governed before we reach the chaos we've been fumbling towards."

"We've already reached it, my friend," Rainwater says. He turns to me. "Just look around you. We're sacrificing the children. After the Feds incinerated those folks in Waco, do you remember seeing pictures of the children in the papers? Hell no. Bet you saw plenty of pictures of bleeding children after the Oklahoma City bombing."

"You don't think local government would improve things?" Nancy asks me.

"I'm not sure breaking the nation into bits and pieces is a solution," I say. "I'm a Texan, but not like I'm a doctor. I've never given much thought to politics. I've never questioned our system of government."

"You don't have to be a professional Texan to be concerned," Nancy says, "just like you don't have to be a gun nut to support the right to bear arms. Before we reach what Eli likes to call the chaos, people who are the worst off may have decided not to wait for system solutions."

"The rabble don't scare me. It's the government I fear," Rainwater says. "Our *Federales* are armed and organized, the same as they are in Mexico. The drug laws have trashed the Bill of Rights."

"We'll soon look more like Mexico on this side of the border, with a dictatorship of the ruling class," Nancy says.

A tall woman with gray hair, coiled in a braid, and long, narrow feet in elegant sandals, comes up and announces: "There's an FBI agent in the house."

Nancy and her husband both laugh. The woman looks startled. "Sorry," Nancy mumbles.

"Well, this is no joke," Eli says. "We're holding an open meeting. Why don't they just say they're from the Bureau? We have nothing to hide." He nods to me before hurrying away with the messenger.

"Did you come to hear our speaker tonight?" Nancy asks. I notice she looks exhausted.

"No. I just wanted to find out more what y'all were about."

She steps back. "Well, it's my turn to introduce the speaker— a professor from the University who's going to tell us about the secessionist movement in Alaska."

"We don't condone law-breaking and violence," Rainwater says once we're alone, his voice vehement and his delivery hurried. "Maybe we ought to recognize this man Michael in some way, but nobody's in the mood to give him a medal."

"Do you seriously think there's a chance Texas could secede from the Union?"

"Nancy and I support the Bill of Rights, especially the right to bear arms. We're not extremists, just serious about holding on to our own individual liberty. People tend to lump all activists together, but you can see the people here are not young hotheads." We look around at the group. We could be at a church social. "We see what's happening in the country. We don't intend to sit by and do nothing." He smiles at me, showing fine teeth, then reaches over and clasps my arm above the elbow. I pull back, startled. "There will come a time when even doctors will have to take sides. A time will come when you yourself, Dr. Dempsey, can no longer find a way to stay above it all. The landmass of Texas exceeds that of Spain. There may well come a time when we once again fly the flag of the Republic of Texas." He salutes me and wheels away, leaving me wondering just how a scattered mind like that of the man who was killed on the mountain might have reacted when first meeting up with such certainty.

I stand by myself out of the way, while my companions of moments before unfold chairs and set them up facing the podium. What have I come here for, anyway? If I've been hoping for some sort of closure, I'm not going to get it. Intervening in a stranger's fate calls for more than lying to the deputy sheriff. I didn't come here looking for a bunch of firebrand revolutionaries as if it were 1836, but I didn't expect to meet folks ready to hang one of their own out to dry.

I need to get out of here. Anything of real interest in this group must happen behind closed doors. While I hesitate, a short Latino woman about my age appears in front of me and sticks out her hand.

"Hello. I've been told I should introduce myself to everyone. I'm Agent Gomez from the Federal Bureau of Investigation," she beams. "You and I need to talk."

"Dr. Dempsey from Doctor's Hospital. I can't talk now; I'm not staying for the speaker."

The beam fades. "I know who you are. We will need to find another time to talk, then." She reaches into her purse, takes out a calling card, and hands it to me, displaying major fake talons in glossy red polish. "Call me, why don't you, Dr. Dempsey. That way we can keep our discussion low key, since you're a doctor and all."

She turns and clumps away, her short back rigid in a blue jacket with a little peplum jutting out over her jiggling hips. I look at the flimsy scrap of cardboard in my hand: Rachel Gomez, Austin telephone number; no physical address. I stow her card in my pocket and go for the door.

Nancy Rainwater accosts me just as I get to the exit. "Duke's talking to the G-girl," she says, gesturing with a toss of her head. "Can't you stay for the speaker?"

I look around. The FBI agent is talking to Rainwater while others are taking their seats. I have an awful feeling I'm off-limits. I shake my head no without even the attempt at a smile. Nancy doesn't pursue it, and I make my escape.

Chapter 15

I t's been three weeks since I've given a single thought to what's going on in the world outside the hospital. Jeff Glover calls me for consults in the most farfetched circumstances just to keep me running fourteen hours a day. Al's life, on the other hand, has been pretty cushy as far as work goes. Finally, when he and Iris go away to a three-day horse show, I start on the drive to Fort Davis as if I'd been planning this trip back to the mountains ever since we left. Even though Anna was all set for me to impose on one of her friends as soon as I let her know where I was going, I stay in the hotel downtown. In the morning I walk across the dirt yard near the Chevron station, past a cluster of propane tanks up on stilts, to reach the unassuming structure kitty-corner from the courthouse that shelters the sheriff of Jeff Davis County.

The sheriff, looking spiffy in a starched white uniform shirt, twill khaki pants, and boots, walks out on the covered porch to greet me. Up until the time of the shoot-out, Texans seemed to view the saga of the sheriff and the separatists as a musical comedy. Still, the man has never looked ridiculous. Now he's something of a hero to both the national and local press for turning away offers of help from the ATF and for calling off his own posse with a man still out there. But what may have started off comically has turned sour, with one man dead.

"Excuse the getup," he says, loosening his black tie before shaking my hand. "I've just been to a funeral over in Valentine." He's a whole generation older than me—he was out of college over at Sul Ross before I started primary school. His wife was my fifth-grade teacher. I have always heard it said that her husband is a straight shooter, a phrase that in the circumstances suddenly sounds sinister.

"I've been wanting to talk to you for weeks," I say, sitting down in the visitor's chair. He merely raises his eyebrows and settles himself behind his desk. The room looks like the kind of private lair all men seem to have back beyond the shed.

"I went to a meeting of the separatist folks in Austin. Just to get an idea of what they are all about. They seem supportive of how you handled the whole . . .

"Unfortunate incident?" he fills in.

"Yes."

"Tell me, what is your interest, exactly?" His tone is mild. Reporters from all over the country have tried to chase this guy down for an interview in the last month. He's turned every one of them away. He's not about to let me rattle him.

"I'm most interested in the part of the unfortunate incident where the man was shot on the mountain not far from us." I can hardly tell the sheriff I *met* the man on the mountain and then misled his deputy a couple of hours later.

"Your husband's not from around here, is he?"

"No. I met him at UT in Austin," I say politely to his change of course.

"I had a chance to visit with him when he was judging at the Science Fair last year."

"Oh! That's nice," I say. "Al knows how to fit in better than I do."

"I can see how that might happen. My wife Alma tells me you were destined to go away and make us proud."

"I know I'm no sort of a stakeholder in Jeff Davis County any longer, but this place is still home to me. What happened on the mountain? I need to know." Of course I know what I'm saying is utter nonsense—I'm not anywhere in the same ball park with the people who have a need to know in this situation. But my grandparents were people of stature in this community. I sit back to discover how far that will take me.

The sheriff steeples his fingers on his chest and leans his chair way back to gaze at the ceiling. He comes back down with a thump and splays his hands on his heavy thighs.

"You ever had a man shoot at you, Dr. Dempsey?"

"No. I never have." I keep my eyes focused on his, as if I could discern the man behind the bushy eyebrows and the weathered skin and know if he's telling me the truth.

"Well, I have. More than once." He turns his head and stares out the window so long I begin to wonder what he's looking at. When I lean over to look with him there's nothing to see.

"Anybody who shoots at another man is desperate. Those folks back at what they called their Embassy let off a few shots. But at the end of the day, that old boy who ran the outfit—he wanted to live. Firing off them shots upped the ante. He knew he was in deep, taking hostages. For what? To get us to recognize a ragtag bunch as a sovereign nation?" The sheriff shakes his head. "He acted the fool for sure. He faces about 99 years in jail." The Sheriff looks at me as if expecting some confirmation from me, but I sit tight. He chews on the corner of his moustache. "On the other hand, the man who run off—the dude from California—what he did was make up his mind to die. Can't say as I blame him."

"The dude from California," I repeat. Sometimes it seems to me we get tangled up in our own fairy tales. This is *Giant* country. Old movie posters of Rock Hudson and Elizabeth Taylor are pasted all over the Paisano Hotel in Marfa, just to the south.

"The Californian who went to live at the compound was a dude," the sheriff says, "like a lot of others who come here to West Texas to play cowboy. This one stayed long enough to find out the rattlesnakes were real. But you—you knew that already. You were staying up at Clayton's when it all come to grief."

"Yes. Uncle Clayton was sheep ranching down near Mason. We went back to Austin just as the roadblock was put up. To go canoeing down the Guadalupe River." I stop myself and smile stupidly. Our life sounds ridiculously privileged. "It was spring break."

"Yeah, I recall. Anyway, Dr. Dempsey, the stranger from California didn't know a thing about our ways. The folks he joined up with made him into some sort of security guard. He'd walk around out there all day in a cocked-up uniform, like a grown-up kid playing cops and robbers. He'd come into town for supplies. I don't know what was driving the poor son of a bitch, and I'm sorry as all get-out he came here to Jeff Davis County to die. But he did. That's what he come here for, all right. He was set on getting himself killed. He went for the dogs! He got his wish, and now everybody's on my ass."

"Oh please, spare me the poor dogs angle," I break in. "As much as I love dogs, the man was driven to the rim of the world! It didn't have to happen."

"Where did it *not* have to happen?" the sheriff shoots back, his face contorted. "Not here, not on my patch. By the time he got here, his fate was fixed. Can't you see?"

"No, I can't see. But I hear what you're saying. For him, it didn't start here in the mountains. It was in all the papers. He felt like he'd been screwed around before he got here. But here's where it ended." I pause. I'm on shaky ground. "The man lost heart in America long before he ended up shot dead."

"Yeah, well, we all lose heart some days. He was an outlier, Zoe. Beyond our help. He didn't have the sense God gave a possum."

"What bothers me the most is he was shot in the back."

The sheriff shakes his head back and forth and then thumps his belly with his thumb like you would a melon to see if it's ripe. "That pains me. I can't explain why he took his bullet in the back except to say it's got to be a damned hard thing to decide to die." He heaves a sigh. "My guess is, after he provoked the sally of return fire he threw down his gun and turned and ran. He was already on the outs with his own *compadres*. Now I'm talking to you . . ."

"Like any prosecutor even just out of school would tell you not to . . ."

"Hell, my *wife* told me not to. I'm more afraid of her than I am of any prosecutor!"

This remark startles me into a bark of laughter. The sheriff joins me. His wife Alma's a formidable woman, with a hairdo like Governor Ann Richards'. The sheriff smoothes back his own impressive thatch of hair while he rumbles to a stop. I briefly picture him and Alma over dinner after a hard day's work running the county.

"My jurisdiction stops at the county line. I'm surrounded by six counties. On the other side of every one of those borders somebody else has to make decisions. But on this side of the border, it's my job. When you take on the job you know you have to make the hard calls. And then you have to live with them. You're a doctor. You've been on the line. So that's why I'm talking to you."

"Yeah. Hard calls. I've had some of those." I pause. "The man was shooting at you and your men? You give me your word on that?"

The man pulls himself around to his desk and leans on his massive forearms. When he speaks, looking straight ahead of him, his voice is hoarse. "Dr. Dempsey: my job is to protect." He shifts his body away from me and looks out the window. "In Nam, my job was to kill the enemy. I did not choose that man who got himself killed for my enemy. He chose me and my men. End of story."

"Why are you letting the Texas Rangers do the talking?"

He turns to me and smiles. "Better PR; way better'n some little old piss-ant sheriff from a mountain county in West Texas. All along I was afraid of something happening here like it happened in Waco." With an unhappy look on his face he raises his hands palms out—*don't shoot.* "But don't let's get started on that."

We stare at each other, recalling the shoot-out and killing fire at Waco. Unlike the Alamo, something Texans would as soon forget.

"The Rangers don't have a better rep with me," I say to break the silence. "I grew up here."

"Well, thank you, ma'am. Now I've been fair with you, why don't you tell me the real reason you're so interested."

I'm tempted to tell him. The story of how the stranger and I confronted each other on the mountain slouches like a dog on the rug in the space between us. "We were up here when it all came down. The event struck me like a prophetic dream. I couldn't forget about it."

The sheriff slams his hands down on his desk. "I'm Sheriff of a Texas county named after a dead president of the Confederate States. Every day I walk into the courthouse, a relic of another era. There are some things I can't afford to forget." He gets up and starts pacing. "A gun-brandishing nutcase was running around the mountain shooting at my deputies. If you don't think I've thought of everything you have, twice over . . . I wasn't the man who shot the stranger and I'm sorry the son-of-a-bitch is dead, I truly am. Don't go thinking I might have *forgotten* who I am, or where I am, or what-all went down, because I damn sure haven't."

I give time for his proclamation to settle. "Why *did* you let the whole outfit make themselves to home like you did?" I ask at length.

He gazes out the window again, his face as placid as a baby's. "You're not the first to ask that. I guess if the truth were known, their whole project kind of tickled me." He looks back at me, studying my face. "For the most part they were earnest, decent, educated people. The leader—the one who started the place everybody around here ended up calling the Embassy— him I mishandled, let him go too far with his silly proclamations. He got to thinking he was outside the law and started making his own. I should've come down on him quicker, served him the arrest warrant for his refusal to appear at my office in regard to the nuisance liens he filed. Instead I dallied around. Bloodshed is just what I was trying to avoid. The poor bastard from California got caught up in the playacting. Now he's dead for real."

"What about the other guy? The guy who's still on the run?"

The sheriff shuts down like a snapping turtle. "Can't rightly say. Far gone from these parts, that is for sure."

I say goodbye to the sheriff, aware that the part of me Al can't deal with is captured perfectly in the sheriff's quixotic taste for the outsiders who settled in his county hoping to restore the Republic of Texas. Nuttiness is catching. It's not so much because the mythic essence of what it means to be a Texan has morphed into one more icon of pop culture. No, it's because this Texas is visceral, backward, and primitive, composed of a love of immense space, blinding light, shadows black enough to make a horse shy out from under you, and critters trying to eke out a tolerable existence in a hostile environment. Al can't reach me when I'm hunkered down in that particular place. Maybe that knowledge makes him lonely, maybe it makes him mad. No telling. It sure doesn't leave him indifferent, anymore than I could be when confronted with a stranger caught up in the Texas myth where, like the sheriff said, the rattlesnakes turned out to be real. Maybe in running into the stranger on the mountain I came face to face with myself only to find out I'm more of an outlier than I let on.

Chapter 16

Back in Austin after my weekend away, Iris recounts how well she did at the horse show; I admire her ribbons. It's easy to put off telling Al about my visit with the sheriff. We're both frantic to make time to forget the world together. Maybe he's right, maybe in general I am the one who is secretive, but he's definitely shown an aversion to discussing the events in West Texas. Although I'm still at a loss to explain the meaning of my chance encounter with the man who was killed, at least I no longer suspect that someone from my own tribe slaughtered him for no reason. Maybe I don't know any better than the fool on the mountain just where I belong, but I continue with my duties at home and at work nevertheless.

Al leaves early for surgery in the morning. It's barely light, but Anna goes out to the garden to enjoy a morning without rain. After a breakfast of juice and a granola bar I peek in Iris's door. She rears up on her elbow with a sweet look on her sleepy face. I step inside her room, negotiating around the clothes and shoes dropped on the floor along with an impressive pile of show ribbons. She's already turned over to go back to sleep. I drop a kiss on her head.

The Suburban hulks in the driveway where I left it. I'm soon speeding down the Southwest Parkway, all three luxurious lanes in each direction stark empty at this early hour. The view from the top of the known world, a mass of greenery falling away from the ridge, the expected development still lurking beyond the rim of the hills, takes me out of myself. But it's only ten miles to the Lamar Street Bridge, one of three downtown bridges over the Colorado connecting the workers from South Austin to the city where traffic begins to back-up shortly after 7:00 A.M. Speeding along in the extravagant morning, I can see in my mind's eye what it was like when all you could see from this distance was the pink granite Capitol and the infamous UT Tower, while in my present view a dozen different downtown buildings and huge houses begin to punctuate the sea of trees. We live on the Edwards Plateau, an ecologically fragile area west and south of town where limestone encases the aquifer providing the inhabitants with most of their water. Water percolates upward to limestone aquifers like Barton Springs, fed by a creek lined with cypresses that runs right through the property owned in common by Al and me and about a hundred neighbors. We live in Eden, but after the fall—this is a gated community.

A cop car looms up on my bumper, red light whirling. I pull over and get out of the car, grabbing my purse to stand in the wide breakdown lane, my back to the car. The sun's coming up behind me as I focus on the young policeman walking up, looking from my face over my shoulder into the car.

"Do you know how fast you were traveling?" he asks, touching the brim of his hat. He's wearing sunglasses in the gray morning.

"No, I don't know the exact speed, officer. I was thinking of getting to the hospital."

"May I have your driver's license and insurance card, please?" I have them ready, and smartly hand them over.

"Is this an emergency?" he asks, not looking up from his task of fastening my papers on his clipboard.

"I'm a doctor responding to a call in regard to one of my patients in the hospital." The cop already knows I'm a doctor, it says so on the vanity plates Al put on the car for my birthday last June. I stare down at the ground while he writes on his pad.

"Here you go, Doctor Dempsey," he says, handing me a yellow slip of paper, along with my license and insurance card.

"I'm only issuing you a warning this time. Please watch your speed from now on. In all likelihood you are called to the hospital quite frequently. The next time you're caught speeding you will be issued a speeding ticket. If it turns out to be an emergency you can sort it out at the courthouse."

I take the papers, smiling humbly, and step into the car. My legs are shaky as I take my place behind the wheel. I pull back out on the road apprehensively, aware of his eyes on me and that my reprieve is conditional. What difference does it make how fast I go, on this road, in this car, under these conditions? I put the car on cruise control and try to relax. While the trooper's still following along behind me, the clouds open. Soon the wipers can barely handle the torrent. The black and white finally pulls around me.

The smell of chemicals catches in my throat the moment I push my way through the heavy door into the morgue. As far as Travis is concerned, our friendship stops at the threshold to his professional domain, as it should. I need to tread carefully, but I always feel a surge of excitement walking in here. Doctors are burying mistakes without a post-mortem way more than they used to, not giving Travis a chance to find out how accurate the diagnosis, how useful the treatment, or what could have been done differently. Indisputable information originates in the morgue. Glover demands more post-mortems than anybody else does, but he is not called upon to share his findings with the rest of us except on rare occasions.

Travis gives instruction to an assistant and beckons me to follow him over to his desk.

"An unauthorized person has been visiting the morgue lately," he says as soon as we sit down knee to knee in the corner harboring his desk, computer, monitor, printer, fax, phones, chairs, water bottle and electric kettle.

"What?" My voice booms in the echoing basement. I rein myself in and start over. "Sneaking in? How's that possible?"

"Maybe it's somebody masquerading as an intern."

"Wearing white polyester, an arrogant look pasted on his

117

face?"

"You got it. But I'm betting it's a patient I've seen hanging around in the basement, somebody from the gastro support group. You know him? Post-op kid racing around dragging his IV pole?"

"Tommy Arbuckle, I'd guess." I push my chair back from Travis, shake off my clogs and put my feet up next to him on the oak swivel chair. He politely makes room. "I do not know how you can wear those boots all day, as much standing as you do."

"Is he one of your patients?"

"No. Cynthia Hagan's. He was a big help in getting the gastro support going. We've tried it before but it never caught on."

"He'll probably turn out to be a doctor. But it's no good him sneaking around. It's disrespectful to the dead." Travis hunches his shoulders and looks around, as if he expects the dead, none of them visible, to overhear. "Could you speak to Tommy—tell him to come see me? I'll give him an informed tour."

"I'll do what I can."

"Thanks. Now tell me what *you* need."

"We don't have that much time," I say. I was only trying to be funny, but Travis's face bunches up like I socked him. I pull myself back on track. "Help me debunk Glover's report and defang his f-ing graphs. He was showing morbidity stats, but left off mortality figures. Morbidity at least shows we're *doing* something. Immune system interventions are strong stuff."

"Better to be sick than dead," Travis says.

"Exactly. Can you tell me where to find the original mortality data for the whole gastro pod? Skip the Byzantine need-to-know baloney. I need to know."

"It's not baloney, Zoe. It's meant to protect the patient's privacy. What if an employer finds out somebody's got a propensity for some disease and on that basis denies them a job?"

"You're right, of course. I'm as secretive as the next person, believe me." I pull my feet off his chair and stuff them back in my clogs. "I promise to keep the files under tight security. I need them to counter Glover's assertions."

"I can give you copies of some original files stored down here and get one of my scut-monkeys to retrieve M & M tables for you."

"How do you know what to get?"

"Simple. The same files he wanted plus his own."

"Fantastic." We stand up at the same moment. I grab him by the hand and pull him into dance position.

"Learn to prioritize," Travis says, turning me in a little fifties-style swing, "and don't expect to find redemption at the hospital." We stop, facing each other chest to chest.

"I hate that word *prioritize*. It sounds like a disease." But I love kindness and comfort. My body softens against him. He lets go of me like he's been stung, taking away his body heat and his own comforting odor, faintly discernible behind the drench of tobacco. "No, come to think of it, it sounds more like a drug," I say to cover my confusion.

"You can't always get what you want by grabbing it, Zoe."

"You can't always get what you want," I sing, snapping my fingers to the Reggae beat. "Speaking of wanting what you can't have, I went to a meeting last night of people who want Texas to become a Republic again."

"The people who want to *take back Texas?*"

"Those are the people defending private property. They get into disputes with the environmentalists. These folks want Texas to secede from the Union, so they get in trouble with the Attorney General."

"Be careful about your new buddies, Zoe."

"They're not my new buddies." I watch him as he cobbles together over a dozen fat files. "You're a prince, Travis," I say when he hands them to me. He mutters something I don't catch as I go out the heavy door. I walk down the hall, feeling a surge of energy. Working shoulder to shoulder with my best friend, I can play dirty, too. Yippee.

By the time I get to my office with the files, I have no time to sort through them. Travis is sure right about one thing—my need to prioritize. I seem to be losing the knack for putting different aspects of life into separate compartments, a capacity a doctor needs to survive. I'll have to come back later to look through these case histories on patients Glover or I have treated since I started working at Doctor's Hospital. I'll sort them according to diagnosis and analyze the whole path, from diagnosis to treatment to outcome, from mild relapse, to full-blown flare, to death. What was it Merla said about unprecedented events and unpredictable outcomes? It's time to grab hold and defend myself.

As I gather my stuff to go home I notice the plants are doing better. The once dying lily's in bloom. Even the violets disclose shy new leaves. Maybe Lydia's treatment worked.

Chapter 17

Turning too fast into the drive, I have to hit the brakes to keep from crashing into the garage door, opening at a mockingly slow pace. Al and I have built a house for all of us, for him and me and Iris and Anna, on a five-acre lot loaded with trees, a refuge from the world. I punch the electronic garage-door gizmo to send the door back down. The house, built out of weathered wood and stone, has a down-home Texas feel, fantastically expensive to create. Parked in the driveway, I ponder how Iris's life is set apart from the lives of ordinary people in a way mine never was. In the mountains, I'm still an ordinary person in a county where everybody knows everybody else, while here in Austin I'm a rich doctor. I can hear our new dog Grendel barking in a constant harsh yelp, like she's treed a possum. But no, it's not a possum. Two strangers come out the door of my screen porch and stop awkwardly for a moment on the steps, taking their wallets out of their breast pockets and dangling their badges in front of them. They descend the steps to stand behind their out-thrust badges on the pathway.

"FBI, ma'am. Are you Dr. Dempsey?" the older man asks.

I get out of the Suburban, holding my phone in one hand and my purse in the other.

"Very official looking," I mutter, my eyes skittering over the shields held out to me, then back to the men's faces. Dark protuberant sunglasses make them look like insects.

"Can we talk?" asks the older of the two men, pocketing his wallet. I take my keys out of my purse, while I study the intruders. One has regular features and closely cut hair. The other one is colorless as a grub, the sort women everywhere call a creep.

"Give me a minute."

I go through the porch to the front door to free Grendel, who rushes out, hackles raised in a satisfying orange ruff running down her back from neck to tail, growling from deep in her throat. I put a hand on her collar and pull her back inside with me, then close and lock the door behind me. Hurrying through the front hall, I pick up a pair of socks from the floor and a coffee cup from a table piled with mail. Theresa comes two days a week to clean. Today's not one of her days. These guys strike me as comical, characters out of a bad play. Grendel disagrees. Better not to let them see anything personal.

"I'm coming," I yell before running to the bathroom to pee. While I wash my hands, I study my face in the mirror. Still looks like me behind the eyes—at least somebody's on my side. I've got myself centered by the time I open the door to the two unsmiling men. Grendel holds her ground next to me, guarding the threshold with a continuous rumbling growl.

"Hang on a minute," I say, taking the leash off the hook inside the door and fastening it to her collar. We lead the way to the porch, Grendel voicing her concern with her lips drawn back in a snarl, nose wrinkled up, fangs showing. She flicks an eye my way, registering her disapproval as clearly as if she could speak. The last time I remember handling my rifle was when I put it on top of the car, up in the mountains. Always aware of the possibility somebody could get ahold of firearms belonging to me, I mentally trace what I did with it until I'm sure it's locked and safe in the gun-closet upstairs. I turn to the two men, still standing on the spacious porch.

"Is there some place we can sit and talk a moment, ma'am?" the older man asks, watching me intently, ignoring Grendel. His lack of concern for the dog scares me. No doubt he's got a lethal deterrent.

"I can't talk to you when I can't see your eyes."

"Yes ma'am," the man says, removing his glasses and pocketing them in one swift gesture. "I'm Frank Green from the Federal Bureau of Investigation, and this is my assistant, Mr.

Collins." Mr. Collins doesn't even pretend to smile, but watching Green for instructions, bobs his head at me mutely, his mien a mix of aggression and servility, and removes his sunglasses. Is he the hired help or the killer guard-dog?

"How long is this going to take? Why not talk right here?" I stand my ground, an ancient defense, hard-wired into my brain from early childhood. The dog still growls low in her throat; I put my hand down to pet her without dropping the leash. "Tell me how I can help you."

Grendel sits close to my feet and leans against my leg. She gives me heart.

"You're a doctor." Green says. "Would you mind telling me your specialty?" The younger man checks his equipment in rapid pats and pulls out a little notebook. He starts to take a step closer but retreats when the dog growls.

"Immunology," I say, watching as the word is duly recorded in the notebook before returning my attention to my questioner.

"You go often to the Davis Mountains?"

"Once or twice a year."

"When was the last time you were there?"

"Last month. April. The cruelest month."

"Pardon?"

"It's from a poem. 'April is the cruelest month.'"

"Yes, ma'am."

"Why?" asks the note-taker.

"Why what?"

"Why is April the cruelest month?"

"The weather promises to be kind, then turns cold and cruel without warning."

His face tells me he's pleased with my answer. I get it. They teach you that about selling—get your mark to agree to something, that gets her halfway to the sale. I kick myself.

Green takes over again after our digression. "You spoke to one of the county sheriff's men last month. He asked you if you had met anybody hiding out in the mountains?"

"Are you asking me or telling me?"

"I'm referring to Deputy McDermott's report. I'd like to hear your version of events."

"Is Gilberto in trouble or something?"

"We'll ask the questions," Collins cuts in. I try not to snicker. Who writes his lines?

"No, of course not," Green says, quelling his sidekick with a look. "You may have heard: the individual missing since the action near Fort Davis has been apprehended. He's in the custody of the Texas Rangers."

Another man left the compound ahead of the sheriff. It was in the papers. But they called off the manhunt after Michael was killed. Grendel looks up at me with a piercing whine. I pet her until she drops her head back on her paws.

"Now, back to your conversation with your friend Deputy McDermott . . ." Green begins.

I interrupt. "Gilbert and I barely know each other. I no longer live in the mountains."

"Yes ma'am: about your *acquaintance*, Deputy Sheriff Gilberto McDermott. I'm just curious. Why did you ask me if he was in trouble?"

I don't say anything.

"If he was in trouble, it wouldn't be with us," he continues. "McDermott works for the Jeff Davis County Sheriff's Department. He reported asking you if you saw anybody that day."

"Gilberto told me they were looking for somebody, yes."

"What did you tell him?"

"Not much. The place was jumping. As you say, we kinda know each other. Since he was a kid. That's how it is in the mountains."

"Yes, ma'am. Doctor." This man Green, evidently the senior of the two, is a perfect specimen of what shrinks call *without affect*—he comes across as if nothing has *ever* affected him. A curious condition. His eyes are expressionless, opaque. I knew a kid in grammar school whose dad worked for the Secret Service. Same look. Doctors do it too. Hide behind the professional mask. The Percocet did that and more—it granted me immunity from the unbearable.

"But you did meet with someone in the mountains," Green says at last. "A man evading arrest, who was later shot in a gun battle with authorities."

"Are you telling me I met somebody? Or saw somebody?" The image of the man I encountered in the mountains, his look of pain and puzzlement, flames into my mind.

"We're asking you to relate your memory of events," the man says.

But the man is not asking. He knows something I don't. I slow way down inside. Everything in the room freezes, including my interrogators, like I've hit the pause button. After my man was shot they called off the hunt. Hundreds and hundreds of cops were out combing the hills. But there were *two* guys who fled the compound. One of these men was still at large when the sheriff asked the Texas Rangers to call it quits. What should I tell these guys? Why not tell them everything? What do I have to hide? Why not be honest?

"You guys are badgering me. I don't like it." The words tumble from my mouth, unplanned.

Collins steps toward me, visibly irritated. "We're doing nothing of the sort."

Green puts a hand on his sleeve to stop him. "Take your time," he says to me.

You've got much to learn, my lad, I think, glaring at the younger man. You need to train yourself not to give so much away. His face shows an almost physical yearning to talk to somebody who actually spoke to the man killed in the mountains. Could this be the man who pulled the trigger? Who shot the man in the back? Surely it would have had to be a sharpshooter, not a low-level bureaucrat. My spine stiffens. Tuning in to my reaction to his sidekick, the older man fixes him with a level look, quelling him. Hierarchy's what these agencies and institutions are all about, just like at the hospital. The stripes on your sleeve and the campaigns under your belt contribute to status and confer the right to give orders. Telling other folks what to do and how to do it at the most trivial level is the payoff for a shitty job. These guys can't be making much money. Nobody makes much at this level, visiting people door-to-door and asking questions.

"What do you really need to know? I've just worked around the clock. I need some sleep before I go back to work." Work. This is America. We all respect work.

"How exactly are you involved with the movement to form a Republic of Texas?"

"Involved? How quaint. I think the whole idea of Texas seceding is a pastime, like wrestling alligators in the Everglades." As soon as I say that I feel a thread of shame. Why am I ingratiating myself with these people?

"Why'd you help them out, then?" Green asks.

"What do you mean, help them out? I don't even know them. I wasn't one of their neighbors at The Resort. We stay at my uncle's place, miles away." Why am I insisting on this? Helping out the secessionists, or separatists, whatever they call themselves—what would that mean? Don't we have the right to gather together and discuss anything we want? Except maybe the overthrow of the government. Sedition. "What about the Bill of Rights—don't we have the right to assemble?" I finally ask, feeling ignorant.

"The Bureau is interested in details concerning your relationship with the group *assembling* in the Davis Mountains with the purpose of reinstating the Republic of Texas," Green says, spreading the words out evenly, like beads on a chain.

"You're kidding. I have a patient I still need to check on at the hospital. I'd like to have a few minutes to myself. What's the matter with you people?" My indignation's real, but my tone's oddly fake. Even though what I said is true: I left without talking to Jordan.

Collins, with the unreadable no-color eyes, casts a questioning look at his colleague. Getting the nod, he turns to me and starts talking, glancing over at his companion after every few words, like he's reading a TelePrompTer.

"The man who fled the mountains at the end of April was apprehended. A map was found in his wallet. Drawn in pencil on a piece of paper with your name printed on it. Why?"

"You found something of mine on this guy?" I ask, astonished. "That's impossible."

The two men glance at each other. In my mind's eye I see the face of my mountain man, the look of childlike bewilderment. Did he see me as someone in authority, like the guys standing in front of me? I look away from them, my hands curling into fists.

"Yes," the younger man says on the out-breath. The older man barely moves his chin. Collins leaps into action, picking up a leather briefcase from the coffee table and extracting a glossy eight-by-ten photo to hand to me—a mug shot of a man in his twenties. I look at the photo carefully, holding it in my hand.

"I've never seen this man in my life," I say, handing the photo back. Nothing in the papers indicated that the two men were together. But they must have been.

"You're sure? It's been awhile, like you said. You want to look at it again?" The younger man seems momentarily off guard. He sounds genuinely bewildered.

"I'm sure." He'll catch on soon enough. I look at my watch. "If you need to see me again, make an appointment. Cross your t's and dot your i's before you bother me again. Maybe we can all get our jobs done."

"We'll be back in touch," Green says, taking his sunglasses from his breast pocket and reinstating them carefully to his face before turning to the door. The sidekick has also put his glasses back on. He opens the porch door for his partner and they're gone. The two of them remind me of immune system cells, screening me to determine whether I'm a threat. They can check me out. They'll see me for another component of the self-system, to be tolerated. But I should've called Gomez.

While I was occupied with the FBI clones I barely registered Al and Iris coming in through the garage. I find them sitting in the kitchen already eating. Anna's gone to a movie. I promise Al I'll tell them everything after I take a bath, and apologize to Iris for skipping dinner.

The next thing I know, Al's getting me out of the tub, wrapping me in his robe, helping me into bed—me being a tiny consciousness in a weary woman's body in the arms of a solicitous husband. In bed, we make gentle love. How can Al feel desire for me when there's so little of me? I can't imagine, but I'm grateful. We're back in the habit of pleasing each other in all sorts of ways, in and out of bed. Parts of me seem to be catching on sooner than other parts.

Chapter 18

In the morning, I pat the bed, checking to see if Al's still there, knowing he's not. Remembering the men from the FBI, dread coats my throat, but the cheerful sounds coming from the kitchen help me out of bed. It's Anna who makes sure we all have a home and not just a place to prepare for work, and I'm eager to see her. I dress quickly and head for the kitchen. Strong and scrawny at seventy-two, every wrinkle and fold of her tanned skin revealed by the overhead light, Anna's getting a cup of coffee from the pot on the stove.

"Long time no see, Grandma," I say from behind her.

She turns around to look at me, her face alive and curious. "Good morning, Zoe. Al told me the FBI interviewed you! What did they want?" She hands me my coffee.

"It's about the man the posse caught up with in the mountains near the cabin." His puzzled face appears to me in perfect eidetic detail. "The FBI found out I talked to him."

"Oh, Zoe. So now the Yankees can come tell us who we can talk to in our own back yards?" Anna considers everybody north of the Red River a Yankee.

"They can't help but be curious about someone who's succeeded in the system they've vowed to protect consorting with people plotting the overthrow of the government."

"Consorting!" Anna repeats with a disgusted snort that makes me laugh. "I heard that the sheriff got Janet Reno on the phone. 'No thank you, ma'am,'" she mimics, thumb and pinky to ear, "'we don't need your help right now, we got everything

129

in hand here.' When the FBI and the ATF showed up, they had to wait at the barricades. I bet those sharpshooters were steaming, cooling their heels along with the reporters."

"Yeah. After Waco, the sheriff would be a fool not to have qualms about the Feds. I guess it would be hard for them to swallow, the little old country boy protecting his jurisdiction."

"Standing up to the Justice Department, just like not hassling those folks any sooner than he did, is why we elected him sheriff. He's a courtly sort of man. I knew his father."

"What else do you know, Anna?"

"Revolutions are easier to start than to finish. Everything changes, but not always in the way you hope."

"Did Mother and all those sixties chicks know they were starting a revolution?"

"Maybe. Your mother went to consciousness-raising sessions. That's all we thought they were doing up at the compound: consciousness raising."

"If that's what they're doing, they did a piss-poor job of it. They just get lumped in with the nuts and outlaws."

"Well, don't you go pissing off the FBI. They're the ones you need to watch out for."

"Oh, Anna, don't worry. I haven't done a damn thing to interest the Bureau. The people giving me the most grief right now are my colleagues at work."

"Lives were ruined in the fifties, when the FBI was checking out how *American* we all were. I know it's hard to believe things that happened before you were born are real, but take my word for it. It doesn't pay to get the attention of the FBI."

"OK, Grandma, I'll try not to offend them." I struggle for some perspective. "I acted without thinking."

"You were in real danger in the river. Do you feel you're in danger now?" Anna's serious.

"Go on, honey, go on, tell me," she says when I don't answer.

"That's just it—going on. The river was a lesson in letting go."

"Taking hold might be more to the point. You believed in

God when you were a little girl; up to when your mother died. You could ask for guidance."

"Isn't that pretty much what I just said? Nearly drowning has made me glad to be alive. I feel more like myself than I have in a long while."

Anna comes over and puts her arms around me. "You've never had a problem being yourself," she says, talking into space over my shoulder. "You had a problem connecting to the rest of us."

She steps back to give me a hard look, her hand still on my shoulder. I bite my lip and feel my abs stiffen against the old stories about my troubled girlhood. Anna lets me go.

"Tell me if you need anything, you hear?" she says.

"You bet." I smooth her ropy arm and kiss her cheek, then dig my chin into the place between her neck and shoulder like I did when I was little, making her laugh.

When I leave the house I go all the way over to a drugstore on South Congress, off my beaten path, to pick up a pregnancy test kit. Grabbing one from the supply cabinet at the hospital is not an option. The smell of the store reminds me of buying my first condoms—how startled Al was when I pulled them out of my pocket! They never failed us. When I got pregnant with Iris it was a choice, or at least we thought so. Nature's supply of baby lust may have had a hand.

I'm too busy all day to get a chance to do the test. Do I want to pass or fail a pregnancy test? Too soon to tell.

The following morning, after Al leaves for the hospital, I finally get the chance to use the pregnancy test kit. Results: highest honors, according to the little blue strip. I'm pregnant. Staring at the flimsy sign I'm carrying a child, I'm wildly glad I quit the pain pills. But why didn't I get two kits? The insert in the package, not intended for doctors, doesn't cite statistics on false positives, but I know it's not negligible. I need to be sure before I tell Al. I wasn't thinking like a doctor.

Chapter 19

Not until the weekend do Al and I find time to be alone together. Both Anna and Iris are out, Anna for the evening and Iris on yet another sleepover at Amanda's. Now's the chance to tell Al I'm pregnant, but I hesitate too long. Instead of revelations, we talk about work, like we mostly do when we're alone. We rehash the staff meeting, already so long past that the whole discussion is as appetizing as cold oatmeal.

"Frank didn't stop Glover from crossing the line. That was character assassination," I complain, "not case discussion."

"Forget Frank. Screw Glover," Al says. He leaps up out of his chair and puts out a hand to pull me up. "Let's go to Stacey Livingood's party. There's supposed to be dancing."

He enfolds me in his arms, pulling me to my feet. When we're both standing he leans his weight on me like a boxer in a clinch. We begin to move our feet around slowly, holding on, dancing to music. Al hums under his breath. After a short time he steers me to the bedroom, but not to get ready for the party. Naked and alone, shining and happy, we come together in a glorious enactment of the ancient *pas de deux*. Sex redeems everything. After the interlude, a moment out of time, we put our clothes back on and go out to face the social world.

"Not everyone's a doctor, at least," I mutter to Al as we step across the threshold into Stacey and Bill Livengood's house, where a maid in uniform stands at the door, welcoming us. We've left the car in the circular drive for the promised valet parking—rich Texans love feudal trappings. Our hostess, thin to the point of anorexia and as pale as cream custard in a seemingly transparent party dress, wafts up to us. "Come in, come, come, we're just about to serve dinner, Doctors, you're way behind the rest of us," she says. "I'm told this darling man sings marvelous Scottish folksongs," she says, latching on to Al's arm, "if courted in just the right fashion." She looks at Al as if he's edible.

"Welsh. Welsh folksongs," he says, looking at me helplessly over his shoulder, his opium receptors no doubt flashing pleasure.

"We've all been sipping glorious margaritas," she continues, pulling Al along.

Abandoned by my husband and the siren, I'm rescued by a young person dressed in black, black-dyed vampire hair tipped in silver. "Daddy told me to show the Dempseys to a table. I see Mother's taking care of one of them." Luckily Al's out of earshot—he's a Clyde, not a Dempsey. "And now your escort approaches," the daughter continues, displaying the genetically conditioned smile. The party noise abates as people recede further into the huge house, except for a large, bearded man who proffers his elbow.

"Hello, hello, lovely lady. I'm Stacey's brother, Reid, come to escort you to dinner. Are you who I think you are?" he asks, the family teeth bared in a smile.

"Zoe Dempsey."

"Ah, yes, shall we?" he says. He takes my hand and looks at me with close attention, his lips pursed as if he knows what Al and I have been doing. I turn to look staunchly ahead as we march into the house along a wide hallway paved with Saltillo tile, past the formal living room, out into the courtyard of this marvelous old house on Niles Road. Tables are set up outside on the patio, under outdoor lights casting pools of honeyed light. Many tables are already completely occupied with seated guests, so many doctors in one place I hope there's no civil emergency. Other folks are circling around, laughing, looking for friends or a place to accommodate their number. It's like the high school cafeteria, the makeup of some of the tables mirroring hospital hierarchies and specialties.

My escort steers me to a table where four people I don't know are seated, then disappears. I resign myself to having more or less permanently lost sight of Al. The two men stand to introduce themselves, but I don't know them and don't catch their names, distracted as I am by a glimpse of Jeff Glover cutting through the crowd. In his own operating room he moves with a portly grace. Here he looks rumpled and out of sorts, moving deliberately, his head darting back and forth on his neckless troll's body.

Sitting down quickly, I ask the man next to me how he happens to know Stacey and Bill. He responds with an account beginning at the golf course during a conference for people who work in a family business. He gives me the impression I should know who he is. I have no idea, but I'm ridiculously grateful he's willing to hold up his end of the social game. I am short of breath, almost panting.

"I'm glad you could make it. Did you run the whole way?" the man on my other side inquires, his face falling into Cary Grant folds of unthreatening male virility.

I laugh too loud and too long, putting my hand to my heaving bosom, only to look up to find Glover standing behind the only unoccupied chair at the table, his hands resting on the ladder-back. Inconsequentially, I notice the chairs are all different at our table, none of them meant for the outdoors.

"Anyone sitting here?" he asks in a perfectly plausible tone, his small eyes looking deserted. Oh, screw it. Will I never get any peace from this man?

The others assure him the spot is unclaimed, and all at once he's among us. I can smell the drink in him. Drinking's back in fashion in Texas, but Glover's not known for it, at least not in the brutish sort of way some of the younger doctors indulge at irregular intervals. I want to object to him joining us, but miss the moment I could've claimed to be saving the seat for Al. The caterer comes around with two kinds of wine. I cover the glass with my hand. Glover takes a glass of red, then says something to the server I don't catch. She nods and goes off. He turns to me, baring small teeth in a grimace of recognition.

"Dr. Dempsey. Lovely to meet you again so soon," he says, lifting his glass to me and holding his wicked smile in place.

I'm stuck, backed up to a concrete container filled with carefully tended plants. Glover works on his wine while I insert myself into the desultory conversation going on at our table. Before any food reaches us a large whiskey is delivered to Glover.

The woman sitting at the end of the table asks Glover what he thinks of the city's decision to exonerate private hospitals from treating the indigent.

"I'm seriously considering becoming a veterinarian," Glover says.

The woman looks doubtful, half aware she's walking into a trap. "Oh? And why is that?"

"Every animal brought in for care is truly loved by someone willing to pay for its care. Strays and unclaimed animals are put down."

"Put down?" the suave fellow asks uneasily.

"Where you from, boy? Put down. Euthanized. Made to go painlessly dead. No longer around to take up the time, attention, and resources of the living."

"I understood the phrase. I was just questioning the application," the man says icily.

Glover begins a drunken monologue about managed care, not gaining any friends for the board and its unflagging efforts to get donations from their rich friends. I tune out, wondering why he allowed himself to get so wasted tonight. The man is a notorious controller. Just about the time the four people who chose to sit together begin to make an effort to stem his banal flow of words with not very subtle body language, Glover stops in mid-sentence. A young person brings plates around. Apologizing for not serving ladies first, she starts in the back where we're crammed up against the planter before putting a plate in front of Glover. He stares intensely at the plate of food put in front of him and then opens his mouth to vomit tidily over the mound of white rice, butterfly shrimp, and tender greens. He wipes the back of his hand across his mouth and removes his eyes from the offensive plate. From behind, the server picks up the plateful of vomit with one hand and puts down a clean plate of food with the other. Not a word is exchanged while she whisks away the plate of barf. The woman next to Jeff grabs her napkin and wipes flecks of vomit from his sleeve, a tight smile on her lips, little cooing sounds in her throat. The server comes back and relieves her of the soiled napkin, her face a mask.

Glover, with the same aplomb he displays in his operating room, scoots back from the table to give them room to finish cleaning up while he continues with his lecture on the evils of managed care without missing a beat. Good manners have downplayed the eruption of the physical into the social. I've witnessed a non-event, everyone at the table roped into Glover's take on things. Up to his elbows with the physical world, he is also oddly removed. The other diners drift off as soon as they decently can, and I'm left alone with Glover. With only the two of us at the table I could angle the table back and free myself from my trapped spot between the abandoned detritus and the foliage. But I don't. Instead I watch Glover fork more food into his mouth.

"Are you sick? Have you had too much to drink?" I ask. My throat tastes of bile.

"No." The man looks at me malevolently, his heavy head bobbing almost imperceptibly. He's holding his knife and fork upright in his fists like a giant kid in a high chair.

"Why are you looking at me like that?"

Glover shakes his head a couple of times, his jowls quivering. The cold meanness fades from his stare and he mumbles into his plate.

"Like what, Zoe? You're a bundle of light, a cry of life in a blighted landscape."

"Stop putting me on." He looks scary to me, like a wild boar confronted unexpectedly.

"You know I've always had the hots for you," he says, his

moist eyes glittering. He's right. I have always known it. But I ignored it like he just ignored a plateful of vomit.

"You've always known I'm married."

"So what?" he asks, his hand making a brushing gesture, both brutish and pathetic. "Sex is something you do with your friends. Not necessarily a lifelong contract to make mortgage payments together. Or haven't you heard?"

"We're not friends."

"We were."

"Ah, well. Perhaps."

"You dumped me for the Chief," he says.

"Surely you're joking. We were colleagues working together on a project, which ended when you caved in. *You* decided fighting managed care was a losing battle."

"When you meant to make your mark in clinical medicine, you courted me. Then when you decided to switch to Admin, you started currying favor with Frank."

"That's not true! That's the last thing I'd ever do! I've certainly never courted either you or Frank Hawkins. That's insane."

"Ah, now we're getting somewhere." Glover laughs, looking down at his plate and picking at his food. "Why don't you apply some of your analytical skills to yourself, Zoe? Judge yourself the same way you judge everybody else—by what you do, not by what you say."

I say nothing, wondering what he would say if he knew I am investigating patients who died on his watch. He looks at me with the appraising look he wears when he's about to make the first incision. Somebody comes by and serves coffee. Glover lifts his cup to me in a mock toast, then puts it back, sloshing coffee into the saucer. "We're more alike than you want to admit, Zoe."

I try not to flinch. There's no way I'm like him.

"You don't like to hear that, do you?" he asks. The expression on his face is almost merry. "We're after the same thing. You just like to dress it up differently."

I look down at my hands. "And what is it that we are both

supposedly pursuing?"

"Power and control, whatever it takes. We're nothing without it. With it we hold in our hands the power to cure." He holds up his blunt fingers up, like he's waiting to be gloved. Arrogant bastard. What did Dr. Lerner tell me? *Don't let them make you choose.*

Coffee won't make any impact on his drunkenness. Glover's eyes are hooded, and his distended temporal vein beats wildly. His skin's splotchy, and he's perspiring. He catches me studying him. "Don't look at me like that. You're a very beautiful woman, and I—I have no delusions about how I measure up in the looks department."

"You must!" I explode. "How else can a doctor take such poor care of himself, except by ignoring the evidence?"

"I rest my case," he says, opening his eyes wide.

"Surely you're not suggesting I don't look after my own health?" Again I wonder if he can possibly know about the Percocet.

He smiles happily watching me react. He flaps his hand at me a couple of times. "Don't take such offence over our little disagreements, Doctor D. We both aim to cure."

"If we're on the same side, why scapegoat me? Your statistics won't hold water. Even a large percentage of a small sample is a small number. My patients do no worse than yours. Admit it."

"They're doing no better. No fucking better. Simply acknowledge that in the next staff meeting and we're quits. Your patients may love you to bits, but you aren't making them any better." He's roaring by now. We both look around. No one seems to have noticed.

"OK, Dr. Glover." I lean over the litter on the table separating us. "If you want acknowledgement. We work in the same system with similar results. Remember those quality-control people the hospital brought in? The individual doctor no longer makes much of a difference. The system determines quality of care, especially in emergencies. But no individual patient fits a statistical average, especially when you're talking immune system."

"Everything's run by the insurance companies and the ad-ministrators," he agrees. "We may as well be working on the assembly line at General Motors. At least we'd have a better labor union."

Getting up abruptly, he catches the table on his fat thigh, noisily jouncing the cutlery and laughing as I catch a glass about to go over. "You'd miss me if I weren't around to play the honorable opposition, Zoe."

"Don't flatter yourself. You're not that significant."

Glover looks both triumphant and miserable. "No doubt you speak truth." He turns to walk away, then stops and stumbles back to the table. He leans over his vacated chair, resting his knuckles on the table, to hold me in his gaze. His piggish eyes seem surprisingly sober.

"Lighten up. Don't take everything so hard. This statisti-cal shit's nothing. Just dipping your braid in the inkbottle. Nothing's gonna hurt you." He stands weaving, breathing heavily, a drunken bully in a sentimental moment. I tip my chin in dismissal.

"I'm going. But you tell me—what is your bitch against those of us who practice scientific medicine, who calculate the odds and refuse to brood over our losses?"

"You leave too much out of your calculations."

"Like what?" he asks, swaying back and forth like a stage drunk.

"All those faculties that complement the body: intentions, beliefs, and dreams."

"I serve the body by serving reason."

"You serve a tyrant."

Glover turns with a snort and shambles away. I've begun to get up, but sink back down when he lurches back and leans against the table, propping himself up with one hand, his face so close to mine I see the enlarged pores of old sebaceous-gland malfunction. I press back against the stone planter. "You've got enemies more serious than me," he says, his fetid breath filling the air between us. "Your redheaded pal Merla, for one. She

139

seems to have a thing for Al, your little tin knight." He heaves himself to his feet and stands for a moment as jolly as can be, getting his bearings, before pulling himself together and marching away.

I sit by myself, no longer trapped with my back to the wall but in a chair on the end of the table, staring sightlessly out at the scene before me. Glover's driven to cure illness through domination and control. And why wouldn't he be? That's how we were trained. Doctors wage war against disease while armies carry out surgical strikes; we use metaphors like narcotics to dull our terrors and hopelessly confuse our distinction between killing and curing. Yet my gut tells me there's another way.

What about what he said about Merla? Could Al be Merla's irresistible guy? I'm wishing I could be whisked back home without having to talk to anyone when I hear a familiar voice.

"You look like you've lost your last friend."

I look up to see Travis, wearing his best boots, smiling down at me. "Sit down with me and be my friend," I say.

"I can't stay. I'm meeting somebody at the Driskill to catch the blues singer. But I need to ask you a favor."

"Ask."

He sits down next to me anyway, leaning close enough for me to see his bloodshot eyes. The dance band has been warming up in the background, and now begins to play some generic Texas two-step.

"Can you find a way to show up for Outreach Clinic in Chiapas for me?"

"I thought you were dying to go to Mexico," I say, leaning away from him. He sighs and straightens.

"It looks now like that won't happen. Think about it."

"Sure, Travis. You know I will. What's stopping you from going?"

"We'll talk, but this is not the place. Believe me I wish things were different. I am out of the lineup to help the clinic with the immunizations." He stands up, slapping his hands on both knees. "I need to get out of here, but I will be in touch. Don't look so glum." He lunges over and grabs my head with both hands, kissing me hard somewhere between the nose and the lip. Odd.

"Yeah. Right," I say to his retreating form.

Al finally shows up. "What's the matter, Zoe?"

"Where've you been?" What a stupid question—and what a contemptible role: the abandoned wife.

Al sits down, a stricken look on his handsome face. "I should've found you."

"Never mind, sweetie," I say. "It's not your fault Stacey snagged you. Jeff Glover was over here telling me I'm no different than he is!"

"Why did you sit still for it? You could've come over to our table."

"I never thought of it. You can't believe how awful he was."

"I believe it."

Al's presence comforts me. "He's drunk," I say. "He intrudes on everybody . . ." I trail off, out of words, vaguely gesturing at the now-empty table, as if I can conjure up the whole scene that just passed.

"Yeah. I saw him staggering around just a minute ago."

"He vomited in his plate."

"He did what?"

I go on to recap to Al my battle with Glover, but I don't tell him everything that's happened since we parted at the door. I'm operating on two levels, retelling the experience while at the same time doing what Glover challenged me to do: analyzing my own actions in the same way I analyze others. I don't tell Al my fear of being like Glover, forging ahead at whatever cost. In the politics of medicine, who bears the costs? Such questions make me queasy.

So I don't ask Al about Merla, or tell him how Travis wants me to go to Chiapas, Mexico for him, or ask him if Travis asked him first, or say anything about how I might be pregnant. I don't even know how to begin talking about all that's on my heart, so I end up leaving out pretty much the whole lot. We go home without dancing.

Chapter 20

Sometime around first light I wake from a visceral, euphoric dream, where I flew through magnificent heavens and swam under vast oceans, rendered in exquisite color, only to be deposited on the desert, but a desert of flowers blooming in every direction. Just before waking—I think it's what woke me—I heard an edict delivered in a sonorous voice, by some Moses just down from the mountain: *if you're going to rely on powers you've never dreamt of, you've got to have the faith that they'll be there.* An in-house Freudian joke, since I was possessed of magical powers moments ago in the dream, and extraordinary powers not long ago in reality, running back from my encounter with the stranger. But why argue with a dream?

Fully awake, the euphoria's replaced by memories of last night and Glover's repugnant behavior. I've been such a fool, supposing he could alter his view of reality instead of forever calling mine into question.

Al and Iris have gone about their Saturday chores, taking Grendel with them. I'm getting to like sleeping too much—a classic sign of depression. I pick up the phone and call Merla.

"Have you been seeing Al?" I say without knowing that's what I meant to say until the words came out of my mouth. My voice sounds peculiar, like someone leading a séance.

"What's the matter, Zoe—have you lost him?"

"I hope not."

The silence gathers and billows at the other end of the phone, except for Merla's shallow breathing, the sound of her slight nasal whistle. She could use an antihistamine.

"I'll be right over," she says, and hangs up.

Anna, fixing bacon and eggs when Merla shows up, starts to offer her some, but changes her mind when I catch her eye. "I'm sure you two have plenty to talk about," she says jauntily, leaving us alone in the kitchen.

"Are you fucking my husband?" The words are out of my mouth before the thought has fully formed. Merla, my girlfriend since third grade at Brykerwoods, stares at me in something close to clinical shock, her skin so white her freckles lie on the surface ready to be brushed off with a powder puff.

"Answer me, damn it!"

"Look, Zoe, don't try to make me the villain here."

"Tell me!"

Merla, near the door, spreads her arms out, the palms of her hands open. Then she hunches her shoulders and shrugs before looking down at her feet.

Shoving my plate away, I thrust myself out of the chair and walk up to her in a rush, taking her by the arm and propelling us both out into the hallway. She doesn't resist. I don't let go until we're in the living room, stumbling over something left on the floor. The drapes are drawn and the room's dark. We fall onto the couch together side by side. "You've been sleeping with Al, haven't you? That's why there was no new guy to introduce me to, this time." I twist around to face her, clenching my teeth. I hate being a chump.

"That's not a fair question."

"You've already answered it." I jump up from the couch and start pacing. When Merla tries to get up I lean over and press her back down with the flat of my hand on her shoulder. "It was Al, wasn't it? He was the one you found irresistible?"

Merla sniffles, looking around the room for some way out, but I'm between her and the French doors we came in by. The only other door leading out of the room goes to the patio.

"What's gotten into you?" she asks me, wiping the back of her hand across her nose.

I stop to think. "Something one of the doctors said to me

143

last night at a party. My worst enemy." I make a sound choking down all that I want to say about how I trusted her, how we were the friends. "How did you expect this to all turn out?"

"We were waiting . . ." she starts, but I can't stand to hear what she's going to say.

"Waiting for what? For me to find out? For Iris to grow up?"

She launches herself off the couch but I follow after her. We stand inches from each other in the gloomy room.

"So *irresistible* is simply a code word meaning you lost all your scruples—you wanted my husband so bad you said to hell with ethics or the affection between you and me. You just couldn't help yourself."

"What is it with you and that word? It doesn't matter why I used it. You're always going on about your precious husband, but you didn't give him the time of day for fucking months. Or months of not-fucking."

"Is that what he told you? That it was me who didn't want sex?"

"Let's just say I got stuck on Al for a while. That *happens* to me, you *know* that. I don't have everything you've got, a nice settled life. The three of us were seeing too much of each other there for awhile. Then you were gone all the time, over with the twelve-steppers when you weren't at the hospital."

I go cold. My pulse beats in my solar plexus. I feel hollow. But this won't kill me. I've handled worse trauma. Stop. Retreat. Think. Stem the bleeders. "So Al's just another mercy-fuck to you."

"Zoe, you don't hardly sound like yourself," Merla says. "Forgive me for that crack about Al being irresistible. I take it back. He's not."

"What did you do? Volunteer to be his little piece of fluff on the side?" My voice sounds ridiculous. Like I'm in a playground fight. I loathe myself, but can't seem to quit.

"Maybe Al and I could've been happy together if things were different," Merla says in a shaky voice. "Who knows. They weren't. Besides, I never fancied being a step-mom." Suddenly she looks stricken. "Don't look like that, Zoe. Hell, Al was never really interested in me, if that makes you feel any better. You were busy getting straight, going to your meetings. You didn't have time for a husband–or for a friend, either. I missed you too, you know. Al and I saw each other a couple of times when you weren't around. It's a free country."

"How could you go on about 'the man in your life' to me like that? Play me for such a fool!"

"You asked me who I was seeing. When I said a married man, you were shocked. You made me feel ashamed."

"You jumped to the wrong conclusion. I wasn't being prudish. What shocked me was the notion any man could be irresistible."

"Anyway, it's over."

"Since when?"

"Since y'all came back from your trip to the mountains."

Merla looks out the window for a moment, then turns to me to reveal a face I've never seen before. She looks bereft, an expression set-off by the mascara smudges under her startling clear green eyes. "I'd do just about anything for—whatever it was I thought I'd found, the key to the treasure. A glimpse of what life might be like if it were whole. You and Al always give off some sort of incredible energy. That's what I wanted."

I snort, wiping my nose on the back of my hand.

"I suspect you've been aware of what's been going on for some time."

"What horseshit. You don't know anything about me. Or about being married."

"You may not remember, Zoe," Merla says, moving away from me, "but I was married once, for eight years. Anyway, what's the use of going over it? I told you before, 'do nothing which is of no use.' Which, by the way, is from an ancient Japanese book on war."

"What are you telling me? Now you're a Samurai?"

"If Al hadn't already called it off," Merla says, "I might have been the one. We had no future. He's got a lot of conflicts."

"Well, yes. It stands to reason when your main squeeze is

your wife's best friend you've got conflict. Who seduced who, anyway?"

"What do you want from me, Zoe? Do you want to be girl-friends talking about my crush on a married man? About how I end up sacrificing the two people I most value for a moment's foolishness? Or do you want to be the wronged wife telling me off? From what I heard, you hadn't slept with him in months." She pauses, panting. "I'm sorry I said that. Al could've lied. Everybody lies about sex."

"No, he didn't lie," I say. I turn my back to her and turn on a light.

When I turn around she's coming towards me, her arms flopping around me in a hug. For a second I want to choke her, but instead I disengage with exaggerated gentleness. There were so many signs something was going on between Al and Merla, but I chose to ignore them all. Hoping they were spoof-ing, like me and Travis. And it's true I was numbed out and not up for sex after coming off the painkillers. I'd lost the knack of connecting.

"Are you all right, Zoe?"

"Cut it out. Listen carefully. You will not talk to Al about what we've said today. I will not have it. You go by different rules from mine. I'll talk to Al in my own time and my own way. Let's just say what you had with Al was yours and his. Now whatever you had going together is over. What happens next has nothing to do with you. Go away. I've got to think."

"What's it going to be like with you and me?" she asks. "People don't always stay in the slots you put them in. We don't have to be enemies."

I fall back on the couch without answering, waving her away. She looks like she's going to try to shake my hand and then thinks better of it.

When I'm sure she's gone, I hurry to the bedroom I share with Al, not wanting to run into Anna. Sometimes I think this is more her house than mine, even though she never intrudes.

Somewhere in the background the phone rings. Anna answers. After a few minutes she tiptoes to my room, where I'm hunched up like a gargoyle on top of my pillows in the dark. When there's no response to her knock she goes away. Why did I ask Merla about her and Al, the one woman in America who would tell me the truth?

Every morning of our life together Al has woken up with a hard-on, his cock a sightless little animal yearning to burrow in female flesh. When we were first married we treated his cock as a pet we shared, one that brought bliss in return for all the countless little duties and attentions.

When did Al's morning hard-on become not a celebration but more like a chore? It wasn't as if I didn't enjoy our early morning pokes. But after awhile it came to seem like an answer to his need alone, and for me, a chit to cash in later when we had more time. How often that morning coming together would create a bloom of desire that would stay with me all day, reminding me of my beloved. Ah. Sex tied us together even when we were apart. I never stopped wanting that. Reason and desire—each demands its due. What do I want? Al has always been so clear about his wants and only secretive about his disappointments. I know what I didn't want, after medical school and internship and raising a child: always to take care of somebody else. About the time Iris was bursting into our room in the mornings I got in the habit of ignoring his morning hard-on as if it were one more creature importuning me for solace. But our erotic life didn't disappear. Even after Anna was living with us we found ways to be alone and to explore my body like the lost continent. Al was the kindest lover in the world.

Why does it seem so long ago, those years of physical passion? How long have they been gone? There were times I couldn't look at any part of Al's body—even his wrists sticking out of his starched cuffs in a meeting, uncompromisingly virile, blue-black hair against white skin—without getting aroused. Back in school before Al and I were married, Travis told me later, there were times he couldn't bear to be in the same *room* with me and Al because the erotic charge between the two of us made him feel so left out.

Merla and Al's secrecy and betrayal gall me. Can I blame Merla for ensnaring herself in Al's luster, the erotic shine he carries with him everywhere he goes? Maybe everyone has a right to have sex with anybody they want, as long as they don't lie about it. What would I have said to Merla if she had told me *your husband came to me, cock in hand. He's irresistible. Want me to take care of it or would you rather do it yourself?* More likely it was Merla who seduced Al.

I can't bear my thoughts chasing each other around like squirrels. Is this what it feels like to go insane? I get up from my place curled up on the bed, crouched against the headboard, turn on the lights, and pace around the room. I catch a glimpse of myself in the oval mirror and go stand in front of it, staring at my face. Why don't I look more changed? I stare until I get dizzy, the reflection in the mirror totally disconnected from the feelings inside.

I want sex, I want to desire and be desired. Does being a desirable woman mean being erased as a particular person? Do men who desire women desire all desirable women? Ah, there's the rub. I do not desire all desirable men. But Merla never seemed to want to get close to a man, only to get laid. She's as much as told me so. All she ever wants is a happy ending, but only for the time being. Maybe that's why she makes her living bowdlerizing old films, making up happy endings to fool kids. In marriage, there's no such thing as a happy ending, no easy way out. Death, divorce, desertion are the only ways out.

What did I ask from Al that changed everything, that led to Merla? Time-out from the routine of need. Time to regroup, maybe find myself in the eye of the whirlwind. So sure enough, he gave me time. Al's given me nearly everything I have ever asked him for. He took over giving Iris the attention she craved when I was in pain all the time, and didn't know why, and it wasn't getting any better.

The Percocet seduced me. When I wrenched my back and was in such agony, I had to keep working; neither Travis nor I had any reason to consider the fact it's a controlled substance.

The drug did something for me I didn't even know I needed done until I started taking it: changed my consciousness, and made me more aware, not less, of the pain I was feeling—not only the physical pain, but also the pain of discovering the holes in the fabric of certainty cloaking modern medicine. At first, it then fulfilled its promise, as drugs so often do, and whisked away the pain, and with it, my ability to discriminate between delusion and reality. I began to doubt myself. I no longer believed I could save anybody, anymore, and couldn't bear knowing the limitations of all human effort. The drug dulled that pain as well. Just like I had to know at some level that the day would come when somebody would look over Travis's schedule C. It was bound to look suspicious—Travis hardly ever writes prescriptions; I may as well have taken out a full-page ad in *JAMA*.

Al must have known I'd find out about Merla, as well. Illicit sex must act like a drug. I've got to stop going over all this. My heart hurts. When did my heart become as brittle as hard candy? I look back and watch the years unfold. It's like I shrugged my shoulders and averted my face from Al for one moment, the time it takes for the pulsation of an artery. An eternity. Instead of pursuing me and coaxing me to tell him what ails me, he looked the other way, pretended not to be hurt, and found someone else to spend time with. It's not the mystery I'd like to make it out to be. I can't afford to let myself be distracted from the whole arc of my life, from what still might be possible. What if I'm pregnant? I groan out loud. All this thinking about sex has made my foolish cunt blossom and tingle. I put my hand between my legs and squeeze hard. What did I want Al to do? What I did not want was for him to go away and leave me alone. Sex with Al, all that grand physical passion through our twenties, acted like developing fluid, making me the person I am, bringing me into focus. Then—wait. Let me see. Give me a moment. What have I been doing in the last few years? Practicing medicine, honing my craft, concentrating my attention on my patients. Needing time was not the same as asking to be deserted.

Come back Al, I whisper. I miss you.

Chapter 21

After having arranged my duties so as I can get to the appointment with Glover and Frank, I can barely remember why I asked for it. At this moment I'm hiding out in the hospital courtyard—a neglected void with a forlorn huddle of sorry olive trees in concrete planters beneath a lowering sky. It's illegal to smoke anywhere in the hospital, including where I sit, but the blighted landscape's littered with cigarette butts. Who can be generating them? How many doctors besides Travis still smoke? I thought only young people and outsiders still dared to smoke in public, but you can see the courtyard from the hospital rooms, littered with forbidden trash—an open secret, like a lot of things.

Days have come and gone since my come-to-Jesus meeting with Merla, days of routine and drudgery and small victories at the hospital. The record-breaking rain continues day after day. The weather is the favored topic wherever people meet. Local talk radio features experts warning us the dams are a danger to us. Helpless, angry citizens reply by telephone. At home I plan my schedule to see nobody but Iris, not difficult to do during the week. Al leaves early for surgery; Grendel sticks to Anna; I'm pretty much free of domestic duties.

Travis came all the way up to my office to talk to me about going to Chiapas in southeast Mexico, bordering on Guatemala. I badgered him to tell me why he couldn't go himself. All he'd say was that self-administered blood tests revealed sub-clinical signs of disorder. He won't provide enough specifics for me to attempt a diagnosis. He claims to be asymptomatic, but can't in

150

good faith travel out of the country to administer immunizations. I go cold all over. That's all bullshit. If he were asymptomatic he wouldn't know squat. He asks me sweetly to take this gig for him and instructs me not to fuss over him. He will tell Al about the blood test when he's ready. Which makes two of us, I guess, who have a fool for a patient and keep secrets from Al. I'm afraid he has Hep-C, but it could be anything. Why didn't I see something was the matter with Travis?

I continue to brood about Merla, but say nothing to Al. I resent the role of the injured spouse—the oldest story ever told. Al and I are in love again, ever since going to the mountains. I'm trying not to push the river. Since I did the pregnancy test I have said nothing to anybody on that score. Maybe I'm just ducking down. Merla has been leaving messages for me on the phone and e-mail. I haven't answered. I'm putting everything on hold to be ready to take over Travis's commitment to immunize children in Mexico. But first I have to clear it with the chief.

Frank waves me to come in from where he sprawls in his leather chair with his feet up on his precious rosewood desk, charming the hell out of somebody on the phone—some board member like Stacey Livengood, judging from his end of the conversation, rich in laughter and flattery. It takes me a minute to notice Glover standing by the window with his arms buckled across his chest, back hunched, a troll dressed in a lab coat. He ignores me, his head lowered so the folds of his chin drape over the knot of his tie. I circle around the office, wondering if he and the chief have been having a pre-meeting meeting.

"Could you stop that pacing?" Glover asks, turning from the window without dropping his defensive stance. I stop practically in mid-step, peeved at myself for displaying my agitation. Pacing is also one of the signs of anorexia, but Glover's not likely to know that.

"Let her be, Jeff," Frank says, hanging up the phone and unfolding to his full stature, powerful looking in his beautifully tailored suit, drawing the ugly energy out of the room like a commercial air-scrubbing machine. Glover drops his arms and

151

wiggles his shoulders like a prizefighter warming up.

"Shall we all sit down and try to work something out?" Frank asks. "It disturbs me to have my doctors feuding."

I sit down on a polished wooden side chair and almost slide off again, my silk skirt swishing on the polished wood. Recovering my balance, I watch Glover locate a club chair for his squatty frame. We both wait while Frank eases his body back into his chair. He looks arthritic—hardly surprising for a former athlete. His body must talk to him every day. Is that why he objected to the pain meds for me? He notices me watching and flushes beneath his mahogany skin.

I look away, sorry to have been caught staring, for seeing this man naked of the trappings of his role.

"Zoe," Frank says, "would you like to start out?"

"Yes." I swivel my hard chair around to face Glover. "How are you getting the numbers? Or do you just manufacture them to make me look bad?"

"I do not manufacture numbers that make us *all* look bad."

"Dr. Dempsey, Dr. Glover," Frank steps in, "let's back up here a moment. What has happened to you both? Not long ago you joined together in the crusade against managed care. You two were prominent among those bucking the tide, trying to make Doctors' Hospital a place I'd send my own people for medical treatment."

What does he mean, his own people? This isn't the high school cafeteria. The differences between black and white don't apply at Frank's level of the bureaucracy. He must mean his family.

"Tell me how I can help you settle your differences," Frank goes on. What he's doing is warning us: resolve your differences or be ready to pay a price for displeasing him.

"Just call him off," I say.

"Let me do my job," Glover says with a loud snort. "Like I told you in my memo, Dr. Dempsey will soon become known as some sort of alternative healer, a Shaman perhaps. It's going around the nursing staff."

"If you're going to take that tone, Dr. Glover," I jump in,

"let me bring five or six people in here from the Office of Alternative Medicine at NIH. For thousands of years nurses and healers have treated patients with therapeutic touch, and other hospitals . . . "

"Yes, yes, yes," Glover interrupts, waving his hand, "I'll grant you all that, but you're too involved with one of your patients. Counter-transference, Dr. Lerner calls it."

I'm not thrilled to hear Glover's been discussing me with a psychiatrist, even if he is old and addled. These people have too much power to damage your career. Better to have patients dying willy-nilly than to have questions asked about one's own mental balance.

"That's a cheap shot, Dr. Glover," I say.

"I agree," Frank says. "I'd back off on that one, Jeff."

"I'm not making accusations," Glover says, "just trying to put things in perspective."

"There's a library full of hard evidence to back up alternative medicine," I say, fixing my eyes on Glover, keeping my voice steady. "The meridians of Chinese medicine, empirically verified for five thousand years before we in the West got interested, are quite likely anatomical pathways for the immune cells."

"Are we in for more lectures on hot topics in immune theory?" Glover says, making an appeal to Frank, who holds up his hand and frowns.

"You can't cure everything with a knife! Immune cells are affected by body chemistry. Triggered by the emotions. The body-brain barrier's permeable. Since we can kick-start the immune system with touch, maybe touch can instruct an overactive system in tolerance."

"You make a unique contribution here, Zoe. You'd be hard to replace," Frank says, giving me a hard look.

"We're doctors, Frank," Glover says, shrugging his shoulders and lifting both hands, palms up, in elaborate pantomime, "and as such we are morally required to remain within boundaries of accepted practice."

"What's on the line here, Jeff? Skip the hype."

153

"This little cluster fuck is about Dr. Dempsey thinking she can practice medicine while not playing the game," Glover says, swinging his head back and forth like a bull about to charge. "It's about her not being a team player. About crap like her getting a massage license so she can touch her patients without getting sued. About you standing by and cheerfully letting your doctors revert to superstition and black magic."

"Hold up there, Jeff," Frank scolds, his voice reverberating. "Some of the modalities included in alternative practices are undoubtedly mumbo jumbo, but science does not approve condemnation prior to investigation. With Lydia Flores, *curandera* or not, we're talking about TP: therapeutic touch. Basically, old fashioned massage. What's *your* problem?"

Frank has apparently delivered some sort of top-dog signal to Glover, whose entire demeanor changes. "You're mistaken if you think this is a personal vendetta," he says in an ingratiating tone. "It's not. OK, let's ignore the Lydia issue. But since arriving here on the house staff, Dr. Dempsey has made claims for immunosuppressive drugs over steroids in the treatment of intractable Crohn's disease. She has shown us study after study, some backed up by her own clinical practice, proving these drugs control symptoms, with side effects insignificant or reversible in most cases. I am not so much calling these claims into question, as asking for equitable comparisons."

I close my eyes for a second, going back to that moment in the river, the moment before I took hold of my own life. My eyes pop open and I start talking. "Fine. Jordan Wilson has simply asked that medical treatment, or surgery if it comes to that, is augmented by a form of spiritual solace combined with therapeutic touch."

The room is still, both men attentive.

"We have tried certain approved interventions with her. Some have failed. Others are working, but slowly. A life hangs in the balance between treatment and response, orchestrated by the entire immune system, not only within the patient herself but also in her milieu, the context of her healthy functioning.

These are facts, not notions. The part the patient plays, her own faith, her experience of chronic illness, her belief in her place in the world, cannot be ignored. Jordan Wilson is an adolescent, a tricky life stage in any case, and more so for a person with a chronic disease. She wants to see Lydia Flores, RN, MSN, Shaman. In times of danger, a person relies on us, the experts. Nobody should be encouraged to hand over her entire life force to our keeping. If Jordan wants to see Lydia, I want Lydia to see her."

"I have no idea what you mean when you say something like that," Glover says. "What possible grounds do you have for such a statement?"

"Never mind, Jeff, this isn't your decision," Frank says. "Lydia Flores will be added to our list of spiritual advisors, as per your request, Zoe."

"Thanks, Chief."

"You seem to have lost faith in the practice of medicine," Glover says to me.

"Patients make decisions based on the story we tell them. If they are disheartened by the story, it acts like a toxin."

"Nobody's arguing," Glover says, looking at Frank, "about the placebo effect. And you are very much mistaken," he twists his head around to me, "if you think my concern proves some sort of personal vendetta." He turns back to Frank. "Dr. Dempsey has hammered away at the efficacy of immunomodulator drugs. Now she's switching horses."

"We've run out of time here," Frank says when I take a breath to reply. "Dr. Dempsey, what are your present intentions regarding Dr. Glover's concerns?"

"I have been looking at Doctors' Hospital mortality rates, using primary data we keep stored in the morgue. Meaning dead people." I pause. The two men wait for me to continue. I take a breath and go on. "Not all the data's been analyzed, but it looks to me as if Dr. Glover's done some creative reporting. Specific patients who died under his care have been attributed to other doctors."

Frank speaks first. "That's a rather nasty allegation, Zoe.

155

Are you ready to back it up?"

"We're dealing with inferences here," I say. "Assigning cases in which the patient died to doctors no longer at the hospital skews the numbers. You'll find the record of immunomodulator drugs matches that of other interventions, including surgery, when the data isn't fudged."

Glover's face begins to go purple.

"Everything depends upon the initial coding of primary data, which is the judgment call in statistical evidence," I say. "Garbage in, garbage out." I sit back down.

Frank speaks in his most sepulchral voice: "Consider the matter tabled."

"I'd like a chance . . ." I start to say when Glover butts in with "I'd rather resolve. . ." and Frank trumps with: "I could form a subcommittee to review the materials and come back to me with their findings."

"That won't be necessary," Glover says.

"What about you, Zoe?"

"A non-partisan investigation would not hurt my feelings."

"Committees cause more trouble than they cure," Glover says.

"Like some medical interventions," I say.

"Shall we all try to benefit our patients with the best means at hand?" Frank asks. My adversary's face knots up. I squirm with the desire to physically hurt him. "Put a lid on your battles," Frank says into the silence, looking at me like he can read my mind.

There's to be no punishment for all the trouble Glover's unfounded harassment has caused me. The little porker must have an idea he's lucky to get off so easy, for he salutes the chief and trundles out without another word.

"He gets away with making me look bad," I say.

"Don't push it, Zoe," Frank cautions. "Dr. Glover is a respected member of the tenured faculty and a senior clinician. He considers you a heretic. You have called scientific materialism into question. You want to push the envelope to include alternative therapies. You question authority and hierarchy.

Glover's unquestionably a sinner. Sinners can be forgiven."

"While heretics are burned at the stake," I say, leaning my hip up against the desk.

"You can always make a formal objection," Frank says, leaning back in his big chair. "We have administrative precedent for putting together a tribunal to investigate the controversy between you and Dr. Glover."

"I'm already tainted just by being the focus of the inquiry. I'm tempted to go ahead with a formal objection."

Frank's big body slumps. "Have you ever considered what a pain in the ass you are?"

"I've busted my ass and neglected my home life to play on the team. You're no prize to me either." We look at each other for a long moment, and then we both erupt into laughter.

"I need to ask for a favor," I say when I've composed myself.

"Go ahead."

"Travis wants me to go down to Mexico in his stead. You know, the project to immunize children through the Outreach Clinic."

"Yes, he already talked to me about this." Frank leans forward. "He came to tell me he's unable to go—and you agreed to go in his place."

"So it's OK?" I ask eagerly. I wonder if Frank knows about Travis's ailment.

"Yes. I can accommodate you while Dr. Duluth, our Aussie visitor, is here to help us out. You see nothing to prevent you from going?"

"Jordan Wilson has gone home, ready to go back on a more or less regular diet. Dr. Hagan can cover for me. All she has to do is stick to the protocols I'll provide. Iris is still in school. I'm covered."

"I'll have my secretary set you up with discretionary leave," Frank says, beginning to dismiss me, "so you won't need to use your vacation allowance."

Out of his office, I review my wins and losses. The QC—quality control—people say system design determines outcomes rather than the individuals who fill the slots. If they're right, all of this was foreordained many moves back, when medicine became thoroughly materialist and different parts of the human body were assigned to different specialists. At least I can remove myself from the struggle when I go to Mexico, a place of gorgeous light and possible transcendence.

The last four days before going to Mexico are hectic. Tommy Arbuckle has checked out of the hospital, but is still coming back to run meetings in the basement. The kid's only seventeen, but already he's made a difference. Jordan has agreed to go to the meetings—hospitals breed romances as readily as superbacteria. She also says she'll get in touch with Lydia Flores.

Escape is never easy. I sneak the second pregnancy kit into the bathroom like I used to sneak smokes as a teenager. The positive results don't cause the elation I felt after the first test. The timing is all off. Both Al and I have wanted another baby. Powerful words, but not as powerful as the strip of blue paper I stare at in my hand. I decide not to say anything yet.

Al turns out to be a pussycat about me going down to Mexico. Iris doesn't want me to go, for very adult reasons, but when I don't relent she gets little-girl sulky. I stifle my fear and spend a lot of time trying to reassure her. She's not buying it. Maybe my motives aren't as pure as I'd like to think. I want to do as I please and yet have everybody approve, like investing money in environmentally sound companies.

I try to mollify Iris, expounding on how the Outreach Clinic in Mexico delivers health care to the descendents of the Maya, how Travis has been their Texas connection for eons, how since he can't go I've promised to go for him. But Iris won't shift from her position. Nothing will suit her but me staying home.

PART IV
THE BORDER

Chapter 22

Suspended in a small plane over a featureless sea of cloud on my way to Chiapas, I peer through the cleft in the nubby green drapes hanging between me and the cockpit. I feel my stomach lurch as the tiny aircraft drops towards earth, spraying the cabin with oxygen masks. The pilot wrestles the plane level while the co-pilot gets on the horn, reassuring us in three languages. From where I sit, his audible baritone voice is shadowed by a slightly delayed mechanical version, exposing the flimsiness of the whole venture. The oxygen masks dangle and dance; a baby lets out a howl; everyone in the plane explodes into talk.

The plane descends steeply into jungle so impenetrable it seems without a scrap of habitation, but Villahermosa appears at the last possible moment. We land with decided impact on the concrete runway at the bottom of a bowl of dense greenery before chuttering to an abrupt stop. Already standing at the door as the co-pilot wrests it open, I'm forced to wait at the threshold for the gangway to be fixed into place before I can disembark. Given the time to gaze out over the small airport, I'm blasted back to a moment in childhood when I stood exactly so, too big to carry, beside my mother as we arrived at one of Dad's job sites in just such a jungle. I start down the steps sniffing the air, the sense of familiarity snatched away like in a dream, but family history telling me it must have been Manila. The co-pilot, who has put on his uniform jacket with braid on the cuffs, walks in front of me, carrying my luggage. He turns when we reach the tarmac to hand me the two small bags, looking at me with a conspiratorial smile that startles me out of my self absorption long enough to smile back, in recognition of a shared real moment snatched from the general unreality of events.

I make my way over to the terminal in the midst of starched, helmeted and booted soldiers, guns at the ready, standing around gazing at nothing, their faces preposterously young and vacant. I had not expected so many soldiers. My fellow passengers scurry along, eyes fixed to their feet. Inside the building people seem subdued. A mesh fence separates arrivals from the rest of the terminal; sounds of conversation are muffled and vendors conspicuously missing. The Mexico City airport, much of it under construction, was crowded and full of cheerful life, but this place has the feel of something going on visitors are not permitted to notice. Forging ahead into an unoccupied aisle marked off by ropes on short standards leading towards a customs table flanked by traffic lights, looking past the surrounding fence for someone who might be here to meet me, I'm stopped in my tracks by an unnerving, frenzied bleating. The traffic light at the customs station switches from green to red and blinks in time with the blaring horn.

People glance at me, then look away. An official in khaki gestures to the line forming on the other side of the ropes. Still gripping my bags, I scuttle behind the small clot of people from the plane. As long as I've lived next door to Mexico I can do no better than read the newspaper in Spanish and catch the drift of conversation. I seldom venture into speech, with my lousy accent and halting delivery. I should have asked someone to explain the drill or simply paid more attention: in my profession, chance outcomes signal trouble. This system, no different from the one in Mexico City, operates somewhat by chance. The lights are on a timer. Officials in quasi-military gear with pistols on their belts open bags at random when the red light comes on. Or they can activate the red light and blaring horn when they choose. I was cutting in on someone else's green light when I got blasted, not thinking we'd be searched again after a domestic flight. A uniformed man glances my way. The traffic light is green when I reach the head of the line and he waves me through.

162

Outside the customs area, on the other side of the fence, a man in a starched shirt and suit pants, and a woman in a dark print dress approach me.

"Dr. Dempsey? I'm Dr. Tomás Leon," starched shirt says when I reach them, "and my colleague, Dr. Alicia Wagner." With a courtly gesture he gathers us together into a threesome. "Dr. Meacham described you perfectly."

"By all means, we are friends with Travis," the woman says, shaking my hand. "Alicia."

Tomás hurries on. "We are sorry our friend Travis cannot be here. Most happy you have come to assist us. What is the saying? Any friend of Travis Meacham's will be *muy simpático.*"

"Any friend of Travis's is a friend of mine," Alicia says. She cuffs Tomás on the arm with her fingers, and then takes a firm hold of my upper arm, her grip surprisingly reassuring.

"Call me Zoe. The original Dr. Dempsey was my grandfather." The social niceties always throw me.

"Con mucho gusto," Alicia says, letting go of my arm. "How fine. So you are not the first doctor in your family."

Tomás picks up my luggage and takes the lead. We make our way toward what looks like a receiving line made up of customs officials and soldiers. An older man of considerable girth, perspiring freely, dressed in a uniform trimmed with braid, gestures to me to open my purse. It takes me a minute to understand his gesture. I claw my purse open with obvious haste. He glances inside and then up to my face with a sweet, consoling expression. Perhaps because he's not accustomed to causing fear in well-dressed gringos, he takes no pleasure in it. He solemnly waves us through.

Alicia suggests we go for coffee while Tomás expedites delivery of the shipment. She tells me the equipment used to immunize in the field under non-sterile conditions is crucial. A local pharmaceutical company has offered to provide serum if we fall short, but they can't deliver supplies. All that was left to Travis, whose high-caliber donation has been at the airport since before Tomás and Alicia left Palenque. Tomás says again how he himself must be the one to facilitate the paperwork. Alicia and I are happy to agree.

We proceed to the café, where Alicia pulls a typed itinerary from her bag the minute we sit down at a table. I begin to feel myself relax while she flicks through the calendar of events with a beautifully manicured nail. She speaks rapidly in idiomatic English, describing the difficulties of coordinating all the doctors who come to help and confessing that the official-looking plan may well change. She pauses while the waiter takes our order, then goes on to tell me about the other volunteers: some regulars from the States, like Travis, and a steady stream from Europe, mostly through *Médecins sans Frontières*.

Recently, the Clinic's big push to immunize more children from the indigenous communities has attracted other doctors like me, with no previous volunteer experience in this environment. She doesn't actually say this makes her job harder, but it becomes obvious as she explains how many different conditions determine the itinerary, and how quickly conditions can change. It would be a big help if I were fluent in Spanish. The waiter arrives with Alicia's drink and my Perrier in its little green bottle just as Tomás comes back to tell us we must wait for some honcho to show up, the only person permitted to release the supplies. They lack some customs declaration that was supposed to be attached in Mexico City.

Tomás orders a Tecáte and lime and settles back with a smile. "We can't leave without the shipment. If it takes too long you ladies can go to dinner while I remain here."

"We will stay with you," Alicia says to him. She turns back to me. "Sometimes I think we're simply 'doctors of the pills' to *los Indios*. Without our medicines and immunizations we would not be especially welcome." She looks back at her companion, but he's busy with his beer, salting the top, squeezing the lime, and drinking straight from the can, like a Texan.

"We used to have the same expression in English—pill doctors," I say.

"We are delighted you have come," Tomás says. "The poor people, in the towns, they are glad. But *los Indios* look to their own healers, the *curanderos,* as much as they do to us."

"I've been thinking about involving a woman named Lydia Flores, a first generation American, as a consultant in one of my cases."

"You're serious about this?" Alicia asks, dismay showing in her face.

"Nothing to be ingested," I add hastily.

"Don't misunderstand," Alicia says. "They do a valuable service. They treat fevers, menstrual problems, and headaches and so on with very effective herbs; besides they provide *limpias*–incantations and spiritual cleansings–for whatever plagues you. I was just surprised."

"They also use massage, poultices, cupping and body puncturing," Tomás says. "I don't know about you, but I missed those in medical school."

Alicia frowns at her companion. "Healers worldwide believe that when the body is sick the soul is wounded. In some ways I can see what they're saying. Surely the soul suffers when the body is sick. On the other hand, a Maya mother may think her child's diarrhea is caused by the evil eye, or *sustos.*"

Tomás makes a comic face and shrugs, still sipping his beer.

"What's *sustos*?" I ask.

"Something like soul loss," Alicia answers, giving Tomás a stern look. "Children, especially, can be spirited away, so to speak, particularly if they're frightened. The human spirit may play some part in illness, but it distresses me when a mother with a sick child goes to some ignorant old woman to be treated with eggs and feathers. The child can die of dehydration, when sugar water, another old standby, could have saved her."

"We'd probably call *sustos* something like disassociative disorder," Tomás says. "I'll just stick to using some tried and true old remedies, like the poultices for sports injuries."

"I have in mind a nurse trained in therapeutic touch who is also a *curandera*; a patient of mine wants to investigate alternative healing."

"You know what such a practice has to offer," Alicia says. "I didn't mean to offend."

165

"You didn't." I sip my warm bubble water; I don't trust the ice even in the airport. "Midwives and other alternative healers have made a huge comeback in Austin, where I'm from."

"Artists, environmentalists, slackers," Tomás says.

"You got it," I laugh. "How do you know about slackers?"

"I went to the University of Texas for two years. Besides, Mexican universities are much the same. Have fun while you can. Now, if you will excuse me?" He stands up. "I must go look after the supplies from our man in Texas."

"You're probably right to worry about mixing folk medicine with modern medical treatment," I say. "In our culture of success, chronic illness challenges everything we believe in. I'm way out of line introducing treatment outside my discipline."

"Oh, no, please don't take me wrong," Alicia says, smoothing her heavy hair with shapely fingers, making me aware of how grubby I am after the long trip. "This is Mexico. Here we believe in more than you can see with the naked eye."

"Indigenous people want modern health care for their children, don't they?"

"They want better care for their children. They do not want to have to pay for it by giving up their identity as a people—or at least many of them don't." She hesitates, looking me over carefully. "Children die because the community is unable to provide basic needs, like clean water. We doctors can do so little. You're not political, I hope."

"No. I don't know enough to take sides on political questions." I squirm with dissatisfaction with myself. "That sounds stupid. How can anyone not be on the side of clean water and healthy children?"

Alicia touches me on the arm. "I know. But don't get caught in the crossfire down here." She frowns. "It's fashionable to advocate helping indigenous people in some vague way. Concrete help, including the immunizations we propose to dispense, can attract unwanted attention. If you must talk to people about our activities, speak only of the medical benefits to children. That will be the best."

I catch Alicia's alarm. "I specialize in autoimmune disorders. I'm beginning to think all medicine is social or environmental medicine."

Tomás comes back with the news that we can't pick up the shipment until tomorrow. He seems to have no trouble shrugging off the momentary setback. Alicia bustles us off to a nearby restaurant, where an attractive mix of Mexicans and foreigners—archeologists from the look of them—fill most of the small space. For a moment I wonder what it would be like to be somebody else, somebody like an archeologist digging in the dirt, looking for treasure.

"We could use you here, Zoe," Tomás says. "Intestinal disease is common among the Indians. But not to mind," he interrupts himself, waving the stemmed wine glass in his hand to forestall discussion, "tomorrow will be soon enough to think on these things."

"All right. Coming down here on such short notice, I know very little of the situation or what in the way of public health care is provided for rural people."

"Please, do not imagine yourself alone," Tomás says. "All the plagues of the poor are coming back—in the city, in the country, in the temporary settlements. Effectively, the cause is lack of knowledge of domestic hygiene. Still, washing hands means nothing when the water is polluted, and when there are no latrines. When pigs and turkeys raised for food eat filth." Frustration shows through his carefully constructed social mask.

Alicia watches him closely. I wonder if they are lovers. "People who are willing to keep their eyes open are many, many," she says.

"I'm not sure I follow."

"It's true that cholera and TB are coming back," she replies. "Some people think the return of cholera is no accident. Disease keeps populations in control. I don't believe that, but the material lives of the indigenous people are worse even than before the 1994 rebellion."

"You've lost me," I say.

"Intimidation, disease, hunger, and displacement are weapons," Tomás says. "We have here in Chiapas what's called *low intensity warfare* since the Zapatistas occupied five towns and five hundred ranchos on New Year's Day in 1994. The revolution is not only symbolic."

"Your government gave TB-infected blankets to the Indians," Alicia says, her earlier caution against political thinking apparently forgotten.

"The indigenous people show courage and dignity," Tomás says, making a placating gesture towards me with his eloquent hands.

"I'm not offended," I say. "We have a history of injustice to our own native Americans."

"*Claro,*" Tomás says. "It is true that here in Mexico many Indians are worse off *materially* than before the uprising, yet there's no sign they are ready to give up their stubborn resistance to the countless aggressions and ever more heartless policies used to scatter them. Resistance has been the case for five hundred years."

"When villagers are driven from their homes by the military, or by the paramilitary organizations, or even sometimes by the police, they do not get the planting done," Alicia says. "Many of the people we will be seeing in the days ahead have no permanent shelter. They never get dry: they live in the rain. All the old people suffer from rheumatism."

"Earlier immunization campaigns in Mexico have never reached enough people from the many different indigenous populations," Tomás says. "The money runs out, or the supplies, and the doctors go back home and forget. This time we have commitments for everything: the people, the permissions, the medicines!"

What they are telling me makes me cringe. How naïve of me to think by showing up here in Chiapas I could stand in for Travis. "I hope you accomplish all you plan," I say.

"Ah!" Tomás says. "It is the problem of Mexico since the beginning, since we became a country. Many, many things can come between the plan and the act." He snaps his fingers for the waiter.

"Something always deflects us from our aim," I say. "I seem to have to learn that lesson over and over again."

"In Tzotzil, *to teach* and *to learn* are the same word," Alicia says.

"Perfect! The best way I've ever learned anything is by teaching it."

"What do you teach?" They ask at the same time, then look at each other and laugh.

"Basic immunology. Occasionally I offer a course in medical ethics."

"Here's one for your ethics class: *to say* and *to do* are the same in Tzotzil."

"Where I come from, the gap between the word and the act seems to keep growing wider." I recall how Glover challenged me to judge myself like I do everyone else, by what I do. "Here I am, acting like I'm bringing the gifts of civilization when I'm here to perform a simple task. I'm sorry. *Yo lo siento,*" I say. Sorrow wheezes out of me. I feel strangled with the pain of awareness.

Alicia pats my arm, untroubled by what I have to be sorry about. I heave an uncharacteristic sigh. The pain around my heart region leaches out. The waiter appears long after Tomás's strenuous appeal. I join in the ordinary rituals of dining, and the meal passes quietly. We end up staying the night in Villahermosa.

Alicia and I meet in the lobby of the hotel the next day. Tomás shows up with the van and the supplies before we've had time to have breakfast. He waves off yesterday's delay and launches into the plan of the day.

"We are hindered from administering the immunizations in Palenque for the time being," he tells us, "but do not worry. We will go on to San Cristobal, a very beautiful old town. You will be most comfortable there," he says, turning to me. "We will travel most of the day and start tomorrow. We are to be given an Army escort."

"What do you mean?" Alicia's voice sounds shrill.

"I am sorry, Alicia, but we will be accompanied by a single vehicle," Tomás says, "with two officers and two soldiers. There is nothing to be done," he says in a tone of finality, splaying his hands out in front of him. He doesn't look her in the eye.

"We have a long trip today," he says. He darts a look at me. "If I had known we would be going to San Cris and not Palenque, you could have flown into Tuxtla Gutierrez, but that can't be helped. At least we will not suffer delays as long as we have our escort."

We start out traveling in a spiffy rented van complete with a driver who is never introduced to me, and a translator, Hector Piña, who is.

"Hector is a Linguistics professor at the University of Guadalajara in Oaxaca," Alicia says happily. "He is an authority on indigenous languages."

"A very tired authority," Hector says. "I hope you won't expect much in the way of discourse in any language, at least until we reach our destination."

I shake Hector's hand, and then introduce myself to the driver, who looks shyly at his knees as I climb in next to him. Everybody else claims a bench seat to himself. The Mexico that begins to roll by out the window is lush and green, nothing like the Texas border towns I'm familiar with. Alicia sits all the way in the back. She keeps watching out the back window where our military escort trails behind. Hector promptly goes to sleep, as promised.

After nearly an hour Alicia moves up to the seat behind me, next to Tomás.

"Before the new roads," she says, "many of the people lived far in the highlands. Only a few ever got out. The roads make it easier to bring the children to a central location for injections."

"It's true we didn't reach the people in the *selva*," Tomás says, "but that's not why the government's building these new roads. They build roads so soldiers can come fast when there's trouble."

"There aren't many clinics," Alicia says. "In the temporary

settlements, none at all."

"It would be better if doctors went to the people in their homes," Hector says, sitting up. "In indigenous communities, everybody must agree. Taking your child out of the village to a clinic causes problems. Who is to decide if a child is sick enough?"

"Now that's a good question," I say. "How deep must consensus go?"

"Traditionally, anything to do with outsiders was agreed upon," Tomás says. "But now a village might have many different factions besides the Catholics and the Protestants."

"I thought the Catholics absorbed the ancient religions, and had more or less a spiritual monopoly in Mexico," I say.

"The Evangelicals have performed a modern miracle," Alicia says, "by getting many of their converts off alcohol. Catholic custom requires everyone to support the fiestas and other rituals." She rubs her thumb and middle finger together in the universal gesture meaning money. "The village headman, the *cargo,* has many costly duties. Protestants offer another way."

"Ah, yes," Hector says. "But religious disputes don't account for all the changes in Mexican habits. Professional people don't take time for *siesta* like we used to."

Hector's interrupted by the driver in a tone of voice that demands attention. We have come to a military checkpoint. As soon as we come to a stop Tomás gets out, leaving the door open. Alicia grabs my camera and stuffs it in a colorful woven backpack, zipping it up before handing it back to me. Two soldiers come up to Tomás. Hector gets out; after a short exchange he turns to beckon to the rest of us. I jump out, disguising an unwelcome feeling of vulnerability. Tomás stands a little distance away in the doorway of a guard hut, built with raw wood, bright yellow in the surrounding green. An army officer sits nearby on the porch of what looks to be a tiny country store. Across the road soldiers construct what must be a latrine with the same bright new wood.

Alicia comes up to assure me we should not be delayed for

long, since she and Tomás prepared a list with our names and bona fides to leave at checkpoints.

She turns out to be right, for the officer appears to do no more than look at the list and count heads. Nobody asks me for identification. Alicia and I walk side by side, stretching our limbs, saying little.

The four men from the army escort trail after us, smoking with exaggerated gestures. One soldier goes barely out of sight to take a leak before we go back to the van to return to our journey.

Chapter 23

We reach San Cristobal at dusk, too late to set up operations. We had been promised a corner of the courtyard inside the massive doors of a charity associated with the work of the Catholic Bishop Samuel Ruiz, a lifelong friend of the Indians. This vigorous old man, a historical monument in his own person, is attempting to negotiate an end to the dispute among the Indians, the Federal Government, various political factions, and the Zapatistas.

We are staying at a hotel on the *zocalo*, near the building occupied by the Zapatistas in the 1994 uprising. After going to my room just long enough to clean up, I meet my new friends in the lobby and we head out for dinner at a restaurant said to be nearby. The tourists we pass on the street appear noticeably European—something about their clothes, or maybe they look smaller and slimmer than vacationing Texans. Alicia tells me the Mexican government recently deported a prominent American who entered the country on a tourist visa but involved himself in the plight of the indigenous people. She and Tomás attempt to fill me in on the situation we face, coming in under the umbrella of the Outreach Clinic, one of a number of non-governmental organizations attempting to help improve the living conditions of the poor and the indigenous people.

I'm told how the peace talks held between the Zapatistas and the government had led to agreement signified by the signing of the San Andres Accords. But then the entire process broke down last year at the implementation phase. The military presence continues to grow while armed gangs, paramilitaries with quaint names like *Peace and Justice,* carry out acts of thuggery and violence against individuals and communities who align themselves with the rebel Zapatistas. Paramilitaries are made up of people from the indigenous communities recruited by the anti-insurrectionist branch of the Mexican military, often made up of men trained at the School of the Americas.

Alicia was so busy filling me in, with occasional help from Tomás, that we pass the restaurant. We retrace our steps when the discovery's made, and at length we settle in for dinner. The menu offers more classic French dishes than traditional Mexican food. I order chicken molé only to discover it takes two hours to fix. Nobody minds. Tomás regales us with a story about Travis scoring a big donation from the governor's wife the last time he was here. He cautions us in a bantering tone about all the risks we might encounter while we go about our work. Iris may have known more about the situation here in Chiapas than I did—at least enough to be worried. Taken up with my professional life, fortified first by the pain meds and then preoccupied by the need to find a way to do without, lonely for Al and worried about Iris, I didn't have much left over for what was going on next door in Mexico. I have no doubt why Travis asked me to go instead of Al. Al would have said no.

Back at the hotel, I buy a phone card at the desk and call home from the phone in the lobby. Al sounds remote and uneasy, and I'm not all that forthcoming myself. Neither Iris nor Anna is around to say hello. Since I have no idea how Al will be able to reach me, I tell him I'll check in again soon. I almost call the hospital but decide against it. It's not as if they can't run the place without me. I go to bed strangely glad to be cut off from everything familiar.

We have arrived days earlier than planned, since we were supposed to spend a day immunizing children in Palenque first. The courtyard promised to us is not available, so in the morning we set up in a shabby storefront near the bus terminal. Hector brings me and Alicia fresh orange juice and mango, with the promise of coffee to come. We are far from the *zocalo,* closer to the outskirts of town where most of the indigenous people live. After driving around the community announcing our location through a bullhorn, a member of the Outreach Clinic, Dr. del Vecchio, shows up to assist us. When he tells Hector he speaks some Tzotzil, Hector embraces him.

Nobody shows up. Alicia speculates that people may fear reprisals.

"Who from?"

She shrugs. "Anyone could be a threat. Perhaps we look too official. This town is the middle of everything. Not only of the Zapatistas, but of the Salvationists as well."

"Now who are they again?"

"Those who believe God will deliver the Indians from oppression. Exactly how is still unclear, but perhaps with a leader like Moses, who led the children of Israel out of Egypt to the Promised Land. I don't know where they place the Outreach Clinic in this scheme. *Yo no se.*"

She smiles at me.

We don't have to wait much longer before people begin to arrive. Many of the children and most of the women come dressed in their finery, colorful traditional dress made from beautifully woven tops over dark wool skirts tied with sashes. The men and older boys wear little trace of traditional costume. They look like other poor Mexicans you meet outside the cities, wearing work pants, short-sleeved shirts, and sandals.

Mothers stand in line with their children. First we weigh each child on the dilapidated scale we brought along, packed on the roof of the van; then we measure, assuring and exclaiming over their cooperation; and then we inoculate the child as off-handedly as we can while surrounded by people waiting for the next bus. Small raggedy barefoot boys dart around selling Chiclets and lottery tickets. At first we begin with all the youngest children, but our plan changes by mid-morning, when it becomes obvious mothers are going to be hanging around all day to get their whole brood attended to. The announcement of our decision to vaccinate all members of the same family at one time is accepted without fanfare.

Even taking into account their small stature, many of the children are underweight. When Alicia speaks to one of the mothers about her youngster's nourishment, she summons an older sister, who gives the child sugar cane. Alicia shrugs and soldiers on. Mothers hold babies inside their shawls, giving them the breast at the least sign of fussiness. We draw the line at inoculating the teenage boys, based on a complicated set of criteria, but give the injections to the teenage girls, who may soon be mothers. The crowd is mostly female, and we only have to turn a couple of boys away. The men waiting for the bus don't even glance at us.

Neither Alicia nor Tomás speaks any indigenous language. Besides del Vecchio to help him, Hector enlists a young man dressed all in white who speaks Tzotzil and Spanish. It's important to explain to the mothers what we're doing, and to impress upon them what they need to watch out for after going home. Alicia's adamant about us all continuing to tell them, in whatever language we have at our command, how much good the shots will do, perhaps to keep up our own spirits. In the most crowded part of the morning we vaccinate so many children without a break our injection guns heat up. We wrap them in bandanas to keep from blistering our hands. The children watch with solemn eyes. Nobody shows any fear, suspicion or hostility towards me or the other doctors. The women, who seem to find me especially amusing, giggle behind fingers pressed against their mouths, their darting eyes merry. These people who make room for me among them in our borrowed space touch my heart.

Finally back at the hotel at the end of the day, I discover I'm dead tired. Everything hurts. I'm ready to go my own way for a spell. My immensely polite colleagues could probably use a break from me, too. After showering I go down to the lobby, decorated in seventies' modern except for a display of regional crafts in the gift shop. I notice a *retablo*—a devotional painting on a piece of tin—of the Archangel Michael, dressed like a gladiator in a Roman skirt, laced boots and breastplate. He carries a sword in one hand and a set of scales in the other. His skin is pink. I find the icon unsettling, reminding me of my run-in with the man in the mountains. I understand superstition—our brains are designed to make meaning out of all the elements held in mind at one time. I look for a connection between this primitive painting—combining myths from ancient times with beliefs now current—and my recent experience in the Davis Mountains, but can't put my finger on what's disturbing me.

Another *retablo* depicts Our Lady of Guadalupe, whose image you can see all over Mexico, reminding me of my near-death in the Guadalupe River. Maybe what disturbs me is that the matter-of-fact allusions to a spiritual dimension prevalent everywhere in this country are finding a match in my own recent experiences. I'm glad when Alicia comes up and stands beside me, her eyes alert.

"Do you know the story of Guadalupe?"

I shake my head no.

"Guadalupe appeared as a vision to Juan Diego, an early convert to Catholicism, ten years after the *Conquistadores* marched on the Aztec capital. Many people believe she is both the Virgin and Tonantzîn, a pagan goddess going back to the Aztecs."

"The Great Mother," I say. "There's nothing like her in the Protestant pantheon."

"Guadalupe has been taken over as a symbol by the conservative elements in Mexico," Alicia says, looking at me with the calculating eye of a diagnostician. "You think professional women need such a symbol?"

I laugh. "Not when you can get the real thing. My grandmother looks after us, all of us—and she's practically raised my daughter Iris."

Alicia puts her arm around my shoulder in a quick squeeze and walks away. I look back at the figure of Guadalupe, a dusky Madonna in a blue cape covered with stars, standing on a golden crescent. Maybe my baptism in the Guadalupe River will help me connect the discordant elements of my life. It takes me a long time before I can concentrate enough to enter the numbers needed to reach Texas; when I do the international line is out. Some things never change, despite the hype. After a perfunctory dinner, this time alone in the hotel restaurant, I end up going to bed without having spoken to Al.

We have a good show of people the following morning, but siesta seems to hold sway in San Cristobal despite Hector's concerns about modernization; no one else shows up in the afternoon. Tomás and Alicia decide to go on up the mountain to Ocosingo, but our driver argues against it, saying we have delayed too long. Alicia attempts to sweet-talk him, but he remains stubborn. Tomás points out all the advance work done by the clinic to smooth our way and suggests that Alicia and I take the afternoon to go shopping. We both look at him so fiercely he takes a step back. I vote for pushing on—I'm beginning to have misgivings about what I left behind me in Texas. If we finish up early, maybe I can switch my airline tickets to an earlier flight. Alicia goes to talk to our Army escort and returns in a hurry.

"We can go to Ocosingo today, the Colonel says, if we leave right away. But in that case they shall not be able to escort us back to Palenque. The escort still has business here and can't leave with us now."

"You mean we have a choice about them coming along?" I ask, startled.

"The escort's for our own protection," Alicia says. "We are permitted to travel like anybody else. Some of us in Outreach considered an escort necessary."

"That's fine, Alicia," I say. She seems to have forgotten her initial reaction to our Army escort. "However you want to do it."

"If we go straight on to Palenque after Ocosingo, Dr. del Vecchio will come with us. Tomás wants to stay on here to help out at the Outreach Clinic for the next few days."

Just as it appears everything has been arranged for our departure, a tiny Indian woman appears with three small children. She looks incredibly old for these youngsters to be her own children. We're not supposed to immunize children unless one of the parents brings them. "Do you think she's the grandmother?" I ask Alicia.

Alicia asks the woman, *"Tus ninos?"*

The woman nods and smiles, revealing several missing teeth. Alicia talks to her in Spanish—it sounds like she's trying to persuade her we're not giving any more immunizations today—but the woman just keeps smiling. I doubt she has a clue what Alicia's trying to tell her, and Hector is out packing the van. I wrap my jean skirt between my legs and squat down on my haunches next to the smallest child, a girl who looks barely two year's old. I start to converse with her just like I do with any child who comes for an injection, quietly, in English. I'm afraid I would sound unconfident if I tried my rudimentary Spanish.

She looks into me with wise, inquiring eyes. We stare at each other, noses practically touching, her brown eyes capturing my blue ones, both of us equally mesmerized. She touches me on the cheek with her small grimy hand, then taps on her chest and says "Sofia" quite clearly. Staggered with the desire to connect with this small soul, happy to be in this moment in Chiapas, glad I have made the journey to Mexico, I tap my own chest and say "Zoe."

Balancing on my fingertips on the floor, I sketch a gesture to enfold the child with my other hand, but before I can complete the gesture, I'm shoved over on the hard tile floor with a painful thump. Someone snatches the child away in a flurry of skirts.

All hell breaks loose. The place is in an uproar. I get up off the floor slowly, my back so bad I have to pause a moment on all fours. The little girl twists her head to get a look at me over her mother's shoulder. I heave myself to my feet. The mother, screaming in a mixture of languages, wrenches the child's head around and down into her shoulder. In no time everyone is shrieking, except for the little boy, about eight, who stands glowering, stationed in front of his mother, his feet planted wide and his fists clenched.

Alicia tries to talk the mother down out of her tree, but

she won't shut up. Del Vecchio shows up and speaks to her sternly. The woman stops the shouting but continues to sputter in a low hoarse tone. There are no tears. Tomás and Alicia are both trying to speak to her at once, saying the same things over and over in soothing tones, until finally Alicia goes out to find Hector. Tomás comes over to me.

"She's afraid you did something bad to her child," he says, looking as miserable as a man can look, faced with a melee of distraught women and children.

"I can see that."

"Please, Dr. Dempsey, I am sorry. Of course you did nothing. These people are very superstitious. And this woman has very little Spanish."

Alicia returns and resumes talking to the mother, one moment placating and the next scolding. Hector explodes through the door like a *deux ex machina*. I feel giddy with relief. Finally there's someone to talk to the mother and the little girl.

We have here the makings of an international incident, but Hector first solicits a report from the other children. The little boy puffs up earnestly in response. The middle child, a girl, wraps herself up in her mother's skirts and watches everything intently.

"The mother's afraid you gave her child the evil eye," Hector says over his shoulder.

"What do you mean? How could she think such a thing?"

"You have a very strong *ool*," he says, coming over to me. "How shall I say—the *ool* is like what you call the soul. But also maybe more like what you would call will. Or heart." He turns to Alicia, lifting his hands in perplexity.

"Your personal power," Alicia says. "Your essence."

"Yes, good, that is correct," Hector says, standing up and coming over to me. "The Indians believe adults who desire something from a child, especially people with a strong *ool*, can damage the child. Make her sick." Hector's demeanor is intense and serious. The mother clutches all three of her children to her and watches us intently.

All at once, tears begin to slip from my eyes. I don't think I've cried since I was twelve years old. I want to stop. Or find a place to hide and cry as much as I want. No one looks at me directly until I compose myself.

I take one step toward the mother then stop. *"Yo lo siento,"* I whisper with all my heart. Her face softens a tiny bit. She speaks urgently to Alicia, gesturing in my direction.

Hector heaves a sigh and goes to join the women. He comes back shortly.

"I'm sorry," I say again.

"No, please do not apologize," Hector says. "Your tears are the best possible *cosa*—I don't know how to say it, the best thing you can do. Your tears give us a way to mend our trouble. Since you have such a strong desire to touch her child, the mother says you must have your wish."

"She wants me to touch her child?"

"Yes. Not for long," Hector says. "For a moment. So as to end your craving. So you do not curse the child. You may hold her, and blow into the cups of her hands, very softly. And also here," he says, touching me minutely on the temple. He opens his hands and shrugs, shy, like Tomás, a man caught in women's affairs. *"Entiende?"*

I nod, closing my eyes and praying for help. *If you're going to rely on powers you've never dreamed of,* I recall, making an effort not to shudder. When I open my eyes the fierce mother stands inches away from me, clutching her child around the waist in front of her, face front. Without warning she thrusts the little girl toward me like a package. I press the child's pliant body to me. She's more solid than I expected. She pushes her hands against my chest and grabs a button, bending back and giving me an impish smile, the ruler of her world. I take her hand and open her fingers and blow into her palm. She laughs while I try to catch her other hand, waving in a bright stutter of motion. I purse my lips to blow on each temple. She twists around to her mother, letting out a small animal squeak. Her mother snatches her back and inspects her. My whole body feels empty. How could her mother have known how much I craved contact with this magic child? For the first time in days I remember I'm pregnant, and my spirits lift.

181

The mother insists on Alicia giving the child her immunizations. The woman talks to both the men in a bossy voice while Alicia administers the shots. I hang in the background.

"She says she'll have to burn the child's clothes once she gets home. Maybe you can give her some money to get new ones," Tomás comes over to tell me.

I'm happy to dig in my purse for money. The woman accepts the dollars, all the time smiling her toothless smile, a face with such power, such a combination of innocence and guile I have to laugh. It feels like she's bolstered my heart by letting me touch her child.

"You gave her too much," Alicia says disapprovingly, finished with giving the shots, "she can outfit the whole village with what you gave her."

"Amends never come cheap," I say.

"But after all, you didn't know."

"Know what?"

"How to protect children from getting knocked off balance from your cravings," Alicia says with a curious hand gesture, rubbing her thumb against the other fingers. It's hard to tell if she believes there's any truth to the mother's fears or not. "Don't look so stricken. The village *curandero* treats dozens of cases of evil eye a year. Usually, of course, when the child's actually sick," she says with a cynical grimace. "Never mind. It's over."

My relief is immense. Alicia and I hug like sisters. I'm beginning to catch on that whatever's in the works for me is still far from over.

"Those three were her youngest children. She has six more living," Alicia says when we are alone again. "And you, Zoe? Do you have children?"

"Yes. One. A girl."

"What do you call her?"

"Iris. We call her Iris." I want to ask her the same question but find I cannot.

Because of the fiasco with our last client, we pull out later than planned. We're also losing Tomás Leon, who stays behind with some supplies. I tell him he's been a great expediter. Hector, it is decided, will stay with him. Distressed by the day's events and cut off from my responsibilities back home, I am glad to get on with our mission.

Chapter 24

We drive back on the newly paved road to Palenque until we reach the minor emergency clinic we've been invited to use at Ocosingo, a small modern town on the side of the mountain. We spend the long day working, with few breaks. Del Vecchio's shyness is no longer apparent. I sip a cold *Coca* one of the scurrying boys brings me. Afraid to meet the eyes of the women for more than a passing moment, I stare at their feet. Wide, strong, and dusty, the feet of the mothers and grandmothers tell the story of a life far different from mine. Most of the women wear sandals. The children run barefoot except for some of the more carefully dressed little girls. The elegance and refinement of the brightly colored woven and embroidered blouses contrast sharply with the bare feet and crudely made sandals.

We run out of clients before we've used up our supplies. At del Vecchio's suggestion, we immunize a few of the young men who've been hanging around, somehow convincing them it's the manly thing to do. There's a lot of laughing and wisecracking going on before everybody's gone. After ceremoniously thanking the clinic staff, we ourselves pack up and get in the van to continue the journey up the mountain to the next hamlet, where we plan to spend the night.

Dr. del Vecchio retains his dignity even asleep on the benchseat at the back of the van, his skinny legs, concluding in neatly shod feet, hanging over the end of the seat. Alicia sits behind me. We've run out of small talk. My mind's on the problems awaiting me when I get back to Texas when the sight of an old

VW bug hurtling toward us in the oncoming lane, its lights flashing on and off, startles me. I instinctively brace my hands on the dash as the van lurches onto the wrong side of the road into the space just vacated. It takes only a moment to figure out the Volkswagen wasn't what was endangering us—it was warning us. We swerve around a pile of trees and brush barricading the whole right-hand side of the road.

We careen back into our own lane to evade an oncoming truck. Making little grunts of fear and effort, our driver frantically switches our headlights on and off. I catch a glimpse of a huddle of men on the side of the road, half hidden beside the pile. "Maybe somebody needs help," I say, touching the driver's elbow. He throws me a look so caustic it makes me recoil. He understands more English than he's let on.

Alicia scrambles to the front and hangs over the console, speaking to him in urgent tones.

"Those are banditos," she says, turning to me. "Maybe they are not finished putting their trap together for the night. Otherwise we could not get by. We were lucky. They take everything—money, jewelry, cameras, passports. It was thoughtless for us to start so late."

How naïve I was, ready to get out and help people who regard us as prey! I go hot with embarrassment. "I'm sorry, Alicia. We shouldn't have departed so late."

"No, no," she says, eyes glinting, "It is my responsibility. I am so very sorry. I hate to know what you must think of us, how we are such barbarians."

Ignorant as I am about what's going on here, I've been no less blind to what's happening back home. "There are plenty of dangers in America," I say to Alicia, touching her on the arm..

Her face seems to close against me. I search for words to make it better, but find none. What has brought me here to the other side of the border, speeding down a narrow road among strangers?

In the aftermath of our adventure we trip all over each other in two languages, laughing and giving precedence to the other only to interrupt with another remembered detail, eager to relate to del Vecchio what he's missed. He goes into orbit, embarking on a riff about the difficulties of the professional class in Mexico: people want doctors to help them, but they also resent them for what they have in material goods, which is next to nothing, not enough to live well, at least when compared to landowners or to politicians. Doctors here in Mexico enjoy nothing like the good life doctors enjoy on the other side of the border, in Texas. His whole outburst constitutes a non sequitur for Travis to add to his collection. We fall into uneasy silence. It would be folly to debate with him in these circumstances.

We finally arrive at the utilitarian motel, where Alicia had booked rooms for us in advance. I'm looked after like a child. We start early the next morning to continue on to Palenque, a modern city built on the famous Maya site, where the palaces, temples and houses rest like jewels atop steep terraces built by the ancients. For believers, the temple provided a sacred entry to the underworld. For vast numbers of world travelers, Palenque's a vacation spot. Archeologists from Mexico and around the world are still unearthing treasure and the record of ancient knowledge. I'm sorry I won't have time to see much.

Nobody has much to say for a long stretch. I'm dozing when we stop at a military checkpoint just before reaching Palenque, an inconvenience Alicia says wasn't here a few days ago. A dozen soldiers surround the van as soon as we come to a stop. Alicia struggles awkwardly until she gets the door open and tumbles out of the van, the rest of us close behind, to be confronted by unsmiling soldiers garbed in new green uniforms at least a size too large on their bird-chested frames. They motion us out into the hot bright afternoon with jabs of their rifles. I leave my camera but grab my purse. Alicia, rumpled but haughty, goes towards the guard hut, while Dr. del Vecchio mills around with an apologetic look on his face.

The soldiers swarm through the van, looking more thoroughly than at any previous checkpoint. Alicia, who carries all the official papers, is presumably going through the same drill she has gone through countless times.

Some enterprising Indians have set up shop along the verge. I take a few steps toward them. Two men and a woman take tentative steps toward me. We are all smiling, suspended for a moment in time. One man, with a face like an ancient Maya warrior, carries a long staff strung with masks. One mask depicts a snake eating a frog like Iris found after my baptism in the river, the sight eliciting a small whoop of glee from me as I stride towards the man and his masks. Before I can reach him he turns and vanishes. I stare, uncomprehending. He might have sunk into the earth, but it's more likely he popped into a ditch behind the band of vendors.

I wheel around to confront an Army officer on my heels, decked out in gold braid, wearing dress shoes. He must've popped out of his hut, accounting for the vanishing act of the mask vendor. The soldier's eyes slide over me before he turns and beckons sharply to Dr. del Vecchio, who slinks our way with his eyes on the ground, like a dog expecting to be kicked.

"You are a doctor for the Zapatistas," the officer says in a nasty tone.

"I am a doctor for the poor people," Dr. del Vecchio answers, gazing down at his shoes.

"It would be better for you not to help *los hijos de la chingada*—for your own good I recommend you get out of this line of work."

Dr. del Vecchio wags his head and hunches his shoulders, looking miserable, but he answers with dignity: "I am a doctor. This is my line of work."

"Watch out. We don't want anything to happen to you. Watch your path," the officer continues, his voice comically cruel, glancing towards me, his selected audience. His simple, slow, short sentences begin to scare me. Suddenly convinced his message is meant more for me, to understand and take to heart, I clamp my teeth shut to keep the fear from showing in my face. Del Vecchio says nothing. The officer's voice ranges higher, and his cadence quickens. He's deliberately working himself up.

"Your studies are useless. Why waste yourself for these

people? They are not worth your life." He darts up close to Dr. del Vecchio, causing him to step backward, trembling. The bully snickers, his chest heaving behind his starched shirt.

Alarmed, I walk up to them, smiling as if I do not understand a word of the Spanish I've been straining to follow. "So we'll be back in time for a good dinner," I say inanely in English, smiling at the officer, who looks me up and down with a puzzled frown on his face.

"Don't get nervous, Doctor. Doctor," the officer says in English, mockingly wagging his head back and forth between me and Dr. del Vecchio, "what I tell you is very simple. These people are not worth your trouble." He saunters back to yell orders at the soldiers still making a show of inspecting our vehicle.

Another soldier comes over and asks Dr. del Vecchio a string of personal questions—where he lives, where he works, the name of his superior—but del Vecchio answers only by pointing to the guard hut. The soldier asks again. As if they're playing an elaborate poker game, Dr. del Vecchio shrugs his shoulders and looks puzzled. The soldier shambles away.

Back in the van, it is just like yesterday after the bandits: we all start talking at once. Except this time we give way to Dr. del Vecchio, who speaks in an indignant voice: "I am going to register a most earnest complaint for this treatment."

Alicia knows nothing about what was happening outside while she was dealing with the officer in the hut. I try to explain, but am interrupted by del Vecchio, so recently insulted for caring for the sons of bitches, understood to mean Zapatistas. His former passivity has been replaced with an equal and opposite ferocity.

"I will denounce this treatment in the name of the Outreach Clinic. The Government uses the Firearms and Explosives Law to search everybody, to do whatever they please. It cannot be accepted by people of conscience."

"What can we do?" Alicia asks. "We have had to provide personal information to travel in this region for a very long time now."

188

I don't say anything. You'd have to have been living under a rock not to know that the Mexicans have learned some tactics of control from us, from the war on drugs or at the School of the Americas, located somewhere in Georgia or South Carolina, I can't remember which.

Dr. del Vecchio looks around somewhat blankly. "The Army in Mexico oversteps its proper function. I must deplore that."

"I wish very much for you to write this letter, my friend," Alicia says. "Make sure to get it published in all the papers. Make clear to people the work the Outreach Clinic undertakes. It is not as some people think, meant for only one locality or only for certain people. The clinic is open to all of the population."

"I am not a political person," del Vecchio says to me in an earnest voice. "We at the Outreach Clinic bring medical attention to those who need it the most. We are independent of politics and religion. We care only about health. Others, *ideologues* for the most part, see us as political. They consider us a threat to their interests."

"But it's all connected, isn't it?" I ask. "Look what happened to me with the mother of the little girl."

"The reason you are experiencing such difficulties, Zoe," Alicia says, then stops. "Let me begin again. The fact Dr. Meacham has been able to come down from Texas and bring with him supplies for us at the Clinic depends on the efforts of many, many people. The Secretary of Health must say he can come. Other officials must cooperate to allow him to bring supplies, sometimes even medicine, and ensure they are not 'forgotten' at some airport, but get all the way to us. This takes time, a little *mordida,* what do you call it, a bribe . . ."

"Or lobbying, or campaign contributions. . ." I help out.

"Yes," Alicia goes on, "we here in Mexico tend to operate on a very personal level. We exercise influence through family connections. This takes time. The permission once given can be taken away at any time. That is why it is so good that you come when Dr. Meacham cannot come, so the connection with the Texas hospital doesn't break down. What I am trying to tell you, effectively, is that the Captain, who does not know the people who have given us the go-ahead, should not try to interfere. It could be very bad for him."

"But like everywhere else, we have what you might call factions," Dr. del Vecchio says. "The Army is not the same as the health organizations. Only in the case of inoculations, like we have been doing these last five days, have we been given permission. We have no authority to direct patients to seek more treatment when they require it. I want very much to do this. We also waste your skills here. I see you," he hesitates, wincing, "would wish to do more for the children. *Yo lo siento.*"

"*De nada,* Dr. del Vecchio," I say. "I know you would like to do more yourself. It's frustrating."

"Yes. I will write to the Secretary of Health himself. Attitudes like that officer's are a long way from what is required if the government wishes to ease tensions here in Chiapas."

"The Army is prevented from exterminating the troublemakers only because of the spotlight on what is happening in Mexico," Alicia says. "We have help from the Italians, the French, the Irish and the *norteamericanos.*" She smiles at me.

"How can the government say it is searching for peace, and the army is here to protect the people? He threatened me!" del Vecchio says, as if he didn't hear her.

"Clearly he did not know who he was talking to," Alicia murmurs. "Will you censor him by name?"

"Alas, I do not know his name, but no matter. No doubt he is not the only rotten apple," Dr. del Vecchio says, recovering his earlier manner of bland assurance. "I am sorry we have made your stay with us so—how do you say, full of frenzy, Dr. Dempsey?"

"My being here with you has no doubt added to the frenzy. It's a good word. It describes what we experience when the different components of a system are out of balance."

"Yes. Exactly. We are *simpatico,*" he says to me with a little bow, one hand across his midriff, from where he is seated behind me.

We get to Palenque at full dark and tumble out of the van, every one of us rank with sweat and frustration. We are all eager to separate. This time I get through on the telephone and speak to Al, Iris, and Anna, which bolsters my spirits. I leave out the business about the evil eye and the log across the road. What else am I not telling? Oh, right. I'm not telling Al, and now can barely comprehend myself, that I'm pregnant.

Our last day together ends like a perfect dream of Mexico. People in the streets dress and walk and talk with the special verve of a Mexican town, making life back home seem arid, and making it easy to forget the seriousness of the low intensity war going on all about us. Maybe del Vecchio was right. Interest in ancient civilizations is widespread, and the Mexican government doesn't want world attention focused on the ill treatment of the living descendents of the ancient Maya. Maybe visits from outsiders do cast a little light.

Alicia and I toast each other and the missing Tomás Leon and speak ebulliently of the future. The Outreach Clinic has heard from Frank Hawkins. Everything's looking good. A French doctor from the *Doctors without Borders* bunch is scheduled to show up about the time I leave. I've missed out on a visit to the Maya temple at Palenque and never found the time to shop for gifts, but remember to ask Alicia about the frog-eating snake on the mask. She tells me the frog is one of the Maya rain god's cohorts. The serpent is associated with the underworld, the place of enlightenment. We talk about what we know and what we do not know, about science and magic and human connection. We go to bed late.

After breakfast the following day I'm provided with a new driver to take me back to Villahermosa. None of my new friends are able to accompany me.

As wired as I am, I don't have much to say to the two strangers, both doctors, one from Sweden and the other from the Netherlands, who share the van to Villahermosa, where we'll catch the plane back to Mexico City. The trees that have been polled into fence posts surrounding the pastures are sprouting leaves and flowers not in evidence only a few days ago. That's what I came to Mexico to find: the tremendous thrum of life energy. Still, I'm anxious to get home.

Even greater numbers of sullen men in green crowd the airport at Villahermosa. I proceed through customs tense and worried, but this time my anxiety doesn't trigger any bells and whistles. I'm flying straight from Mexico City to San Antonio. Unable to sleep, I replay images of Mexico in my mind's eye. My car's parked at the airport; I should be back in Austin a couple of hours after landing, with plenty of time to swing by the hospital before going home.

Among the happy bustle of mostly Latino faces waiting to greet the plane in San Antonio float the pale impassive faces of my FBI Twinkies. I stand rooted to the floor, a metallic taste in my mouth, watching them walking towards me side by side, then flanking me. The one who talks, Green, takes a grip of my arm just above the elbow and tells me I'm under arrest, muttering the Miranda, enunciating clearly, bead by bead: "You have a right to remain silent." An animal sound bleats from my throat.

"Just walk along naturally with us, please, ma'am," he says in a low voice, "and we will not need to cuff you."

I go still. I turn my face to him, my body stiffening. He pulls a pair of handcuffs out of his pocket and speechlessly suspends them between us, the way you'd dangle a rattle in front of an infant to divert it from howling. It works. Each man grips me hard around the upper arm, Collins fingers gouging into me, Green's thumb practically in my armpit. I dig in my heels and glance from my arm to his face. Without altering his expression he moves his hand down towards my elbow and eases up a tad. The other one, Collins, looks to him for instruction, and when he gets the nod we march off three in a row. I crane my head around me and catch the eye of a woman pushing a stroller. She takes in the men hanging on my arms and abruptly looks away, wheeling her child away from trouble. A man about my age takes a look and steps towards us, his arm rising in a tentative motion, but backs away when Agent Green flips his badge at him disdainfully. The rest of the crowd parts around us like the Red Sea for Moses. I am definitely not headed for the Promised Land.

Chapter 25

The vivid male face on the other side of the wall of glass doesn't match the controlled voice coming over the telephone gripped in my hand, as if the rude data of the senses filters through a prism, sorting messages into separate streams, one for each sense organ.

"Dr. Dempsey, I'm Phillip Speck from the law firm of Brooks-Dunlop. We are going to get you out of here with the least possible delay."

"Now would be good. I'd like to get out of these ugly hot clothes." I look down at the day-glow orange polyester of someone else's clothes and feel subtly diminished.

"Yes, you're right," he agrees, his face mournful, his voice crisp and impersonal.

"So where's Brooks-Dunlop? Why isn't s*he* here to help me?" My eyes cling to him.

He studies me for a minute, unsmiling. "Your husband picked *me* to come. My partners are doing what they do best."

"What's that?"

"Making calls on your behalf. I won't lie to you. We're not likely to have you out of here before morning." His eyes skitter from left to right as if he's afraid of being overheard. Silly—of course he's overheard.

"Why did Al pick you to come see me?" I want to keep the link between us alive, but can't seem to help acting like a shit.

"Al and I play squash together. He knows me."

"What does he know about you from playing squash?"

He sighs and sits back in his chair. "More germane is what

he knows about you. Al's worried about you spending a night in jail." He checks his watch and glances around. "Frankly, he's in worse shape than you are."

"I doubt it, Mr. Speck. I'm the one in jail." He looks crushed. I laugh. "You might consider taking up another line of work," I say into the phone.

He smiles: a jolly young man, fit and healthy and helpful, and on the other side of a pane of bulletproof glass. What happened to seeing your lawyer in a nice private room? There's to be no touching, no more closeness than we have here. I am already being punished.

"I'm good at what I do, Dr. Dempsey," he says, an expert with some power to budge the system, someone paid to help me. "Now let me apprise you of the situation. You were apprehended on suspicion of *unlawful flight to avoid confinement*. UFAC for short."

"Unlawful flight? I was coming home!" I'm in a cold fury; I can feel my internal organs dropping temperature.

"Yes. We expect to get you out of here before you are transferred to a federal facility."

I have pained him, I can see by his face, by not cooperating, by not helping to hide the agony of my situation or to make it easier for him. Silly me, he's my lifeline to the outside. I adjust my expression. Speck continues. They can legally keep me here. The law allows it. It is possible I am a threat to others. It is possible I could flee. I have failed to comply. Beneath the rattle of words the subtext is clear: the only power at this moment resides in the criminal justice system. I am now *in* the system and can do nothing for myself, by myself.

Only my representative, Phillip Speck, attorney at law, the one who has paid his dues in this context, passed his exams, paid for his license, who is privy to this particular system—who was already part of it before I fell into it, and who will remain part of it after my case has been resolved—only he has any leverage in this system. Not me. Maybe somebody else also in the system, somebody who owes my lawyers a favor, can be

found. Maybe Speck's partners are already on the phone trying
to find somebody else to smooth the way. Here I am, locked up.
On the wrong end of the social caste system, not the one I normally occupy. I'm here so the criminal justice system can teach
me a lesson. It sucks. And nobody has to tell me I brought it all
on myself.

"What's one night?" I interrupt Speck's monologue.

He takes the receiver from his ear and looks at me, surprised for a moment, then puts the instrument back to his ear.
"Do you do any kind of yoga or meditation, Dr. Dempsey?"

"No."

He looks disconcerted by the flat no. He was only trying to
help.

"Hiring a lawyer's supposedly more useful than meditation
and prayer."

He leans forward. "I'm sorry I can't move the stream of
events along faster. Since I won't see you until morning, please
treat yourself kindly. It's going to be a long night."

My jaw juts out. He reacts as if no barrier lies between us.

"Please, Dr. Dempsey. Nothing in your training has prepared
you for this. Try to cooperate. I'd like to see you looking just as
chipper in the morning as I see you now."

My body temperature drops even lower. I make an effort
not to shiver as I look at the darkness in the young man's eyes.
"You're worried about me!" I exclaim into the phone.

His professional voice floats back over the phone with perfect pitch, but from behind his goodlooking young face he's
making wild signals of distress and sympathy.

"You'll be fine. Sorry we can't do more for you, more
quickly. Just wanted you to know we are unlikely to move the
mountain before morning. False hopes don't do anybody any
good."

"You sure? Many hopes don't pan out. Doesn't make them
any less comforting."

He smiles but looks up over my head. The guard has mate-
rialized behind me. The telephone goes dead without a goodbye.
Speck nods and smiles and gestures through the glass. I miss

him already.

My instant crush on Phillip Speck has me vowing never to tell another lawyer joke. As soon as I am escorted away from the visitors' area, cuffs are placed on my wrists, my arms in front of me. In minutes, I am walking down the hall toward my jail cell. Speck falls from favor. My patients do the same, running hot and cold towards me at warp speed. I never understood that before. Now I do. What a difference a day makes.

"Don't get ahead of me," snaps the truculent woman striding next to me.

"Pardon?" I say, bringing the guard into focus. The ugly look on her broad white face stuns me. Her name badge says Audrey Crunden.

"What did you say?" She grabs me forcefully by the upper arm.

I yelp, shouldering away the fingers grasping my upper arm, hampered by the cuffs binding my wrists in front of me.

"You do NOT ask the questions here, missy," she says, shaking me in her grasp. She's huge. My vision blurs. I consciously go slack. When her grip softens I jerk my arm out of her grasp and spin. As I do, my elbow catches her somewhere between bosom and chin. I've hit my funny bone. A small matter, until I feel myself spun around, my arm twisted so painfully she may have dislocated my elbow. I have no luck stifling the cry that roars out my throat.

"You think I have to treat you nice, you being a doctor? Well, missy, you keep on punching me, you're the one going to need a doctor."

I don't say a thing. How did this happen? Why didn't I think? Oh boy, Phillip Speck the boy-wonder saw this coming. My heart's thudding. Her fingers poke me in the back sharp as a stick. Maybe it is a stick.

"March," I'm told. I'm already lurching forward.

In front of my cell I exhale slowly. Looks like home. She opens the door, pushes me in, follows, turns me around, and flings me against the bunk. I have to struggle to remain upright.

She whips out another piece of equipment and shackles one ankle to the bed in one balletic motion. I look up at her, the bile in my throat choking me. Her eyes gleam.

"You say one thing to me, just one, and the other foot's strapped down too. You decide."

She waits, hands on hips, panting slightly. Barely exerted. A lot of weight in her midriff, the worst thing for future heart trouble. She's red in the face, displaying her disposition for all to see, the sort medieval doctors referred to as choleric. What a fool I've been. She's having a good time. She goes out, slamming the cell door home.

It's a sound that reaches deep inside, a sound I could've gone my whole life without hearing. The odor of the place confronts me—an old-lady smell. Mare's piss. I do an inventory. I have to pee. My temple's throbbing. I don't remember hurting it. It. Me. Just go on. I check myself for damage. The bruise on the temple must've happened in the scuffle. Dry mouth—blurred vision—heart pumping a mile a minute, at the mercy of a maniac. Tears threaten but I fight them back. This situation's temporary. It's not going to whip me: death before dishonor. I am not letting the fucking guard see me cry.

I go back over what the lawyer told me. They can keep me without a charge. What charge is there to bring against me? I haven't done anything unlawful. Phillip Speck tried to prepare me for the hours ahead of me. I've put in longer shifts, but never in this situation. I notice a spirited drone, like cicadas, and listen for the longest time before deciphering it: women talking cell to cell. It's after dinner, before lights out. Ha. Lights are never out.

How long have I been sitting here, cuffed and shackled? I lost myself in a reverie of Mexico. I was hurrying home with those experiences in my heart, ready to share them with my family. Now those memories will be covered by whatever's in store for me now. Judging by my physical state, I've been here an hour. I need to micturate. Micturition refers to the *desire* to make water. How fine the words of my profession, how they give weight and importance to the body's everyday activities, acknowledging the mystery. Put all notion of desire and need out of mind. Like on long car trips when I was little, make it a game. Don't think about it. Get points off every time I do. I can go a lot longer than this. I'm a camel when I need to be. I've had no coffee or sodas. I can see the toilet, but no telling when I'll get to use it.

I can't prevent worse sensations than the need to piss from tormenting me. I scrunch around trying to find a position that will put less strain on my muscles. My elbow throbs. There's some swelling. Would be good to wrap it. Lucky not to have it twisted behind my body. The ankle shackle's demeaning, but it doesn't hurt as bad as the cuffs, which have already chafed my wrists. At least my hands are in my lap. Me and my body; in the happy times I can't tell them apart. Joy comes to me in my body. Music. Sex. Horses. Iris. A gulf of unknowing divides me from my body at this moment, but I feel tender towards it in its present plight, like it was my pet, say a lap dog. It. Now I've become an *I* and an *it*. I giggle. What happened to *I* and *thou?* Martin Buber said address the other as *thou,* and the whole picture changes. I try it on my body: thou art hurt. Tears seep from my eyes, easing up the knot in my womb.

Think about something else. Picture what Al's doing. Going nuts, no doubt. In some ways worse to be him. In other ways not. Al, thou art hurting for me. It's such an easy concept, spending a night in jail. Why is it so awful? You're completely at the mercy of others and there is no mercy, only punishment. Others have taken away your freedom, your right to be human like them. Someone who after the day's work goes home to someone who cares. What did I do to forsake this right? You're supposed to think about it. I cannot comprehend what I did for them to put me in here, tethered to the bed. But of course I can. I mocked them. Ah.

A wave of shame heats my body from top to bottom. I wouldn't want Iris to see me like this or to know how lax I have been. How did I let this happen? I wanted to be invincible for Iris. Wonder Woman keeping harm from her; from me; from us.

This is so damned stupid. I've done nothing deserving this treatment, strapped down. Indignation wells up in me, the heat now rising until I feel I will explode. How dare they! A sound erupts from my throat, almost a roar. Satisfying. I try it again. Then I stop. What did the guard say? What would she do if I called? I cannot remember! How can I not remember? It was a very short time ago. Strap my other foot to the bed. That's what she said she was going to do if I called out. With my free foot I prance in a circle. Having this foot free makes a difference, but still it's torture. Not good, not good at all. I won't think about it. Surely there are some rules of treatment. Surely she can't leave me like this all night.

The cicada song of women talking between cells dies down, hollowing out my insides with a whiff of fear. I go back to the moment in the river. What constitutes the light in the place where I am now? I glance out to the glare of the fixture spewing light outside my cell and close my eyes to shut it out. The light must come from inside when you're locked up. No one in this building cares about me. My plight is not personal. I am an inmate in a prison. I am no longer Zoe Dempsey, M.D., mother, wife, sentient being.

I check myself out, more like a mechanic doing a tune-up than a doctor making a diagnosis. My physical, emotional, mental and spiritual bodies—all suffering. I am matter. To be human is to matter, to know you mean something to somebody. To *be* anybody we need purpose and recognition. I see del Vecchio's hangdog look in my mind's eye while the bully tells him his life's work caring for the Indians *does not matter*. A stupid oafish man was empowered to challenge another man's significance. I wish I had felt more compassion for del Vecchio's suffering. Ha! I was so eager to get home, where I thought I'd be safe. I was convinced things like this just don't happen to people like *us*. Does taking away my freedom make me less human? No. I am not at their mercy in my mind and spirit. Power of will got me everything I ever got on this earth. But maybe not—maybe I've outsmarted myself.

Will may be akin to pride, the fallen angel. Is this what it's like to be chronically ill—to occupy a place from which we must question the foundation of self? Everybody working at the hospital says they're devoted to the well being of the patients. Is that true? I've got to think. Everybody's devoted to the smooth running of the institution. We study where to apply pressure to get the ego rewards and sense of omnipotence that comes with beating back death.

I haven't thought about the need to pee for some time. Warmth oozes from my crotch and onto my thighs. Horror fills me. Surely I'm not peeing in my pants! I've had no conscious volition to pee. No. I check myself. The terrific urge is worse than earlier. I'm not peeing. What's going on? The more scrutiny the body's given, the more information it yields. Or not. Too much attention on my body may make everything seem odd. Happens to my patients with IBD; inflammation's the first line of defense. Spooked and uncertain, we defend ourselves by attacking the first tissue at hand. We betray our bodies in many ways. Think of something else.

What are Al and Speck doing to get me out of here? When I was in labor so long with Iris, with my cervix holding fast, refusing to dilate, I told Al to go on home and get some sleep. He asked me how could he sleep when I was in such pain? He's thinking the same thing this very moment. He's got to be. We're connected now at this moment far more than we are in ordinary time. They will need to contact a judge, to get judicial attention, to get me out of here before morning. The judge is probably at dinner. Then going to a concert or something. What does a judge do on a Friday night? Al and I know a district judge, Peter Chapa, the man who married us. Does this fall under his jurisdiction? Peter's had some very interesting cases. Now I'm an interesting case.

Chapter 26

Why am I acting like such a baby? This is nothing. A bit of discomfort, like I tell patients all the time. Nothing compared to the losses Indians in Chiapas have experienced in the last few years, or the last twenty, or the last five hundred. The Maya themselves practiced human sacrifice. The people I met in Mexico, the present day indigenous people in Chiapas, are mostly descended from the Maya. Blood sacrifice is an ancient practice. We're connected to the gods through blood. Look at the Christians—same thing. The universal intuition: the gods crave life just as we do. Go ahead and appease the gods! Sacrifice someone else, if you please. What about the Latino lady, poster girl for the FBI, Rachel Gomez? I'd sacrifice her. Flout her. I'd be happy to blow her cover. Is that why I'm here?

Something inside of me sends out a little signal. Ping. Something's going on in my body. I quiet my mind so I can pay attention to my body: stickiness in my crotch that should not be there. Meaning this is a medical emergency I have no way of investigating. I call out.

"Guard!"

Nothing. Again I call. Not a soul.

"If you keep saying *guard* you will never get an answer," a clear voice announces from somewhere nearby. "The term is CO, as in corrections officer. No use hollering until after the shift change, anyway."

"Where are you?"

"Next cell. Other side of the vent," the voice answers.

"When's the shift change?" My voice sounds loud and hoarse.

"About a quarter of an hour. Can't you hear the sounds picking up?"

"No, I didn't notice. Thank you." Startling comfort in hearing her voice. But fifteen minutes. The stickiness in my crotch demands attention. I'm miscarrying. No other explanation comes to mind. I'm still strapped by one leg to the bed. Earlier I was foolish. Far earlier in my life, I was a fool, walking down the hall at six o'clock, stupidly pissing off the god who has total control over me. Now wise and cunning, I wait.

When the sounds have died down, I call once. "CO!"

I count to a hundred before calling again, as superstitious as a child. Twice more before someone booms: "Shut the fuck up! Hold your mud!"

I hush, not even breathing, waiting, but the blood still comes. I can't wait. I holler again.

"What the fuck do you need the CO for?" the voice comes back with a volume I'd give anything to muster for myself.

"I'm losing my baby," I shout back, causing a commotion all down the line. "What did you say?" the woman close by says sharply.

"I'm miscarrying. I need help," I repeat, my voice stronger.

The sound of rhythmic clanking starts up. It gets louder. They are making a racket for me, a rocking sound that swells to a crescendo before it diminishes to a clatter, delivering a guard to the cell door, a pint-size woman half as big as Audrey.

"I'm sorry," I say in my smallest voice. Suddenly I *am* sorry. Sorry and ashamed, sorrier than I remember ever being in my life. I gulp. "I'm pregnant. I was pregnant," I correct myself, then pause, swallowing painfully. "I'm a doctor. I'm not wrong about this—I'm miscarrying. I need to see a doctor." I wait. She doesn't move. It's like she's planted. No wonder she's frozen: *I'm pregnant, I'm a doctor,* means nothing to her. What I am is a prisoner. She continues to examine me without speaking or changing expression for what seems like forever. Her long dark hair is wound in braids around her head.

"*Por Dios,*" I say. "Please help me."

Finally she backs a step away from the cell door, the frown growing on her face, a miracle of human feeling to fill the empty official mask.

"Audrey wrote you up," she says in a soft voice. "She said you was dangerous and I was not to go into your cell. You injured her."

"I won't hurt you. I'm bleeding. I shouldn't be bleeding. I'm pregnant. I need to see a doctor," I say, trying to coax a cat out of a tree.

"You just told me you was a doctor," she says with a gotcha! smile.

I smile, afloat with endorphins. We have all the time in the world. I'm in no hurry. Juiced on nature's helpers, I watch myself from a short way away, some cold remnant of survival instinct coaching me on how to handle this ignorant woman and her power over me.

She smiles back at me.

"Yeah. I'm a doctor. I'm also four, maybe five, weeks along."

"How do you know?"

"I did a pregnancy test."

"If you was having a miscarriage, you'd be hurting more. It happened to me. Fool doctor told my mother I was having a 'spontaneous abortion.' Took all I could do to convince her I didn't do it to myself."

"Oh, that's bad," I say. "But you know, you're right. I *would* be hurting more. You're one hundred percent right." I'm sorry I ever thought this woman was ignorant. "I'm cramping, but not so bad. I'm losing blood, but not gallons. Something can still be done to save this baby."

"Nothing before morning, except what Audrey said," she says. She speaks carefully, like she's dealing with a retarded person.

Audrey again! One tiny unguarded moment I can't make go away. "Could you take these cuffs off me?" I ask, my voice coaxing, like a nurse getting a urine sample. "Make it possible for me check to see what's going on down there?" My voice quavers. This woman's not stupid. I was wrong about her. But she's no independent thinker, either. She doesn't want to do anything different from what Audrey the sadist left orders to do.

"Please," I whisper, "I want this baby." And all at once I do want this baby, this bit of matter that turned a strip of paper blue, soon to be a baby with the power to transform and bless.

She looks doubtful. "Audrey could of done you worse than she did, what with you hitting her. You should've thought about the baby before you got yourself into this fix."

"You can say that again."

"I can undo your handcuffs, but I can't take off your leg cuff. You want me to check what's going on down there?" she asks.

"Terrific idea," I say, feeling a spurt of hope. "I'll tell you what to look for. Maybe you'll decide you want to go into nursing."

"Why would I want to do that? This job pays good. Why would I want to be a nurse?"

"No reason. Forgive me, I'm just babbling. I'm afraid I'm losing this baby."

She finally uses her key and comes into the cell. She's very small, smaller even than I first thought. Her skin is perfect, her eyebrows two fine wings of black, her mouth curvy. A beautiful girl embedded inside a guard's uniform, equipment hanging all over, her eyes luminous in the semi-dark.

"You're not going to hurt me, are you?"

I shake my head back and forth. "God no. You're the only one who can help me," I say, beginning to perspire. Not a good sign. The miscarriage must be well along.

"Can I touch you?" she asks, matter-of-fact.

"Yes, of course, fine, I've got to see how much I'm bleeding." She removes my cuffs and fastens them to her belt. "Also I have to pee," I say while I rub my wrists and hands.

She looks over at the bare toilet in the corner of the cell, then back at me, taking in the whole picture. She loses her nerve.

"I shouldn't be doing this by myself," she says, departing abruptly. I start to plead but the slam of the cell door drowns me out. "Maybe somebody else can help you," she says from the other side of the door. "What is your chosen faith?"

Staring at her through the bars, my mind's unable to comprehend her question. How can you choose faith? I feel the sweat beginning to run down my ribs and know I'm losing ground.

"Do you have a church?" she prods. "We have visiting ministers. Or would you like to see a priest?"

"No. No, thank you, no priest. A doctor would be better. Or a nurse." Science, my chosen faith.

"I'll see what I can do."

I figure it will take my lady of the braids at least an hour to get back. She'll be obliged to locate somebody with more authority, whoever it is she reports to, a person still low on the chain of command, probably not eager to interrupt her chores to tend to me. Once my guard gets this person's attention she'll still need to persuade her to come back here. By making the request she already loses points, gives herself away, and labels herself incompetent to handle the problem on her own. And I'm the problem. Hunching over to touch my inner thighs, a hot snake of despair and shame writhes through my body, emerging out of my throat in an unearthly sound. The bleeding does not seem profuse, but the subjective experience of blood loss is extremely unreliable—up until the moment of losing consciousness. All my life I've worked and struggled so I would never be at others' mercy or contempt. I beat back the temptation to holler. The guard with the braids is my last best hope.

Back to the old dilemma: monitoring my body too closely amplifies the pain. On the other hand, organs are often silent right up until the moment they're about to pack it in. I decide to keep time by counting off minutes. Once I've run out of fingers and toes, I clench and then relax different muscle groups, staying with my body, staying out of my head. Above all, staying out of my imagination. After maybe thirty minutes the cramping steps up. I give up on keeping time and fold my hands over my abdomen. My womb flutters for minutes at a time, between cramps so severe it leaps and thuds against my soothing hand. "There, there," I croon. The cramps continue to intensify, notch by notch. The sweating stays about the same.

How can carrying this baby to term depend on a chain of such inconsequential incidents? The law of life—everything good, everything bad, equally dependent on what has gone before. My personal history, the history people have created on this wondrous piece of land we call Texas. The world we've got is the one we've connived to create. Do we have an equal chance of making a difference? Not likely, even here in the land of the free and the home of the brave.

The guard shows up with a uniformed behemoth, no taller than my lady but twice as wide. I look up to the cell door, smiling as they enter, an ingratiating look stretching my face, like I'm greeting a jealous lover. The little guard left before checking to see if I was bleeding. Now she holds out something, something for me to take from her out-stretched arm, but I lean away, bewildered, while the behemoth looks on impassively.

"Here," the braided girl says, glancing anxiously at her mastiff, who stands in front of the cell door with her arms belted across her massive chest, "take these."

I hold out my hands. She drops three tampons into my palms.

"I don't need tampons," I say, making my voice dull to keep it from trembling. "I need to see a doctor. I need medication."

"Maybe I can get you some IBs for the cramps," she says, bending over to unlock the leg shackle. Her uniform cap perches on her corona of braids, too heavy for her stem of a neck.

"Ibuprofen's good for ordinary cramps, you are so right." I say. "But it won't do much good in my case. I need drugs to stop me from miscarrying!"

"Well, dear me, I didn't see any of them sorts of drugs down in the dispensary, did you Angie?" the behemoth asks.

My body's shaking. I want to hurl insults at her. I want to get the pleasure of calling her an ignorant slut. But I'm afraid.

She reads my mind.

"You do not know how lucky you are you got Angelina here on this shift and not a hundred other girls. You'd still be hunkered down and shackled up. Don't give me any more shit. I have to deal with shift captains like Audrey Crunden every day of the week, way after you be gone, miss lady-doctor." She looms over to where I sit trembling on my bunk.

"I see," I say, my eyes not lifting higher than her belt. Now that I know they're not going to help me, I want them to go. She grunts, taking her time leaving the cell.

The hours go by and the bleeding continues. I change the first tampon after maybe two hours, sometime before midnight. The next one lasts no more than an hour. I put the last one in about the time truly vicious cramps begin, and have to remove it soon after. All my parts are swollen and bruised and I'm drenched in sweat. I feel like I've got a fishhook in my gut. The tampon comes out with difficulty, hunks of tissue along with it. I hold the tissue in my hand, kneading it between my fingers, before bringing it up to my eyes. Fetal tissue. I massage my stomach, pressing my fingers through the muscle and fat, hard enough to feel my womb, distended and rock hard against the tip of my fingers. Weeping begins from that place and spreads through my body to well up in tears from my eyes and low sounds from my mouth, but ebbs almost at once. I shift my attention to how much I'm bleeding. My mind keeps working. How much blood am I losing? I've already lost the baby. Now it's me. I need to stay awake. I could bleed out, here alone, on a prison cot.

How did I end up here? First my mind goes over the events, step by step, leading me here. I catalog the mistakes I made. Thinking I was different. Ha! I didn't think the criminal justice system would crack down on me. In my own mind I was convinced I served the same system, the system that values order and service to your fellows, based on reason and self-denial. Now here I am in some Bexar County facility. What am I supposed to have done?

My mind goes back to the discontent I hoped would end right along with the year I devoted to fulfilling my conditions for continued employment. I was coming back to life up there at the cabin. That's where this journey began, in the mountains. I was willing to take risks again, to embrace desire. Perhaps Michael, a man ready to martyr himself to a hopeless cause to make his life significant, had something to tell me. Maybe beneath my sentimental wash of feeling for a man who gave up his life because he didn't belong is the fear I'm no different, pulled by strings of fate and the plaything of secular powers I didn't deign to notice.

I smell funky and my saliva has a strange coppery taste. Was this anything like what it was for him at the end, alone on the mountain, tracing in his own mind the path that took him there? My body goads me into compassion—my suffering body, locked up and bleeding and now shitting a trickle of evil-smelling diarrhea. I go squat over the toilet. My consciousness no longer emanates from inside my head, but hovers over and enfolds me from outside myself. I go back to lie down on the cot after doing my best to clean off the blood and dung. No nurses to make me presentable or diagnose my distress; instead I'm left to wallow in my own stench. Anger builds up inside my entire body, a migraine of humiliation.

"God save me from myself," my voice explodes into the empty gloom.

In a moment, like the space between the lightning and the thunder in an open field, I am flooded with a conviction that *I have been heard*.

All at once I feel warm, almost placid, bathed and comforted with the sense of another presence hovering beside me, listening.

The euphoria recedes slowly, like a dream of *powers I've never dreamt of*. Stress and punishment have shoved me to the border between sanity and psychosis, or else God heard me call out. Either way, I'm relieved of the duty to play God.

My body does not belong to me alone, not since I married, not since I bore Iris, and especially not now, having miscarried. For the first time in this whole endless ordeal I cry in earnest, without sound, without hope, without ceasing. Time passes. The sense of a listening presence slowly withdraws. Only my taste of myself brings me back to ordinary time and into my body. I'm hungry. There's a lot I need to do. I get up and walk the cell.

Chapter 27

After the shift-change the next morning I stand up and call out in a carefully controlled voice to a middle-aged guard going by—a lady of substantial size, very black. She turns abruptly, her eyes widening when she sees me. I feel like a bloody mess but I doubt that's what she sees.

"I need to see a doctor."

"I thought you was a doctor," she says in a wondering, mellifluous voice.

Here we go again. "You're right. I am. I am also a woman who has just experienced what's called a spontaneous abortion—a miscarriage. I need to go to the sickbay or clinic or hospital or wherever you take sick prisoners. I must order a fetal-tissue analysis from the lab."

The woman laughs so long she almost gets me laughing with her.

"You *gotta order?* The only thing you *gotta* do, honey, is wait for breakfast. The only person giving any orders about what to do wit' you is Audrey. She already wrote you up, and she won' be back until three o'clock this evening."

"Audrey's the only one who can do anything? Who's in charge now?"

"Well, there's the shift captain, but she won't do nothing. Not after what Audrey told her about you punching her. Except maybe write *me* up soon's I start doing what *you* say." She laughs again, holding her fist to her mouth.

"I see your point. I haven't been in here long enough to get used to it. But look. You can do that, can't you, just look?" I put my arm out between the bars. She jumps back quickly. I open up my hand. The products of conception stick to my palm: nothing recognizable as an embryo.

"You want me to take you out your cell and carry you over to the dispensary so they can decide if that's your baby?"

"Yes. Precisely. They look at this matter with a microscope to make a determination."

"Nobody's going to believe this." She walks away, laughing and shaking her head. Watching her go, for a moment I'm pumped with hatred less clouded with doubt than anything good I've ever felt.

Why hate her? How is any of this her fault? But I feel the same hatred for the pretty little guard, who might've been able to help if she'd been a tiny bit braver. I grip the pieces of tissue, the consistency of raw meat, in all likelihood a piece of the placenta—at this point there'd be more placenta than embryo. I search through it again, but find nothing identifiable as an embryo, which might be as big as five millimeters. I grasp the matter in my hand, hard. I'm not letting go of it. Maybe I'm being perverse. What difference does it make? What meaning does it have if I prove this bit of tissue was to bloom into the baby we've been hoping for, or if I show through microscopic analysis how I've been cheated out of a possible future? Why should anyone care except me and Al and Iris and Anna? Oh, yes. Why should any of us ever care—unless we want to stay human.

What I want now is for somebody to hear my story. For somebody to see how wrong it is to brutalize me, to kill my baby to make a point. I want somebody to believe how the system is running over me after I've spent my life in its service. But the people who need to know this won't believe it. How can they? I didn't. Not before yesterday.

Everyone else along the cellblock has already gone to breakfast and come back. I lie in a heap of refuse on my bunk, still clutching in my hand what had been developing in my body. When I get these bits of tissue analyzed, confirming no one came to my aid, shall I sue the jail, the warden, and the mayor of San

Antonio? I now know why patients want to sue. My insides have been emptied out. I have lost my baby.

Belief determines reality. I remember the look on the mother's face in Mexico when she thought I'd knocked her child off balance with the strength of my *ool*. Coiled at the base of our brains, the metaphors of our tribe. Scientific thinking, like all thinking rooted in metaphors derived from our most rudimentary experiences. In my training we battle against an unseen enemy using weapons we barely understand or control. Maybe there's another way. Maybe a *curandera* could put me back in balance.

The guard comes back accompanied by somebody I assume is higher up on the food chain. Not discernibly black, white, or Latino, this one's a smoker with yellow simulated-leather skin. She must be in major withdrawal right this very minute. I keep still while she unlocks the door and comes in to scrutinize me from under lashless lids.

"You are going to go shower and remove all bits and pieces of bloody tripe you've been hanging on to through the night or I will have you medicated and transferred to the psych ward before lunch, where they will clean you up themselves." She speaks in an East-Texas drawl, straight from the lizard brain, reinforced by training and practice. Her eyes survey me without a glimmer of emotion. "Do you understand me?"

I understood her all right. I look over at the bunk, covered with blood and sweat. It looks warm and cozy compared to what I'm facing in this woman. I nod at her, my chin going up and down. I feel cunning. If I'm four or five weeks pregnant like I think I am—I need to go back and do the arithmetic again, where have the days gone since the mountains—more of the products of conception will emerge in time. There has simply not been enough matter. I can afford to give up what's already been expelled.

"Give me verbal confirmation."

"Yes."

"Yes, what?"

"Yes. I understand you. I'm a doctor. I know about the psych ward."

She looks at me, considering. She was waiting for me to say yes, ma'am. We eye each other. She lets it go.

"Do me a favor."

"Yes?"

"Try not to tell us about how you're a doctor 'n all any more, OK?"

I nod. I see her point with laughable clarity. "OK," I say.

"OK. You have a visitor from Admin." She strides away. Probably needs a cigarette. I envy her the comfort. I'm stiff and all knotted up. The middle-aged CO watches me, her eyes revealing nothing. She waits for me to leave first. We start down the hall, our progress painfully slow even without shackles. One woman in the cell next to me stands with her forearms resting on the horizontal bar of the cell, her arms hanging out limply, her head slumped. Without lifting her head she slowly turns her right hand, thumb thrust vigorously up. I glimpse her face as we pass, impassive except for lively eyes. At the next cell, a woman drifts to the front in time to thrust her arm out, thumb up, as I go by. In the next cell, the occupant stands leaning over at the waist, both arms out the cell, two thumbs up, and grins at us. At the next, the tenant, barely older than Iris, puts out her hand, wrist drooping, and then waggles a thumb in a tiny flick. I turn my head back to acknowledge her gesture; her eyes drop. All night she's listened to my lamentations. She cared enough to express herself, to take a risk for me, a total stranger.

Already a different person from the one who stepped into the cell last night, I am made whole by the silent signals from the women I pass by. In my cell, bleeding, I was alone. I felt betrayed by those very people I'd earned a place among. Now I see I made a category mistake. Just like my friend in the mountains, I based belonging on the abstract notions of knowledge and power. How could I have been so mistaken? I feel lightened and strengthened by the regard of these women I have never known, ready to eat my own suffering as an offering to them.

Once I give up the idea of hanging onto the bloody pieces of tissue, I'm allowed a good hot shower, Ibuprofen (called IB's

214

and dispensed from a massive glass vessel like an old pickle jar), and a fresh sanitary napkin—better than a tampon, as raw as I am. I don't know if I'm getting brainwashed into liking my jailers or this bunch in the dispensary really is different. I put on a clean bright orange uniform and am then sent to breakfast, where once again I receive small signs of encouragement from a number of people. I don't know how they've heard about my situation or why they care.

After breakfast a sweet-faced young guard escorts me to a room with windows, lined with books and furnished with comfortable chairs and a small desk. We stand and wait without speaking until an official, a woman dressed in civilian clothes, comes in. She glances at me and mutters her name and title, but I don't catch it. She sits down behind the desk, situated on an angle in the outside corner of the room. She's dressed in sober browns and dull greens, like the social workers at the hospital. She motions to the CO; the Madonna removes the cuffs and looks at the woman questioningly before going to stand with her legs straddled, hands behind her, facing the fat spines of law books. I'm waved to a chair.

"We've spoken to your husband. His testimony indicates a possible conspiracy to delude the sheriff's deputy of Jeff Davis County."

"I have no idea what you're talking about."

"Listen, Dr. Dempsey. Tell me exactly how you are involved with the actions of the Texas Separatists. I'm sure you don't wish to implicate your husband. Dr. Clyde demonstrates a healthy concern for his continued ability to practice medicine. If the two of you are convicted of felonies, neither one of you will be able to practice medicine. Then who will support your daughter?"

"I'd like to talk to my lawyer. Phillip Speck." I can't remember anyone telling me I have the right to remain silent.

"Your husband said you knew the man you met in the mountains."

What is this woman after? The CO turns around to look our

way.

"I refuse to talk to you unless my lawyer is present." I'm dying for a cup of coffee, for some semblance of my own life. The clean clothes and the nice room help more than I would've thought. "Will you get my lawyer, please?"

The woman gets up, gathers her papers, and takes one more shot: "It does not appear as if your husband has engaged a lawyer on his own behalf. Do you want to shunt this off on him?"

My legs shake as I make my way back to the cell. I don't have to wait long before the woman who escorted me to the dispensary comes back, telling me respectfully that my husband is waiting for me, along with my lawyer—she has my civilian clothes in her hands. Al and Phillip Speck have managed to spring me in less than forty-eight hours, and I'm grateful. I only wish Peter Chapa, our friend the judge, could have helped get me out of here before the criminal justice system got its chance to teach me a lesson. I might have miscarried anywhere, but I would not have been so degraded.

PART V
DELIVERANCE

Chapter 28

On Saturday morning I'm delivered out of the criminal justice system as far as the public rotunda. Out here in the public space, the jail isn't noticeably different from a hospital lobby. Among the crowds of the overwrought and the self-important, Al and the lawyer, Phillip Speck, both looking happy, stride towards me. I'm so angry my teeth hurt, but there's nothing for it but to suppress my emotions and take on the cloak of decency of the woman rescued.

"Zoe!" Al croaks, reaching to embrace me. I can hardly bear to be touched just yet, but plant a kiss on Al's cheek and turn my lips up in a smile, staring over his shoulder at the lawyer's face, recalling his warning. He knew I'd be changed by one night in jail. He drops his eyes.

"Do you have your phone with you?" I ask Al. "I want to call Anna and Iris."

"Let's wait until we get outside," Speck says, taking a step towards us and pointing to a sign forbidding the use of cellular phones in the building. He examines me openly. In person he appears younger than he did through the safety glass.

"Since when is everything forbidden in this country?" I say, holding out my hand for Al's phone. He hesitates only a moment before dropping it in my outstretched palm. Speck casts us a worried look. Ashamed at my own irritation, I hurry away as fast as I can without breaking into a run. I bet everybody who has been locked up feels much the same urgency when they reach this spot on the tiled floor. What if my keepers were to change their minds? Outside, I call Anna and tell her I'm on my way. Matter-of-fact and competent, she takes down instructions. She will make an appointment for me with the gynecologist. Al arrives with such a beseeching look I allow myself to be steered into the car.

"You've got to tell Al about the baby," Anna says a short time later. We've retreated to the refuge of her room, redolent with good smells. Dressed in a pale yellow sweatsuit with embroidered top, my grandmother stands in front of me with her bare blue-veined feet dug into the carpet. I rock back and forth in the boudoir chair, clutching my knees. We listen intently to a high keening sound meandering through the room until I realize it's me and chop it off.

"Please, no, Anna. Let's not speak about a baby. It wasn't a baby yet. It was a collection of cells, an early embryo. Not a baby."

Anna squats down in front of me, awkwardly trying to fold her arms around me. This position can't be easy for an old lady, but I go on rocking, locked in inertia, until she heaves herself to her feet. "I'll fix us some herb tea."

Travis or Cynthia might prescribe a sedative if I were to ask, but that would just postpone everything. Besides, if I were to take any drug affecting consciousness I'd be breaking my agreement with Frank, and I don't want to do that. He could have had me hauled in front of a review board, and he didn't. I might have lost my position. No, I won't take any chances on that score. And of course, in 12-step parlance, taking a sedative would qualify as a full-blown slip.

"At least tell Al about the miscarriage," Anna says when she comes back with the tea. I give her a look, but she stares me down. "Holding secrets keeps people apart."

"You might be right." I burn my tongue on the tea.

Anna's face is a pudding of love and sorrow. "You've gone through a life-changing experience. Why won't you ask for help when you need it?"

"What do you think, Anna? Am I getting my comeuppance?"

"No," she says. She looks me steadily in the eye for some time. "For what? You didn't do anything."

"Oh, I wasn't talking just about blowing off the FBI, although that was sure stupid. My reality has been shaken—my belief in myself and my faith in what I do." My voice falters. Inside it feels like catastrophe. "It's as if what I've always feared would happen, has. I don't know who I am." I clap my hand over my mouth to shore up my emotions.

"You're the same person, Zoe," Anna says.

"No. In no way am I the same person."

"Then you will have to learn to believe in this new self," she says. "Listen to yourself." She puts her strong arms around me, pressing her cheek against mine.

"Oh, Anna, I don't know what I'd do without you. But something strange happened to me in that cell." I disentangle myself from her and look down at myself. I'm wearing one of her flannel nightgowns, thin and worn.

"Tell me about it, Zoe," she says, so ordinary just looking at her ties me to the earth.

"The words 'God help me' came out of my mouth." I try to feel what I felt then. "I felt a presence in the cell with me, listening. Like I'd been heard."

"That would change anybody."

"For sure. 'In the twinkling of an eye,' as they say in the fairy tales, I felt comforted."

"Do you still feel it?" Anna watches me for a moment then looks away. She knows what a dyed-in-the-wool scientific materialist I am. Ever since I was a small child she's waited in hopes I would open to the possibility of a divine dimension.

"I felt like I'd been given some sort of a reprieve," I admit. "Like some burden I've been carrying lightened up. Even if it was not exactly whisked away." I shiver. Anna goes to the closet and returns with a yellow robe made from some plush fabric like fake fur. She drapes the homey garment over me. "I've always been afraid of giving in to notions about the soul. Like something I can't spare might be removed, taken away from me, along with the burden." I smooth the fake bunny fur of the robe.

"The answer to our prayers often comes in the form of an enigma," Anna says. "Otherwise we could've got what we wanted without the need for divine grace. There's a part of us hates to give up control."

I sip my cooling tea, thinking about her words. Jail was like the river, teaching me that the way out is the way down.

"Is there anyone you want to see? Iris?"

I brighten. "Yes. I'd love to see Iris. When do you expect her home?"

"I'll find her. You get in my bed and try to get some sleep."

"That sounds good. That sounds terrific." She's still in the room when I fall asleep, so profoundly it's like going on a trip to a far country.

"Mom. I hate to wake you," Iris is saying, smoothing my hair, "but I've got to get over to Amanda's to help her with her math homework."

Layer by layer I come back to what's happened and what we're doing here, like the moment at the river when I mistook Iris for my mother. Struggling to sit up, I yawn hard enough to choke. Iris moves off the edge of the bed. "Oh, don't leave, Iris." I catch her by the wrist.

"Let me turn on a light," she says, patting my hand before slipping away to the lamp on Anna's dresser. The room, which I once thought feminine to the point of silliness, with its boudoir pink walls and heavy drapes, looks glorious to me, and feels like a sanctuary.

"Pop said absolutely not to tire you out," she says, sitting back down next to me.

"What else did he tell you, honey?"

"Not to get in any fights with you," she says, with a wild look, like a feral cat.

"Well, don't stifle yourself none now, you hear?" I reply. Iris smiles, but still looks at me warily. "I have got to get up. I can't sleep here all night."

Let Me See

"Grandma says you had a terrible time in jail."

"Let's just say I'm overwhelmingly glad to see you." With an effort I get up, picking up my clothes from the chair, the outfit Anna sent with Al for my homecoming, silk sweats in a dark plum color. Iris stays on the bed, scowling at me. "What's the matter, pumpkin?"

"The matter, Mother, is I told you not to go down there!" she says. "Everybody did! And don't call me pumpkin!"

"All right, Iris. It wasn't the Mexicans who put me in jail. It was the Americans." I finish putting on my clothes and kneel down to fish under the bed for my shoes, startled by such a grown-up anger coming from my daughter.

"I don't care who it was," Iris says, standing up, "it was because you left. I didn't want you to go. Something awful has happened but nobody's telling me anything."

"You're right—it doesn't matter which side of the border you're put in the clink." I sit back down on the edge of the bed to put on my shoes. "Come back over here."

Very slowly she comes back. "Tell me what happened to you."

I have a metallic taste in my mouth. The words come hard. "I thought I was pregnant. I had not told anyone—not even your dad. In case everything didn't work out."

We both resolutely look out in front of us. We sit side by side on the edge of the bed in Anna's womb of a room.

"You lost the baby in the jail, didn't you?" Iris asks after a long silence.

"That's like one of those sentences they use to teach people grammar," I say with a faint laugh, "misplaced object."

"Mother, don't do this!" Iris shrieks, leaping off the bed. "This is what you always do! How can you talk about the object of the verb! Are you crazy?"

She tears around the room looking for some way to bear what I have told her. "I wanted a baby! A sister! It wasn't just you who wanted a baby, but Pop, and me too! You don't care, do you?"

I stand up, trembling. "I'm sorry, Iris. You can't imagine

how much. . . ”

"What? What can't I imagine? Do you think I am still a child?" Her face is pinched with anguish.

"No, Iris, that's not what I meant."

"Of course I can imagine what it's like," she goes on in a more normal tone, "you are not the only person who has lost a baby. Two seniors came into our Sex Ed class and told us about their abortions. One cried and cried and cried. But she'd done it on purpose. You could've saved the baby if you wanted to."

"How can you possibly think that, Iris?"

"Because you always get what you want. You never, never, never don't get what you want," she says with chilling certainty. "And you're always right and everybody else is wrong!"

Anna comes back in the room as Iris screams these appalling words.

"What are you doing, Iris?" Anna asks, her mouth a round oval of bewilderment. "This is not the time to be yelling at your mother!"

Iris tries to run out of the room past her, but the old woman catches hold of her. Iris draws herself up and sweeps us both a scornful look. I go over and stand close beside her without trying to hug her. Anna slips away. "I'm sorry, Iris. Sorry, sorry, sorry." The deep shadows under her eyes sear my soul. "Please forgive me. Please believe I cared about this baby. You're breaking my heart."

Iris flings herself away and stands panting in the dim light. "Why should I believe you?"

"Maybe because I told you about the baby."

She considers this.

I look at her as if I've never seen her before. "Maybe you're right, what you say. I've been selfish. It's not because I haven't loved you. Until a little while ago you were still a part of me. A part of me that's gone missing and I don't know how to get back. I love you, Iris. Come sit over here with me. There's more to tell you."

"What about Amanda?" she asks, wiping her face with her

arm.

"Give me a minute. I said you couldn't imagine because I couldn't. Some experiences can only be lived through." I take a deep breath before going on. "Before the experience fades into memory, I want you to know: no matter how horrendous this loss, it doesn't change the truth of my life with you and Al and Anna. I wanted that speck of life to grow and become a baby. Nature helps a mother protect the life inside her—every woman feels it. It's a force of nature. If I could feel something like that for a teensy tiny bit of matter not yet formed, what do you suppose I feel about you? I've loved you fiercely. We can learn how to be with each other again, happy as flowers."

Iris turns to me, traces of tears on her face. She's cut her hair since I left for Mexico. It's curly on top and plastered down with gel at the sides. "Do you really believe that, Mom?"

"Well, we're not flowers. Let's use our giant human brains to figure out a way to spend more time together before you head off for college."

"Mom! I haven't started high school yet!" She chews on her lip, trying not to laugh.

"Right. I'm barging ahead too fast."

She hugs me and darts away. "Do you want me to brush your hair?"

"That would be nice. Anna's got brushes on her dresser." I run my hand through my tangled hair until Iris gets back and starts working on it with the brush. I close my eyes. Tears slip down my cheeks. Iris stops brushing and hands me a wad of Kleenex.

"You need to trim your hair, Mom. You've got split ends."

"The scissors are in bathroom drawer. I don't know how good they are."

Iris departs. When she comes back she takes me by the arm and sits me down in the chair in front of the vanity. She leaves me staring at my reflection in the mirror while she gets a glass of water. She dips the comb to wet the ends of my hair.

"I'm sorry about the stupid comment about the sentence."

"It's OK, Mom," she says, her face unclouded, concentrating on what she's doing.

"Forgive me for seeming so removed."

"Oh Mom, it's not that," she says, stopping her work for a minute and meeting my eyes in the mirror, "it's just that you're almost always at work."

"Your dad's been the heart of the family, I guess."

"When nobody would tell me what was happening, I figured it had to be something terrible," she says.

"Can't you call Amanda and tell her to do her own homework?"

"I could, Mom, but then it would be worse tomorrow. Why don't we call Pop? He can take me over to Amanda's."

"We'll do it your way," I say, awed by her resiliency. "You know, sprite, it's not true I always get my own way."

"Oh, Mom, we were just having a word fight. Do you want to see what you look like?" She hands me a mirror to look at the back of my hair. It hangs down to the middle of my back, straight as a furrow across the bottom, Irish hair like my mother's.

"It looks good, Iris." She looks ageless as she puts her tools down to lean over and put her arms around me. We sway together for a moment. No words and no tears. She lets go first.

Maybe I can let go of some of the pain I've been carrying around. Maybe the conventional wisdom has it right: like toxic waste, pain is impossible to bury. Something between Iris and me has changed for good. We're closer, more at peace. But she's not my little girl anymore: she's herself.

Iris leaves the room and I remain, waiting for Al, emptied out, grieving for a life that might have been. I didn't know I had a choice about the baby I was carrying before the choice was taken away from me. I'll see a doctor tomorrow, but I doubt if a little bit of matter will tell me anything I don't already know. I'm aware of my part in the chain of events stemming from colliding with the man in the mountain. I also know for sure I'm not immune to rough treatment from the powers of the State of Texas. It's a bitter pill to swallow.

Chapter 29

In our own room, with Al, for the first time since leaving for Mexico, I appear to be OK physically. The emotional pain has also eased up. At least I no longer feel stunned. Al looks abundant and natural. Our room, austere compared to Anna's, seems bursting with stuff after a night spent in a jail cell. I look around like a kid at Christmas. Everywhere I look I see monuments to our life, from Iris's kid drawings on the wall, to the photos on the dresser, to Al's telescope propped next to the French doors, to the pile of books on my side of the bed. I move around the room touching things while Al sits in the Eames chair near the window. "A detective interviewed me claiming she'd spoken to you and you wanted me to tell her everything," I say.

"That's horseshit," Al says.

I laugh. Al so rarely swears. "She told me to come clean to avoid implicating you."

"Textbook case of the prisoner's dilemma: she told me the same thing about you. What did you tell her?"

"To get me my lawyer. She said *you* didn't have your own lawyer, like that meant something. I remember the prisoner's dilemma, we learned about it in our psych class—rat on your buddy, we'll go easier on you, and he's already betrayed you, anyway. She tried to act sinister, but the whole interview seemed perfunctory, like she didn't have her heart in it."

"Did you ever read the book about the guy in Argentina whose wife was among the disappeared? He kept his wife in mind every minute she was missing. He believed that his concentration on her and what she was going through in his imagi-

227

nation was a way he could help her, to give her strength and keep her alive. I did my best to do the same for you the whole time you were in jail."

I blink and swallow around the lump in my throat. "We need to talk. I need your help all the more now I'm out."

"Any way I can, Zoe."

Iris has gone on to Amanda's. Outside the window, lights illuminate the big Spanish oaks and glint off the horse-head sculpture resting on its pedestal of Texas granite. "I feel your energy blasting away. It warms me up," I tell him.

"This may not be the time to say it, but what you're feeling may be lust."

I laugh and walk over to touch his lips with my fingers, ready to tell him all that I have kept from him. But I can't bring myself to say anything. I am hollowed out. Our bodies speak for us, two sides of a living bivalve. Slowly, gently, we make love. I'm shy. Al's so delicate and questioning I have to keep encouraging him, like the very first time. We couldn't believe my hymen was so strong. We laughed at this trick of nature. I'd say wait, and he'd wait, an agony of waiting, just when the waiting was supposed to be over. We were only nineteen, our sexual energy and longing coiling and growing for months of friendship. And now at last, pledged to marry, Al manfully holding back because I asked him to, until finally I said the words, told him go ahead, and we came together for all time, bonded by pain and blood.

"Is this what you want?" He kisses my cheek and my neck, brushes against my lips. "You're sure? It's all right?" he pulls away and looks at me closely.

The look on Al's face, a mixture of tenderness and desire, is like a balm to me. "It's fine. We're doctors . . . let's play doctor."

He kisses me on the ticklish spot between my chin and my shoulder. I start to laugh, rolling my head back and forth on the pillow. And now it is like that first time. There is nothing I want more, nothing I need more, than to stamp in flesh the glory of being alive at this moment, of coming together again. No question of anything so trivial as pleasure, but there's joy in the two of us, fusing together and letting go. My uterus clenches, but

228

only a tad. Getting the juices flowing will clean out the uterus, but the clinician in me decides against Al's crowding inside, as much as I'd like him to. He tenses when I let him know, worried something's wrong, but I won't let him draw entirely away. When he finally comes on my belly something I've been holding back gives way inside me. I'm crying, and then he's crying. He rears up to look at me with something like awe. He lifts a shaking hand to touch my sweaty face. I'm connected to this man forever.

I'm having trouble getting the words out. Al sits waiting for me, cross-legged on the foot of the bed, like a Buddha. I falter. Every word that comes to mind strikes me as fearsome. "It's hard for me to tell you," I start, and then spin to a stop. "I feel responsible," I say at last.

"Take your time," he says.

"Anna hasn't told you or anything? Or Iris?"

He holds me in his gaze. "Try something different. Do a mental one-eighty. Unburden your heart. Tell me."

"Oh, Al, I love you, I surely do."

"Now don't you go hurting yourself over loving me, darling," Al says in a fake drawl, "when it can't be helped."

"I wish we could just go on laughing and joking. You're not going to take this as well as you think you're going to."

"Spit it out," he says, leaning over and cupping his hand under my chin. He looks fine, lean and tan, with a chest covered with dark hair.

Beguiling as he looks to me after lovemaking, he's a doctor. He's probably figured it out. I tell him. About how glad I was to make love in the mountains. He studies me, his eyes ominous, as if he already knows. I tell him about the pregnancy test. He doesn't interrupt. I tell him how glad I was to discover I might be pregnant. And then, how I didn't think about it for a while. Once I knew for certain, so much was going on I couldn't bring myself to tell him. I try to name everything I was afraid of, hurrying to get to the part about how I lost the baby.

I tell him how all my life I've had dreams about giving birth and then losing the baby, mislaying it, searching for it. I want to go on telling him how bad it was, to go over every hour. But his eyes are sad, and he keeps looking away. His pain is different from mine, connected to his longstanding fear that I'm moving out of his reach. Except for when Iris was tiny, we have both betrayed the early ideal we shared, in some long ago golden age, of how we would be as close as two people can get. Now we each stand on our own; and that can't be helped.

"If I'd done like you wanted me to," I say into the long quiet at the end of my recital of what happened. "If I hadn't gone to Mexico, if I hadn't shot the finger at the FBI, if I'd just ignored the Texas Separatist folks . . ."

"Or if you'd never run into them in the first place," Al says. "There's the element of chance to factor in."

"Yes. I'm not sorry about most of what happened to me personally. Encountering life in ways I never could have predicted let me see where I put my faith."

Al gets off the bed. He brings his face close to mine. "I love you, Zoe, and have a lot of faith in you." He moves away, pulls on a pair of shorts, and straddles a small chair with a caned bottom. "I've never been very good at bearing up to the pain of the world. You took it on yourself to see behind the obvious."

"When what I was allowed to see became unbearable I tried to drug it away." There. I've said it. It was never only physical pain I was treating with the Percocet.

Al abandons his chair and comes next to me on the bed. We fidget around to untwist my robe and get our arms around each other, holding on until our body rhythms are in sync.

Al speaks first. "I wish you hadn't kept your pregnancy a secret."

I move a little away from him. He wipes the heel of his hand in the sockets of his eyes, one by one, then drops his hand and stares at me, his face as grave as a saint in a Goya painting.

"I was always going to tell you, as soon as I could."

"A baby wasn't just something happening to you, Zoe."

Al doesn't seem angry; he appears inexpressibly weary. I could tell him I know about Merla. Ask him if things we've kept hidden are of equal weight. Maybe have the kind of fight only married folks can have—the teeth sunk into flesh, refigure the map of the world sort of marital battle. But I can't bring myself to say anything, and certainly nothing hurtful.

"I've done the same thing," Al says. "Kept things from you."

"I need to tell you what I told Anna about what happened in jail," I interrupt. I want to stop him from saying more. "I remembered saying 'God help me' when I was miscarrying and heard a response."

"You mean you felt the presence of God?" Al asks.

"That's exactly right, Al. That part of it was right. But I'd already forgotten exactly what I said."

"Now you remember?"

"Yes. I overheard my own voice saying 'God save me from myself.'"

Al nods at me, his arms braced on the bed.

"I cut myself off from everybody else who could help me." I drop my eyes from his face. We're still in bed together. I feel an urge to get up and sit on a chair but don't. "It was like I was never allowed to ask for help, I could only provide it. I started to play God, thinking it was up to me to cure people. And my fault when they didn't get well."

"Sure. We learned to play God in med school," Al says, "but it was always meant to shake off the fear. We're annointed; we do what must be done, but death is in the hands of God. You never learned the crucial second step."

"Maybe. But one thing I know for sure: I'm not God."

"You never seemed to like the meetings you were going to."

"I liked the people. I didn't buy the message. Before last night . . ." I blunder to a stop, spellbound, staring over the divide between the person I used to be and the one I am now. I finally swing my legs over the side of the bed and stand up, disoriented, lost between worlds. Al's on his feet, too, barely inches from me. "At one time I believed only in what could be observed and measured." I probe for what's missing, like a child tonguing the gap a tooth used to fill. "Now, I don't know what I believe."

"Promise me something?" Al asks. We are squared off, Al no taller than me.

"I'll try."

"Don't hold out on me. Whatever's going on with you, tell me."

"It won't be easy. But I'll do my best."

"Yeah," he mutters. "I need to tell you some things, too."

"I wish you wouldn't." My voice comes out painfully stilted. "You look like a doctor with a grim diagnosis."

"Do you already know what I'm going to say?"

"About Merla, yes, if that's what you mean."

"I'm sorry, Zoe. More sorry than you'll ever know."

"We'll talk about it," I say. "But not now."

He gathers me against his chest. "Can we go back to being partners?"

"OK, sweetie," I mumble into his neck, "you play the guy and I'll play the girl."

"How hard can that be?" he asks, kissing me. I kiss him back. Later there will be time to clear away more of the debris between us.

Chapter 30

Except for the brief sleep I managed during the time it took Anna to fetch Iris, I've been awake for a long time, clutching too hard on to the blessedness of ordinary reality to fall asleep. Al's usual stamina is spent and he is beginning to look pained. He's ready to give me a sleeping pill so we can both get some rest. Just the threat of intervention seems to do the trick, for in no time I'm pulled into a dream where I'm milling around with others in a public space. We seem to be in the courtyard of a church carved into the side of a mountain, where a mass is about to be said for the living by the dead. I see Jordan, looking healthy and powerful, dressed like she's part of the church hierarchy. I fail to catch her eye to let her know we're sharing the same dream.

Pushed forward by the small crowd, I kneel at the altar rail. From the altar side a woman appears wearing a caftan. My consciousness whirls out of my body to hang suspended over it in a speck of light. Familiar people, some of whom I have loved, kneel down beside my kneeling body. The woman in the caftan comes along to each person. Unmoved as the lens of a camera, I see the line stretches way out along the altar rail. People surge forward and fall back in a wave. The atmosphere is jolly, more like a Bar-B-Q than a communion service.

The woman offers each kneeling figure something to eat, mumbling blessings. When she reaches my kneeling figure I see myself nod vigorously and am plunged back into the figure of myself kneeling at the altar, overcome with emotion, sorry and repentant, heartsick with remorse, heart pounding and knees sore. After an excruciatingly long pause, the word *please* forms and comes out of my mouth. Behind the gowned woman I catch Jordan's eye. She winks and nods. My unbearable emotions evaporate. The woman in the caftan proffers a crumb of bread, holding it out like a dog-treat before she places it on my outstretched tongue. She nods briskly and beckons to Jordan, who hands her a large, imposing cup, which the woman holds under my chin. Looking down into the liquid held before me, I see it's swarming with worms and draw back, my gorge rising. Jordan dashes forward and takes the cup from the other woman and holds it to my lips with both her hands. I stare up at the beautiful young face smiling at me encouragingly. She presses the cup to my lips and holds the back of my head with one hand while she tips the liquid from the cup to my mouth. I swallow hastily, afraid of choking, but the liquid pours like light down my body until it dislodges the lump in my throat, settles my stomach, and spreads to my entrails to dissolve my fear and warm my loins.

The gathering behind the altar surges forward, singing choruses of some sprightly tune I can almost identify, words I'm almost able to decipher—something like *show me the way*—while the head honcho takes the cup back from Jordan. I half rise from my knees and try to embrace her, but I am thwarted by the altar rail. The procession behind the railing sweeps past. Jordan turns around to give me a complicit wink. I come awake, wondering. Were the worms just for me? Did others along the rail see them as well? I fall back into a deep sleep, only to be awakened what seems like only minutes later with Al shaking me and handing me the phone.

"It's Travis."
"What's the matter?" I ask, already alert.
"You need to get dressed and get down here right away."
"It's Jordan Wilson, isn't it, Travis?"
"Yes. She seems to have had an allergic response to an infusion of the new medication, what the hell is it, the mono-

clonal antibodies. The acute stage is passed; she should be fine. But she doesn't seem to be rallying."

"We decided against the new meds," I exclaim. I hang up and get dressed in a clean pair of sweats. Al ushers me out to the Volvo, as speedy and solicitous as when I went into labor with Iris. We race to the hospital, hardly exchanging a word.

I get zero eye contact as I go past the nurses' station on the ground floor, where Jordan is installed in her palatial suite. I step inside the room to find Jordan lying in the Egyptian effigy pose, still as a stone, her arms outside the bedcovers, eyes closed, face composed, like a child pretending to be asleep. Her mother stands between the bed and the chair.

"What's happening?" I ask.

"I decided not to wait," Mrs. Wilson says, "until you got back from Mexico. They convinced me it was OK to go ahead with the infusion."

"Who's 'they'?"

"Dr. Glover and the Australian doctor."

"What happened? Did she have another flare? Did she have a stricture? What?"

Mrs. Wilson sidesteps out the foot of the bed. "I was hoping the new treatment would make her well enough to go back to school."

"Dr. Glover and the visiting Internist gave the infusion. And then?"

"It went along fine for the first hour. I left to get something to eat. Nobody would let me in the room when I got back. The nurse said she was having an allergic reaction—went into anaphylactic shock. What causes it?"

"Anaphylatoxin," I say, the correct answer on an exam, keeping her occupied while I check Jordan's vital signs before picking up her chart. I'm now way back in the chain of medical responsibility for her daughter's condition and must set aside my fury for later.

"That doesn't make any sense," the woman says.

"Never mind. It doesn't matter. In ordinary English, treatment caused a reaction. We'll deal with it." What more can I tell her, and what would it signify? Anaphylatoxin, a postulated substance, cited as the immediate cause of an immunologic (allergic) reaction, characterized by contraction of smooth muscles. A term in an equation with too many unknowns, coined to account for shock, the result of *in vivo* combination of specific antibody and the specific sensitizing material injected as a shock dose in a sensitized subject. Matter, stuff of the universe; to matter, to make a difference. All kinds of matters are in play here at this moment. Does some truth lie behind the concept of *sustos*—fear, and its attendant soul loss—that we can't reach with modern medicine? Crohn's cannot be considered a psychosomatic illness. Cows get it. We're still looking for the intervention that will tip the balance of health in Jordan's favor.

"Dr. Glover wanted to operate on the fistula." Mrs. Wilson voices what I have read on the chart. "Jordan said not with you away. He proposed the new medication as an alternative."

Glover had adrenaline on hand. The reaction was brought under control in short order. Jordan's present lassitude is not recorded in the chart. But something alerted Travis.

"How long has she been sleeping?" I ask.

Mrs. Wilson frowns at me and steps back from the bed. "Pretty much since the serum reaction. If only they'd waited until you got back."

"Well, I'm back now." I continue the physical exam of my comatose patient, glad when Mrs. Wilson goes out of the room to call her husband. After censoring the impulse to bend down and kiss my patient's cheek, I limit myself to smoothing her hair. What have I missed? What's wrong here? I repeat the steps of physical diagnosis: inspection, palpation, percussion, and auscultation. Look, touch, press my fingers against her body to feel the outline of the organs, each with a different energy frequency, tap to set up a reverberation, listen for a sign, for the silent gut to gurgle, to tell me it's doing its job, keeping my ear tuned for disharmony, for the telltale sound of specific distress, blockage, or interruption. I hear nothing out of the ordinary: I receive no sign. Towards the end of my examination, my ear to Jordan's abdomen, I feel her presence. Without moving my head I glance up to her face to find her gazing at me with a look of perfect wonder.

"We need to hook you up to a bigger energy. A saving grace," I say conversationally, straightening up to go to the head of the bed, "to get you back in balance. Otherwise you're fine, you've pulled through the setback. We're going to ask Lydia Flores to come treat you. OK?"

Jordan nods, then looks past me to the foot of the bed where the nurse, Shaunna, stands watching us intently. "They said you might be needing me."

"They were right. Stay here with Jordan. I won't be long."

Outside in the hall, I'm not prepared for the young man walking swiftly towards me. He stops in front of me, his hands clenched at his sides, his jaws working. "You're Dr. Dempsey, aren't you?"

"And you must be Tommy Arbuckle," I say. An edge of bright light outlines his skinny adolescent body, dressed in black.

"You shouldn't have left," he says, his voice breaking, "the treatment was new!" My vision narrows and clarifies, watching his fist rise. "How could you leave her?" he asks, whirling and slamming the wall with the side of his fist, inches from my head.

"Tommy, I'm sorry." My vision widens out until I look down on the two of us standing in the hall, and then floats out still further until I see the hospital in its place near the river. I clamp my teeth on my tongue and come back to the present.

"You're sorry?" Tommy asks, his voice piping in pain, holding on to his hand. "Jordan is dying. Can't you see that? Because those pricks, the cutter and some foreign asshole, want to add a new procedure to their bag of tricks?"

"Stop," I grunt, leading him away from the door, "you're way out of line here. It's not going to help Jordan if you break down. And you'd better get your hand checked out."

"How dare you say I'm not going to help her," he says, putting his hand behind him. "Nobody else is doing anything.

How could you leave Jordan, who totally trusted you?"

I begin to reply, but he continues, furious: "What are you saying, I'm not going to help her? Nobody's helping her." Pity for the boy competes with the urge to defend myself, but there's no time. "Jordan was home, taking care of herself, changing her diet," he says, speaking rapidly. "She needs nourishment."

When I left for Mexico the fistula was slowly healing, the flesh closing. I say nothing, thinking of the anomaly of the fistula in the body, the body's desperate attempt to make things right by inventing a new growth.

"Why can't you answer me? You doctors always know the answers when it comes to telling your patients how to lead their lives. I bet you've never been sick a day in your life, have you?" His anger makes him grow larger as I watch. "You stay healthy by feeding on the rest of us, sucking up strength from the unfortunates who fall sick."

"That's enough, Tommy!" I say sternly, feeling a cleansing shot of anger. "You've gone too far. It won't help to attack me. It won't help in the least."

But I'm wrong, I see right away. The anger goes out of him all at once, shrinking him back to ordinary size. I want to grab him, hug him, and take him home with me, anything to get us past this moment. He saves us both from an awkward gesture by wheeling abruptly and heading for Jordan's room.

"I've got to see her while I still can," he says over his shoulder.

My knees are quaking all the way up my thighs as I turn to head back down the hall to call Lydia Flores. She agrees to come, but needs a ride. Austin taxis are notoriously slow. I'm out in the parking lot in no time, making my way to where Al's sitting in the car with the sunroof open, smoking a cigarette. I'm flooded with relief.

"Where did you get that?" I ask, getting in the car.

"From Travis. Want the rest of it?" Al asks, holding the butt out to me.

I look at the glowing cigarette, imagining taking the smoke into my lungs, the nanosecond of relief from pain, conscious of nothing else but the smell and taste of the smoke filling my lungs. I long for it. But the reel of my imagination keeps running, and I see myself handing the butt back to Al, nothing changed. I shake my head no, my lips pursed in concentration while Al smokes. When I ask him to pick up Lydia from her house in South Austin he stubs the illicit cigarette out in the unused ashtray, salutes, and starts the engine. I brush a kiss on his cheek before inching my way out of the door and sidling along between cars, heading back to Jordan's room while Al goes for Lydia.

What did I tell Al only last night about my experience of the uncanny? What do I think now? We are not only physical. The immune system—the spleen, bone marrow, lymph nodes, all the immune cells circulating along with all the other cells through the body—is affected by emotion, by intention, by purpose, by belief. Jordan has been asking for something to help her connect her body and soul. All along she's believed Lydia can help her. Surely she deserves the help she's repeatedly asked for. How could I not listen to her? She's in need of food for the soul, just as I have been. I asked for help and got it; I have been held safe in another's regard. To be lovingly beheld by another human being may create conditions the very opposite to what happens when the evil eye causes *sustos*. In Jordan's case, to be so beheld by a *curandera* may be enough to change the equation, to shake up the immune system, to change the terms of whatever's going on in an autoimmune reaction, one we see in terms of an absurd battle the immune system wages with an imaginary enemy. The way out between the horns of a dilemma, fancied or real, requires creative imagination—maybe just another way of saying God.

In the meantime, we'll continue to do all we're doing to monitor the serum reaction with the standard tools available to us, already set in motion by Glover and his team.

239

Chapter 31

The nurse Shaunna, bending over Jordan, twists her head to look up when I step into the room. She straightens up, her face coloring in small patches, and shakes her head sharply back and forth, a gesture I take to signal her fear for her patient. I walk up swiftly and pick up Jordan's wrist to check her pulse. Steady. But she looks moribund. There's no code-blue for this type of imperceptible dwindling. I look at her chart, which shows nothing acute, nothing at all to indicate without question that any bodily system is closing down.

"Dr. Glover says if there's no improvement he'll do an exploratory in the morning," Shaunna says. "Any change for the worse we're to call."

What are the medical options? The patient was improving when I left for Mexico. The infusion of the new medication given in my absence wasn't salutary, but the immediate reaction has been dealt with. We should have perceived a positive change by now. What are we missing? Has everything been done that can be done? Yes, at least everything allowed under the orthodoxy of modern medicine and the auspices of approved medical interventions. Jordan looks tiny in the hospital bed.

"All right, Shaunna, take a break. It's going to be a long night."

"You want me to go?"

I flash a look meant to back her off. I need to concentrate.

She frowns. "You're the only one who can do something here, Dr. Dempsey."

"Please go find the mother. Tell her my husband, Dr. Clyde, will be back here with Lydia Flores in a little bit."

She flashes me a smile, paradoxically revealing how weary she is. "OK. I'll be back."

All the instruments agree: the patient's not in immediate danger, but studying her face, I feel a spurt of fear, precise as fuel injection to an engine. Swiftly adjusting the lights, closing the door to the hall, and pulling the curtains over the darkened view to the west, I return to her side. Her eyes gleam in the near dark. I touch her on the arm, and then kneel down eye to eye. "The *curandera's* on her way, Jordan. OK?" Her eyes flutter open and she nods assent.

Lydia appears in the darkening room. "Your husband filled me in on what's been happening," she says softly. The broad planes of her sculpted face remind me of the young Indian mothers in Mexico, but her dark hair's short and stylish. "Tell me about the patient."

"Forgive me for calling you in on this case after so much delay. This is Jordan Wilson, the girl who has been longing for you to come see her."

I give Lydia the lowdown, a case history suitable for a nurse, and show her the chart. If there's a different version of the girl's history she needs to hear, I am not privy to it.

Lydia studies the chart a minute and puts it down briskly. "Let me ask Jordan for permission to intercede on her behalf."

Jordan responds in an unexpectedly robust voice to Lydia's question, filling the room with assent. Lydia goes on in a conversational tone, all the while taking things from the bag she brought with her. "You've been sick, Jordan. You've arrived at a place where you ask 'Who am I?' It's a fair question. Your doctor has been caring for your physical body, the place your spirit dwells. I am here to help you find a safe place for your spirit to reflect and come to trust in your place on the earth. I help focus the energy you'll need. Do you understand?"

Jordan's eyes open. She frowns with concentration, and

241

then nods.

"Do I have your permission to work through the energy provided for me from the Holy Spirit and the Great Mother?"

Again Jordan nods her head, her upper lip drawing back from her teeth in effort. Lydia's quick fingers assemble an altar on the supper tray. Here she puts candles, a little statue of Our Lady of Guadalupe wearing a star-spangled blue cloth mantle, and a few amulets. She then takes out a whiskbroom— from the lemony scent, made from the plant I brought back from the mountains—and sweeps all around the patient and the bed with the ordinary grace of a good housekeeper.

Standing tall, Lydia stretches her fingers over the girl, who looks as insubstantial as a discarded doll. Pulling deep breaths of air into her diaphragm, she seems to swell up right in front of my eyes, as if unseen bellows pump energy into her body. My body starts to tingle.

Lydia puts her hands an inch or two from the girl's abdomen and makes stirring motions, then moves her hands in rhythmic waves from the top of the head to her throat, chest, diaphragm, before sweeping along more swiftly over her legs and concluding with a pinching-off motion at her feet. These hand gestures remind me of Iris and Amanda playing their teenage version of pattycake.

"My hands act like a magnifier," Lydia whispers as she works like a swimmer paddling purposefully over the girl's recumbent body, "picking up subtle energies, combining your own energy with all the physical and spiritual energy available at this moment in this place, then focusing this energy back on you."

Over and over the gestures are repeated. No telling how long this goes on before I see a barely discernible response, as if wisps of energy are jelling, becoming more solid. Jordan's face breaks out in a sheen of perspiration. Not long after this stirring and settling of energy and intention, Lydia's hands move down to the troubled areas of Jordan's body, hovering over her stomach and hips, making small circles, like she's cleaning or polishing. This motion seems to tire Lydia's neck muscles—she steps back to relax, plucking and pinching her neck, shaking her hands as if she's shaking water from them. She picks up the little broom made of the fragrant flowers from the mountains and whisks around the patient again. A sense of coldness and lethargy coming from the girl troubles me. I wish her mom would hurry.

"Lay on your hands," Lydia says with a jerk of her head, her dark eyes opaque. Lydia makes a gesture with her hands and arms, encouraging me. My hands come within a breath of making contact with Jordan before beginning to move, as if I'm stirring a thickening sauce, side by side with Lydia. I'm working with some sort of sticky substance, like hardening syrup, and make small grunts, then little panting sounds, as if I'm exerting myself to the border of my own reserves. I move beyond this sticking point; the stiffness and hesitation in my own body withdraw. Lydia gives me a nod and I step away. Lydia begins to make vigorous pulling motions, like she's pulling taffy.

"Jordan," Lydia croons, "come to the feast. You are included. The gift of life and breath is yours. You are welcome at the table." Jordan is hooked up like an astronaut floating in a hostile environment to state-of-the-art technology, a picture that would seem to mock Lydia's words. Lydia goes on, undaunted. "You're connected to us all," she sings, "through your mother and her mother and all the mothers who nourish their children through the gift of life. And you're upheld through your father and his father and all the fathers back to the beginning. Accept your gifts."

What's happened to her mother, I wonder. Keeping one ear cocked to Lydia's ministrations, I walk to the door and look down the hall.

"You belong here in this world where you are fed, body and soul, through God's gifts," Lydia says behind me to the sleeping girl. "You belong here and are cared for."

Jordan starts to move and to make small sounds as I watch intently from the door. Where do the instructions to Lydia's hands come from? It doesn't matter. Lydia eases off the taffy pulling and begins to make scrubbing motions, like scrubbing out a dirty oven, over the girl's whole trunk. The expression on

Lydia's face and her movements around the recumbent girl give me the sense we have all the time in the world.

Without stopping what her hands seem to be doing pretty much by themselves, Lydia leans over to scrutinize the girl's face. Jordan rolls her head back and forth against the pillow. Her eyes are still closed, but her skin's rosier. I lean against the wall, bewilderingly tired. It is not yet time for me to step away. It's like when you've been driving a car across the vast empty spaces of West Texas, aware of the drastic consequences of the tiniest moment of lost consciousness. I concentrate on the tableau in front of me when all at once my effort is lightened by an abundant, expectant awareness of a change in the room.

Jordan trembles under the healer's fingers, a soul on the cusp, teetering between life and death, poised but indifferent to whether she falls on the side of this life or the next.

"Don't go now, Jordan," I plead silently from my place of vigil, "you are wanted here."

Jordan opens her eyes and stares at me like a woman in the last stages of labor, pearls of sweat dotting her upper lip, her eyes bright and unfocused, set off by a tiny vertical frown. My arms open wide of their own accord and I take a step toward Jordan.

"Will you stay here with us?" I ask her. "Long enough to look things over? Can you do that?" No longer self-conscious or afraid, I ask her casually, like inviting a guest to linger for refreshment. This decision, after all, is entirely hers to make. "What do you say?"

The girl nods while her eyes fall shut. Her body wriggles, making tiny adjustments. She seems to plump up as I watch her, the beads of sweat on her lip giving way to a glaze over her whole face. I think momentarily about checking her vitals, then decide to wait a moment. Instead, I envelope her in my arms without touching her, just gathering up tons of energy and heaping it on her like soft clouds of life-giving stuff. Like *manna*, maybe. I laugh quietly, no more than bouncy breathing, crooning in a singsong voice, "manna maybe, manna maybe."

Not altogether under my breath, I realize as Shaunna walks

in with Mrs. Wilson. The mother looks inquiringly at Lydia, and then glances at her daughter.

"I'm so glad you're here," Lydia says to the mother. "Your daughter needs you."

Lydia's dark eyes and unwavering voice steady everyone in the room, but now she no longer seems mysterious. She looks like an ordinary, dark-haired woman with a collected mien, maybe a musician listening to her own music. For a moment I'm confused. Moments earlier she had loomed like a giant.

Lydia shows Jordan's mother what we've been doing, and she steps in for me. The three women spend the night tending Jordan, sometimes working together, sometimes spelling each other. I check back throughout the night, catching a nap in my office in the small hours. Each time I come back Lydia is as fresh as when she started. The mother lies in bed with her daughter, cradling her in her arms, totally transformed from the brisk businesswoman into a loving and tranquil presence. Extraordinary. When they're both asleep, the rest of us encompass them with our energy, whispering our mantras, holding the girl on the earth.

"Good morning," Jordan says when she opens her eyes next day.

The mother looks up, startled, and goes over to her daughter. I stand in the background, a witness to how modern medicine benefits from ancient wisdom.

Shaunna answers a knock on the door and opens it to discover Tommy. I nod to her unspoken query and Tommy bustles into the room.

"You will not believe what happened," Jordan tells him in a carrying voice. "For half the night I was like a figure of fire. No, not *like* fire, I *was* fire. Insubstantial. Zinging with light and energy. What a trip. Only I wasn't hot. Maybe it wasn't fire, maybe it was more like light. My body was consumed in this vibration where nothing bothered me. I wanted to tell somebody to find you, so you could feel it too. If you had come in and touched my hand, you'd have been whizzed away too. But I was afraid if I spoke I'd fall out of the spell."

"Hey! I was just down the hall. They said I could stay in the hospital if I promised not to barge into your room. Should've done it anyway."

"I'll leave Jordan in your capable hands," the mother says, looking at Lydia before disappearing into the next room of the suite. Maybe her instincts are right: maybe it's time for separation. The room's peaceful, an island in the normal hubbub of morning activities. I leave to check the lab results.

Tommy's gone when I get back to tell Jordan that her chemistry profile shows safe parameters on all counts. She's alert, almost manic. Dr. Glover comes in, followed in short order by his team of interns. Jordan's energy bubbles steadily. Neither of us makes any objection to the tests Dr. Glover asks permission to schedule. Standing at the door, I watch Glover's clownish energy brighten Jordan's whole aspect, while her girlish flirtatiousness humbles him almost beyond recognition. After Glover leaves, followed by his retinue, I hurry outside to speak to him. Looking subdued, he agrees to meet me in his office at lunchtime.

"What's happened since I've been gone?" Jordan asks when I go back to her bedside.

I don't ask her what she means by being gone. According to the ancient healers, fear can result in the spirit withdrawing from the body. Next, the spirit withdraws from the world, which means the death of the body. Maybe they're on to something. Withdrawal's a dangerous protective strategy when you're already sick. I provide Jordan with a history of the last two days, staying with her until one of Glover's interns comes to update her Crohn's index.

Chapter 32

The nurses' lounge, apparently furnished with furniture culled from family-room castoffs, is empty. I walk in and open the door of the fridge to stare stupidly, as if expecting to see something with my name on it. I shut the fridge and slump into a chair to wait for Lydia.

I don't have long. Lydia comes in and plunks down next to me, dropping her straw carryall, bulging with her candles and saints, on the floor.

"I'm glad you came to help us, Lydia," I say, then nothing more. She just looks at me with a spacey look. I laugh. "We seem to have run out of words."

"Yeah. This always happens to me after giving a treatment. I'm glad you called me."

"I'm the one who's grateful," I say.

"Well, me too. It's not the most common thing in the world, a doctor asking for my help during a patient's crisis."

"What about patients relapsing after going home?" I realize Lydia knows nothing about my troubles with Glover. "I want Jordan to pick up her own life. I hope this recovery will last. I was told not long ago that my patients were leaving the hospital well and then crashing, Jordan being the most obvious case."

"Consider detaching from her."

"Not you, too! I thought alternative medicine was about connecting to the patient."

"Let me explain. Your patients may be piggy-backing on your energy rather than creating their own. It's a tricky business. Healers use their own energy as a booster rocket. Everybody has to hook into the divine life energy on their own. Let me show you a couple of things you can do to keep your patients from relapsing after separating from you. And to help prevent you from getting sick."

Lydia leaps up out of her chair and stands in front of me. "You're not sick, are you?"

"I just had a miscarriage."

Lydia waits a beat and then goes on. "Then this will be good for you, too." She starts making gestures like she's washing herself, standing in front of me dry scrubbing quickly over her whole body, shaking her fingers in front of her, then whirling around and picking up the little broom out of her bag and whisking away. "You have to separate the two intermingled energies, yours and your patient's. Here, you can keep this." She thrusts the little broom into my hands. "Then take a bath as soon as you can."

"I'll work on it. Thanks."

"Good," she says, squinting at me. "Purveyors of medicine are not gods, but our beliefs are made manifest. If doctors believe that without constant medical surveillance the patient will relapse, it would take a mighty strong patient to resist that belief."

"Paul Lundy!"

"Excuse me?"

"A patient of mine, Paul Lundy. He didn't relapse when so many others did."

"OK. What's different about him?"

"He's older. He's been sick longer than I have lived. He knows more about his illness than most of his doctors. He's accepted the reality of his condition."

"Sounds like he uses his energy to deal with his illness, rather than burning it up in fantasy and false hope. I don't pretend to know how all this works on the level of spirit."

"Me either. But I know comfort is a good medicine. Thank you, Lydia."

"*De nada.*" She gives me a big hug, and I find myself hugging her back.

"So hugging's OK?"

"Oh, sure. But let me see if you learned the little cleansing ritual."

"OK. I won't forget. A shower of energy."

"Then get busy," she says, flipping her fingers at me to get started.

Feeling a little silly, I do as I've been told.

I meet Glover in his office, where in the olden days we plotted to prevent the insurance companies taking over our lives. Maybe Glover blames the ignominious defeat of a noble cause on me, his comrade in arms. That would explain a lot.

In marked contrast to Jeff Glover himself, his office is clean and orderly. He looks haggard despite his starched shirt and carefully knotted tie. For the first time since I've known him I notice he's looking old.

"Sit down, Zoe," he says.

I take a chair and look at him intently.

"What?" he asks.

"I am considering filing a formal complaint."

"On what grounds?"

"Supplanting my authority. Choosing to use my patient to test a new medication."

"I might do the same if I were in your place. If it will help for you to know, I regret doing it."

I snort. "Of course you'd regret it now."

"Not just because of the outcome, but because of the precedent. Nevertheless, you know a formal complaint will go nowhere simply because I am the department chair and have the authority to make decisions regarding patients. Period. It wouldn't have mattered if you were not away in Mexico. Her mother wanted to try the new medication. We could have gone ahead despite your views."

"Yeah. I know you are the chairman, Dr. Glover. But it's not a lifetime appointment. Dr. Hagan could do your job."

"Dr. Hagan can have the job and good luck to her, Zoe. But

never mind." He drums his fingers on his desk and looks around. His walls are covered with diplomas and plaques.

When I start to get up he motions me to stay. "Don't go yet." I hesitate, half out of the chair. "Please." I sink back. He fixes his gaze at a point just over my head. "I'm sorry, Zoe. I made a mistake. The girl was in no danger when her mother brought her back in. I would have liked a surgical solution to the fistula formation. But it's true the TPN was doing the job. I should not have pursued the new medication. I know better. You can play the odds for so long in the practice of medicine before coming up against a case like Jordan Wilson."

I stand up and lean on his desk. "Will you tell the whole staff meeting what you've just told me?" He meets my eyes, shrugs his shoulders in his tight coat, and wrinkles up his face like a Shar-Pei. "A simple statement that includes 'I'm sorry' and 'I made a mistake' will do fine."

"And if I do?" A crafty look sharpens his features, but he almost looks like he's enjoying himself.

"I won't file a formal complaint."

He stands up and sticks out his hand. "Deal?"

"Deal," I say, shaking his hand.

He sits back down. "I may ask Frank to appoint Cynthia Hagan to my position anyway," he says, waving me out.

"Whatever," I call over my shoulder, hurrying out, eager for a shower.

Chapter 33

This was the day I was supposed to see my gynecologist, who rearranged her schedule for me. Instead I find myself sitting face to face with Agent Gomez at the FBI annex next to a discount liquor store on Burnet Road. We confront each other silently, me with my arms folded across my chest, she with her hands clasped in front of her on the gray metal desk.

"I'm genuinely sorry about the night you spent in jail," she says, her face puckered with an exaggerated expression of concern.

I say nothing, stumped by all that's unspoken. I consider everything that has brought us here, two women sitting silent in a friendless room. Time stretches out like silly putty between me and this official, a woman who strikes me as no more intimidating than a guidance counselor from the middle school across the street. I remind myself she can intrude into my life in ways I never thought possible. Besides the two of us, the other objects in the windowless space are the desk, a high-tech telephone with lots of buttons, the chairs we're sitting in and my purse, lying like a pet on the floor beside me. None of the doors on three sides of the room lead to the outside. The overhead light, casting no shadows, shines down on her bland face and flawless olive skin. She bobs her head to and fro, like a lizard, her lips compressed.

My hands are stuck in my armpits. I remove them and place them on the woman's desk in front of me, palms down. The two of us form a reverse image of doctor and patient, with Agent Gomez in the power seat. Her office lacks the rugs, books, Kleenex, family pictures, couch, sink and plants that soften my office in the hospital. Still, patients wait in front of me for pronouncements concerning their future in the same way I am waiting to hear what this woman will say. My only identifiable emotion is barely contained rage. Surely my patients also feel trust and hope for what I can do for them? I adjust my face to one of bland indifference.

"I don't have to tell you this," she says at last, "but there was a bomb scare at the capitol in which the Separatists were implicated, eventually leading to you being picked up as a possible UFAC—unlawful flight to avoid confinement. While you were detained, that organization was exonerated." She speaks slowly, as if not expecting me to be fully conscious.

I want to squeal that I was coming back *into* the country, but clamp my teeth and say nothing, sitting with my spine rigid. I wonder if she's trained in martial arts. She pushes her chair back from the desk. "You could have made this a whole lot easier on yourself if you had come to see me earlier. Maybe it would have been me who met you at the airport. Perhaps I would have used my discretion and kept you out of jail. No place, really, for a professional woman, a person of your achievements."

She places her elbows on the desk and steeples her fingers, a position favored by those in authority. "You know why I joined the bureau?" she asks. When I don't answer she goes on anyway. "In the eighties I was a single mother. The Bureau was recruiting minorities. They offered to put me through college. You probably would not understand, Dr. Dempsey."

"What part do you think I would not understand?" I ask, jumping up and standing a few feet back from my side of the desk. She looks at me warily. She probably has a panic button somewhere. My words trail behind my agitation like skywriting. "The part about a secure future for your children? The part about wanting to get an education and a steady income? The part about making a contribution? What part?" I'm getting incensed. "What about you? What part do you not understand about me? What I do in my profession? The part about not having much of a home life? The part about paying back student loans? The part about holding someone else's life in your hands?" I shake my head rapidly back and forth.

"What's *not to understand* about what's happening here in this country, Agent Gomez? Nobody trusts anybody else. We're no longer capable of self-tolerance. We mistake various parts of the self for the enemy. Enforcers like you carry out deranged orders to seek and destroy. I understand you a whole lot better than you do me."

She strokes the air in front of her in a pawing motion, trying to calm me. I've made the same gesture to patients' acting-out in response to bad news. She glares at me with displeasure; my own face hardens in response.

"It's my job to understand why someone like you would get involved with people like the Separatists. That's what I'm on the team for, ma'am."

She smiles a seemingly genuine smile. It does not disarm me, but it gives me pause. I imagine myself on her side of the table, the authority with all the cards, wondering why the person in front of me is so suspicious. Professional distance is created to *prevent* empathy; for the most part it succeeds.

"Are you recording this interview?" I ask. I came here without a lawyer because there is something I have to find out, I'm not sure what.

Gomez beckons me over to her side of the desk with her forefinger, her head hunched down between her shoulder blades, a sly smile on her face. As I walk around she pulls open the middle drawer to show me a tape recorder slowly revolving.

"What does it matter whether our interview's recorded, Dr. Dempsey?" she asks conversationally, then pushes the power button on the recorder, stopping the rotation, and checks her watch while waving me back to my seat and shoving in the drawer. "Tell me what you were doing in Mexico. Whatever were you thinking?"

"Why should I tell you my thoughts?"

She sighs. "Well, I assume you're interested in doing just

253

what you did—improving local conditions for the poorest people with little means of getting health care other than involving the international community. If you want to go back and do it again, the Mexican authorities will scrutinize you carefully. And," here she all-out grins at me, "I personally will have to remove the obstacles for you to travel outside the States. Talking to me now will save you plenty of grief later."

"Don't you just love that power surge, deciding what can happen to someone else's life?"

"No," she says. Her voice drops and she looks away from me. "What I like is having some control over my own life. I'm all for you going down to doctor in Mexico. I have relatives there. I care about the people, although personally I don't think the Indians are going to survive another fifteen years like they've been doing, no matter what the politicians on both sides of the border decide. But I could be wrong. They've resisted assimilation for five hundred years. I'd like to see the people survive, even if their culture does not.

"Just to clarify your motives for my report," she says, back in her professional tone of voice, "where do you stand in regard to the Texas Separatists? Do you plan to work for Texas independence?"

"No."

"Just no? No ifs, ands or buts?"

"I'm an American. From sea to shining sea." I look her in the eye. Even I don't know how much I'm bullshitting her—the tribal instinct lies coiled up with the Kundalini snake at the base of the spine.

"Then what is your interest?" A bewildered look crosses her face. "Surely you were aware that taking an interest would have repercussions?"

"No. I wasn't aware. Whatever happened to the right of assembly, the right to discover what others are thinking, and why? How can we find out unless we ask, face to face?"

She looks at me, eyes narrowed, then frowns at her watch. "Why does it matter whether our interview's recorded, Dr. Dempsey?" she asks, making little quotation marks with both fingers in the air, and opens the drawer of her desk to switch on the recorder.

"It doesn't matter in the practical sense whether our conversation is recorded, Ms. Gomez," I say, my voice coming out oddly stilted, "I object to it on principle."

"What would be the difference between recording our conversation and taking notes?"

"Just ask me what you want to know and let me get back to work."

"Are you planning the overthrow of the United States government?"

"No. I am not. I am planning to oppose the inequities I've witnessed here and in Mexico by making them known to others."

Agent Gomez proceeds through her list of questions, asking for clarification even on the most obvious statements. I answer while the tape recorder whirrs. Would I have saved myself a night in jail if I'd done this sooner?

After leaving Agent Gomez in her office I walk outside and pause under the awning in front of the clock-repair shop, trying to get a fix on where I parked the Suburban. I remember parking next to the huge sign advertising the strip mall, a large plastic masthead on a pole, bolted into a concrete base, situated at the street-side corner of the parking lot. I'd been careful not to bang the door into the concrete when I got out of the car. I take a few steps out from under the shade and am blinded by the light. I stop to dig in my purse for my sunglasses, and then look over to the place I remember leaving the car. When I don't see it I experience something like vertigo.

Agents Green and Collins materialize out of the ether, both of them wearing their ubiquitous shades, dressed as usual in suits and ties, their faces bland as custard.

"Lose something?" Green asks, his lips parting to simulate a smile.

"Maybe. What do you want?"

"Just a moment of your time, ma'am." His voice drops. "I

do not know what Agent Gomez told you, but I wanted to personally remind you that you are now in the book of every FBI agent in the country. We will always know where you are." He plucks off his glasses. His pink-rimmed eyes stare out at me like a possum caught raiding the garbage.

Steeling myself to hold the man's gaze, my interview with Gomez a walk in the park by comparison, I retain my composure, but find no words. Green tilts his chin over his shoulder without breaking eye contact. When a man stares at you like this you know he either wants to fuck you or kill you. This guy is definitely in no mood to fuck.

He speaks to his subordinate. "Check around back for Dr. Dempsey's green Suburban."

"I know the one," Collins answers from behind his superior's back. He mouths the word cunt over his boss's shoulder, as clearly as if he'd shouted out loud. I flinch—the man's stolen my wonderful word and fingered my soul. His boss whips around to see what I'm looking at, but Collins has gone.

They eventually tire of their game and show me where to find my car, now parked behind the building, where I definitely did not leave it. I get in and drive off slowly, my chest hollow. In a time long ago, these assholes and I were all on the same side—part of the establishment. By moving my car they're trying to tell me I've crossed some invisible line. An adolescent gesture, but it chills me.

Driving aimlessly, not knowing where to go, I decide to head over to the Presbyterian Church basement on Ninth and Brazos to catch a noon AA meeting.

Again I find myself wedged in a corner, back against the wall, but this time at an open AA meeting, not a society party littered with doctors. An impeccably groomed businessman reads from the Big Book. I doze off and don't wake up until the moment comes to identify myself.

"Hello everybody; I'm Zoe." I do not confess to being a doctor. Or to being impaired. Meetings for impaired physicians go on somewhere else in this city, but I never seek them out.

People here don't ask what you do outside. Maybe you come here because there's nowhere else to go, or maybe because it's here or jail—or because no one else will take you when you hit bottom. I didn't used to know what that meant, but I do now. Not so bad as I thought. It provides a solid pushing-off place on your way back up to the light.

Chapter 34

I cut out of the AA meeting early to keep my appointment with Frank in his posh office. We stand facing each other in the gracious room, filled with good furniture and flowers, both dancing around the subject of my night in jail like it's dog-shit on the carpet. We've segued from my trip to Mexico to race relations here in the States.

"Women and African-American people used to share something," I say after an extended silence, picking up the heavy end of the dropped conversation. "When we were outside the system, we couldn't help but see its evils."

"You're saying women and black people once had soul?"

"Bingo. We could nourish our souls when we weren't so tempted by the rewards."

"Nonsense!" Frank says, so loud I jump. "Of course we were tempted," he adds, modulating his voice with effort. "We're as much a part of the system as anybody else. Can't you see that? Once you get the hang of how the system works, once you find a way of getting a leg up, the easiest thing to do is to switch sides. It's a helluva lot easier than building a system of liberty and justice for all. Women have made the switch quite handily."

"You may be right. I see what you're saying. We couldn't be corrupted with power until we got some. Once we did, we started to act like everyone else. Remember the quality control people who were all over the hospital before managed care took over? They must've said a million times: the way the system is designed controls results. The individuals in the slots don't count for diddley-squat."

"What's your point?"

"Doctors were trained to be gods like Marines were trained to kill. Now all we're supposed to do is conform. There must be some middle way."

"Why did you choose medicine?" he asks, his broad forehead crumpling into a frown.

"My grandfather was a doctor. At the end of his life, he spent a long time dying of congestive heart failure. My mother died when I was still a kid. I wanted to save people. Why else become a doctor?"

"Your grandfather would be proud if he saw you today. Look, Zoe, I know what you've been through," Frank says, leaning on his desk with one hand and getting our little dialogue choo-choo back on track. "About your young patient's medication: monoclonal antibodies look very promising against Crohn's. It would be a mistake to blame your colleagues for one reaction."

"Dr. Glover apologized to me for interfering. There's room for optimism."

"Good," Frank says, his face smoothing out. "You might try diplomacy before making incursions across the borders of common clinical practice."

"Ah, yes. Diplomacy. I've always been interested in how the ills of society show up in the ills of the body." I hesitate, staring at my feet. My painted toes look cheery in my dress sandals. "Dr. Glover said he would apologize in a staff meeting."

The Chief retreats behind his desk. "Where do you think we went wrong?"

Maybe this man is not hopeless. "We denied our brutality."

"Yes, perhaps." Now the man retreats still further, behind his sleek carapace, taking his Cross pen out of his pocket and flipping it end over end. "One more thing. I hear you refused to speak to our visiting doctor from Australia. He will be leaving soon. He wants to talk to you about Jordan Wilson."

"No, thanks," I say, keeping my voice calm. "You're the

one in that job slot."

"You're right about that, Doctor," he says, his shoulders sagging.

"You don't look so good to me, Chief. Maybe you'd better have a checkup with a medical doctor." I grin at him. "You know, clinicians are now referred to as *interventionists*. What do you make of that?"

He gives me a sour look. "The folks on the next administrative level are all MBAs, not doctors. Maybe it's time for me to step down from this position, give one of the younger people a chance. But not today." Frank rears up like a cobra, cloaking himself in his most stately manner. "Dr. Lerner died last night. I hope you will join me, and many others from our hospital and community, in attending the memorial service. You were a special favorite of his."

"Was I?" I picture the moment on the landing when he told me not to let anybody force me to choose between *either/or.* "How did he die?"

"He just wore out, Zoe," Frank says, returning to the chair behind his desk. "He was well up in years. When his wife died last fall he started prepping to follow."

Frank looks at me intently. The whites of his eyes are yellow. "And Zoe. Concerning your overnight detention . . ."

Ah. The dog-shit acknowledged.

"I will not have my doctors treated so—cavalierly. So *shabbily.*" He looks indignant. "If there is anything I can do, anyone I can speak to on your behalf, please let me know."

"Thank you." That sounds inadequate. "I'll try to get to the memorial service for Dr. Lerner, Chief," I say as I cross the threshold.

What's going to happen now that the sustaining fictions of modern medicine no longer convince me? What is there left for me?

Al drives me back home from the hospital. Too tired to process complex thought, I lean back on the passenger side of the Volvo, massaging my skull. Al looks over when a sound slips past my lips.

"Tell," he commands.

My hands still on my head, I nod vigorously, trying to shake the clutter in my head into some sort of order. "I can't seem to grasp hold of a single thread of this sorry mess," I say at long last. "First I've got to tie off the bleeders. Maybe I don't belong at Doctors' Hospital any more."

"You'll need time to sort things out," Al says.

"I used to be so certain of what to do next. Now old solutions look simplistic. It seems like eons ago Glover accused me of stepping out of bounds. Back then neither one of us had any idea how far out I was destined to go."

Al takes his eyes off the road to sneak a look at me, and then turns back, his body coiled over the steering wheel, head and neck thrust forward. I move closer to him. We're crossing the Colorado River on the Lamar Street Bridge. The familiar landscape looks like the face of an old friend. The billboard in front of the Conoco station has been sprayed with graffiti proclaiming *The People's Republic of Texas! Now.*

"Did you see that sign, Al?" I grab his arm, excited.

"No."

"It says 'the People's Republic of Texas *now.*'"

"I never did understand what that poor bastard you met on the mountain was after."

"Something to believe in. Like the rest of us. I wish I'd talked him out of his folly and persuaded him to come back to town, instead of leaving him out there to die."

Al cuts me a look. "Don't second-guess yourself, Zoe. You've sacrificed enough: don't go building any altars to a stranger's god."

"But what about my own? Why should taking one teensie step beyond the boundries of your place and time be like stepping off the edge of the world?"

"If you stray too far, the tribe won't want you back," Al says. I wave away his concern, my attention caught by a familiar looking car that doesn't belong here.

Al turns into the drive and comes to a smooth stop.

I gesture to the parked car: "It's my old buddies from the FBI."

What business do they have here? Time slows down. I call the house and talk to Anna, who says the car's been there for an hour. I know she's worried by the precision of her words. Next I call the security guard at the gate. He's no help. He's the one who let them in. Al waits, concentrating on me, while I'm riveted on the car. In a flash of glee, I call the Travis County Sheriff and talk to the dispatcher, who promises to send someone out to investigate.

Al leaves the car running and the AC going, but for once I don't complain.

Al and I study each other, with all the time in the world together in this car to sort things out. "I've woken up to a world I don't much like, but it's the one where I'm going to have to act," I tell him.

Al just grunts. Neither one of us makes a move to get out.

"I'm not ready to cave-in to threats and punishment when I've committed no crime. You're not either."

"I'm way behind the curve here, Zoe. I haven't gone through what you've gone through. But it's been enough to make me want to stroll over to that car and ask the occupants to account for themselves." He switches off the engine and opens his door.

"Let's both go."

Our local law enforcement shows up just as we get out of the car—they couldn't have been very far away. I don't know if what I feel is relief or disappointment, my adrenalin is running so high. Al and I barely acknowledge the small band of intruders before we go into the house to reassure the rest of the family and await developments.

I'm ready for whatever comes down the pike.

Glossary

CD: Crohn's Disease
Chronic inflammatory bowel disease, origin unknown, resulting in chronic ill health with abdominal pain, diarrhea, weight loss, intestinal obstruction, and sometimes fistula formation. Treatment varies.

Complement: A branch of the immune system
Acts during the initial stages of a foreign invasion. Complement is a substance found in the blood and can kill cells on its own.

Fistula
Abnormal passage from a hollow organ to the surface, or from one organ to another.

IBD: Inflammatory Bowel Disease
An overall term for disease that causes swelling and inflammation of the wall of the digestive tract.

JAMA: Journal of the American Medical Association

Pancreatitis: Inflammation of the pancreas
"Pancreatitis can be so deadly, so fast, that I think of the organ as the P-bomb." Michael D. Gershon, M.D., *The Second Brain*, (Harper Collins: New York, 1998), p.135.

Peds team: A team of doctors from pediatrics assigned to a particular patient.

Percocet: oxycodone and acetaminophen; street name *perks*

PNI: Psychoneuroimmunology
"The psychoneuroimmunology movement [recognizes that the immune system] does not live isolated—that in fact it is integrated into larger wholes, among which are the neuropeptide system, the autonomic and central nervous system, the brain, the hypothalamus, the interpretive—the cortex, which deals with emotions and feelings and perceptions and stress." Peter Boswell, as quoted in: *Flexible Bodies: Tracking Immunity in American Culture*, by Emily Martin. (Beacon Press: Boston, 1994), p. 86.

TPN: Total Parenteral Nutrition
TPN infuses all required nutrients through a catheter in a vein.

Kirsten Dodge lives east of Austin, Texas, on Wilbarger Creek in Bastrop County, where she writes and rides horses.